About the Author

Former magazine editor Charlotte Butterfield was born in
Bristol in 1977. She studied English at Royal Holloway
University and an MPhil in Gender and Women's Studies
at Birmingham University before becoming a journalist and
copywriter. She moved to Dubai in 2005 and lives with her
husband and three children.

Twitter: @charliejayneb
Facebook: @charlottebutterfieldauthor

Me, You and Tiramisu

Charlotte Butterfield

Harper
impulse
we've got the love

Harper*Impulse* an imprint of
HarperCollins*Publishers*
1 London Bridge Street
London SE1 9GF

www.harpercollins.co.uk

A Paperback Original 2017

First published in Great Britain in ebook format by Harper*Impulse* 2017

A catalogue record for this book
is available from the British Library

ISBN: 9780008216511

This novel is entirely a work of fiction.
The names, characters and incidents portrayed in it are
the work of the author's imagination. Any resemblance to
actual persons, living or dead, events or localities is
entirely coincidental.

Typeset in Birka by Palimpsest Book Production Ltd, Falkirk, Stirlingshire
Printed and bound in Great Britain by Clays Ltd, St Ives plc

MIX
Paper from
responsible sources
FSC www.fsc.org FSC® C007454

For Team P:
Ed, Amélie, Rafe and Theo

Chapter 1

Fate was supposed to throw them together again in Rome, standing in the shadow of the Coliseum, exchanging guide-book-gleaned titbits on the tyrannical reign of Nero. Or often, in another one of her daydreams, they'd be in the grand lobby of the Royal Albert Hall, swapping polite apologies as they jostled into each other a few minutes before the lights dimmed at the Last Night of the Proms. Sometimes they'd be smiling nervously at each other as they prepared for their hot-air balloon to slowly lift off the ground over the sun-soaked sand of Queensland, or occasionally sitting at sunrise on neigh-bouring blankets watching turtle eggs hatch on a beach in the Florida Keys. Jayne had never been to Italy, Australia or America and, truth be told, she didn't actually like classical music. But regardless of these small, and insignificant, realities, not once had she imagined that her reunion with Billy would be accom-panied by a lingering smell of analgesic and mouthwash on a dark February afternoon in Twickenham.

**

Jayne had arrived uncharacteristically late; her cheeks were flushed from getting off the gridlocked bus and deciding to run the remaining half mile with her satchel containing thirty dog-eared exercise books bashing violently against her hip the whole way. The door let in an icy gust before slamming behind her, rudely announcing her arrival to the packed waiting room. Flustered and overly apologetic, she sandwiched herself into the only available seat, which was under a graphic poster screaming the words *Disorders of the Teeth and Jaw*.

She tried to keep her elbows close to her body as she took off her glasses to de-steam them and yelped as her bag slipped to the floor, scattering books and papers across the waiting room. Twelve pairs of eyes looked up at the unexpected commotion as Jayne fell to her knees reaching under the plastic chairs and leaflet-laden coffee table. 'Sorry, sorry, I'm so sorry,' she kept uttering while plunging her hand between boots and shoes.

'Here's a few more,' a man's deep voice uttered to her side. He was holding a pile of books and papers. 'I think that's the lot.'

'Thank you so much,' Jayne replied, accepting his outstretched hand to help her back onto her feet, 'What an idiot.'

'Don't be daft, it's fine.' He looked at the top sheet of paper he was still holding and read its title aloud. '*Terry Pratchett has been called the Shakespeare of today, discuss.*

Wow, now that's the kind of essay I wouldn't have minded writing when I was in school, or even now, actually!'

Jayne blew her hair out of her face as she took the papers off him, stuffed them in her bag and sat in the empty seat next to him. 'A Pratchett fan?' she said.

'Have been for years,' he replied. 'Is that really what kids are learning nowadays?'

'Not officially, but it's a bit of light relief after the mocks. For me more than them, I think, although I may have converted a few of them. What was it he once said, 'The trouble about having an open mind is that people will insist on coming along and trying to put things in it'?'

'My favourite quote of his was, 'The pen is mightier than the sword if the sword is very short and the pen is very sharp'.' They both laughed. Jayne retrieved a bottle of water from her bag and took a big gulp. She'd wanted to nip to the bathroom and give her teeth a quick brush before her appointment, but then she'd lose her seat, and she thought that it might seem a bit rude if she just got up in the middle of her conversation with this random man. She settled for swishing the water around her mouth like a wine-taster; that would have to do.

The man courteously waited for her to swallow before adding, 'So what else do you normally like reading, then?'

'Anything really,' she shrugged. Being in London, talking to a stranger, albeit one that you're touching shoulders with, was a rare phenomenon. She hadn't yet dispensed with saying 'sorry' or 'excuse me' when she mistakenly jostled someone on the tube, which immediately singled herself out as an outsider, even after fifteen years in the city, but there was a difference between proffering up instinctive apologies and actually having a conversation with someone she didn't know. She didn't have anything better to do, though, apart from a quick floss, but then, that's what she was just about to pay someone to do.

'I usually have a few books on the go, which I know you shouldn't do, respect for the author and all that, but, um, biographies, classics, I guess, and I try to read a few of the Booker list each year, because I feel that I should, historical fiction, some science fiction if it's not too weird, a bit of crime, if it's not too gruesome, um, poetry, I do like a good poem.'

'Who doesn't?' He replied smiling. Up until then their exchange had all happened side-on, giving a nod to the unspoken English rule of respecting one another's personal space, quick side glances punctuating the questions and responses. Jayne swivelled slightly in her seat to face him; he smiled and then, embarrassed, they both quickly looked away. This didn't happen to girls like her. Strange men in public places didn't just strike up a conversation about literature.

She started scrabbling through her bag for her phone, under the pretence of checking the time but actually just to break the silence. Thank God he didn't know that without her glasses she could barely see the screen, let alone the numbers on it, but she didn't want to put her specs on and spoil the illusion of being a seductive temptress. She was pretty sure he was incredibly attractive, but admittedly, at that moment he resembled a beautiful pastel drawing that was delicately smudged around the edges. To keep up the charade of having the power of sight she sighed, prompting the man to venture, 'They seem to be running late today.'

She nodded and took one of the essays out, but deciphering the swirled swags and tails of teenage penmanship didn't really cut it as a distraction technique, particularly as she was only pretending to read. Her eyes began straying to the side, at exactly the same time as the man looked up from the page of his book.

'You know, reading shouldn't really be so much of a chore,' he teased. 'If your forehead got any more furrowed you'd start to lose things in there.'

'Is it that obvious?' she smiled, 'Here I am trying to earn an honest living and all I get is mockery.'

She could sense his mouth turning up at the edges at her feeble attempt at being affronted, and he held his hands up, 'Sorry, sorry, I didn't mean to cast aspersions on your obvious dedication to education; it quite literally seeps out of you.'

'I hate the word 'literally',' Jayne rolled her eyes, 'Like it *literally* kills me. And 'seeps', now you come to mention it.'

'I'm like that with 'gusset'.' He shivered theatrically. 'Eugh.'

'I have a theory about that, actually.'

'This'll be interesting. A theory about gussets.'

'Indeed. I think, in the case of gusset, it's purely because of what it describes, so if it swapped its meaning with a nice word, it would be okay – like if Judy Garland had sang 'Somewhere Over the Gusset' it wouldn't be a horrible word.'

'Okay, so by that reasoning, and I grant you, it's a valid theory, we'd be sitting here saying 'I loathe the word 'rainbow', bleurgh. Vile word. Yuck'.'

'Exactly!' They both sat back in their seats smiling. The room had relaxed; it felt lighter, more convivial.

Jayne started to feel butterflies building inside, a sensation she hadn't really experienced since she was a teenager. It was quite an achievement to get to the age of thirty-three and to never have experienced anything resembling a light storm, let alone a thunderbolt. She'd even tried match.com recently, at Rachel and her friend Abi's insistence, which she thought should really be renamed lookingforaquickbonk.com because every bloke's interest had evaporated once she'd made it clear that she wanted dinner first. She didn't think it was too much of a hardship for a man to endure a meal with her if mediocre but enthusiastic lovemaking might be on the menu after, but it turned out that it was.

'Okay, Mister, I'm going to enter into the spirit of this because, well, we're clearly not getting our teeth seen to any time soon. Quick-fire round. Favourite character of all time?'

'Huckleberry Finn. You?'

'Jane Austen's Marianne Dashwood.'

'Predictable, but it's your call. Favourite book from child-hood?'

'*The Magic Faraway Tree.*'

'Excellent choice. I loved Moonface. And Mr Saucepanhead.'

'Saucepan Man.'

'What?'

'His name was Saucepan Man, you said Saucepanhead.'

'You say tom-arto, I say tom-ay-to.'

'Well, no, we both say tom-arto, because we are not from the Land of the Brave.'

'Speak for yourself,' He comically puffed out his chest and affected a deep baritone voice, 'I am incredibly coura-geous.'

'I don't doubt it,' she quipped back without missing a beat, 'but just to prove it, what was the last macho thing that you did?'

Still in character as Johnny Bravo he said, 'well, I asked an attractive stranger sitting next to me in a waiting room for her number so we can meet up and celebrate our clean teeth by drinking red wine and coffee.'

The invitation had been so unexpected Jayne almost had to sit on her hands to stop them from applauding. Quickly composing herself, she replied with what she hoped was a tone of flirty sarcasm, 'Wow, you *are* a charmer.'

The elderly lady next to Jayne who had been following

their exchange with a barely concealed smile reluctantly left her seat after being called by the clipboard-wielding receptionist, but not before giving Jayne a little wink.

Jayne moved her coat and scarf off her lap and onto the warm vacant seat. 'I need to save this for my twin, she's meeting me here after my appointment,' she felt the need to explain.

'Oh my, there are two of you?'

'Yep, non-identical. The only thing we share is a birthday, though, so you can put your seedy thoughts back in their box.'

'Seedy thoughts, indeed. Jeez, a second ago I was a charmer and now I'm a pervert. How did *that* happen?'

'It's a delicate tightrope you walk. Right, back to books. What's your favourite last line of a book?'

'Oooo, good question, but very easy. 'The president of the immortals had ended his sport with Blank.' Who's Blank?'

'So simple you're embarrassing yourself – and the answer is Tess of the D'Urbervilles.'

'She shoots, she scores. Okay, maybe that one was too easy, how about . . .'

He was cut off mid-sentence by a woolly mammoth smothering Jayne in a bear hug. 'Oh my God, Jayney, I'm so sorry I'm late!' Rachel shrugged off her huge fake-fur coat, and plonked herself down on the spare chair. 'Rubbish day, didn't stop, so sorry, were you waiting long? She suddenly stopped, aware that she'd interrupted a conversation. 'Oh Jeez, sorry, who are you?' she stuck her hand out over Jayne, and he slowly took it.

'Will.'

His name was Will. They'd been talking for a quarter of an hour and her sister had managed to get this information in under a minute. It had never even occurred to Jayne to ask him his name; maybe this was why she was still single. Finding out his literary preferences seemed much more important than what his parents had decided to call him.

'I know you – I'm sure I do,' Rachel was peering at him, eyes narrowed.

A little part of Jayne started to wither and die inside. Please, please let Will not be one of the multitude of men she had seen making the walk of shame from her sister's room as she was leaving for work in the morning. The trouble with having a flatmate whose aim in life was to horizontally rumba with all of London's bachelors, and much to Jayne's disgust and Rachel's annoyance, some who were bachelors only in mind and behaviour, but not in the eyes of the law, was that it didn't leave many men who were untouched for Jayne. Not that it had ever bothered her before, but at that moment, it really, really did.

'Will? Jesus, it's Billy!'

Oh God.

Jayne decided that she didn't want any part in their cosy

reunion, so started to fidget in her seat, packing her pathetic little belongings back in her bag before they started doing whatever it was people did after one-night stands.

He shrugged apologetically, offering up a polite smile to compensate, 'Um, sorry, I don't think we've met,'

'Billy, *Billy*, I'm Rachel, *Rachel.*'

Jayne suddenly felt really bad for her sister. Having a person who's seen you naked not remembering, or even worse pretending not to, was really humiliating, and she knew all about that. For it to happen to Rachel was actually quite unheard of; it was normally her sister feigning ignorance in a corner when a dubious pull popped up, never the other way round.

'Jeez, Billy, this is Jayne. *Jaayynne,*' Rachel implored.

'Jayne? *Jayne?* Oh my God!' Before she had the chance to duck out of the way, or at least prepare herself, Will had lunged at her, enveloping her in a huge hug and burying his face in her neck. She had no idea why a conquest of Rachel's would be so emotional, but she let him carry on holding her because he smelt of coconut. She chose to put to one side the fact that he'd slept with her sister, because this was the closest she'd come to male contact for nearly two years, and up until four minutes ago, she was going to marry him.

Rachel suddenly started hugging both of them over the top of his hug, so she was trapped in some strange kind of pyramid embrace. *What the hell?* Jayne started wriggling free of the pair of them and finally extracted herself from their bizarre outpouring of affection.

'Jayne? What's wrong? I thought you'd be really pleased to see him after all this time? Why are you being weird?'

Me? The world has just gone crazy, she wanted to shout, but ever the diplomat, settled instead for, 'Um, sorry, I just think it's a bit inappropriate, and I should probably leave you two alone, to . . . er . . . reminisce without me.'

'Jayne. Put your glasses on.'

'What?'

'For the love of all that's holy. Put. Your. Glasses. On.'

She did.

'Now look at him.'

Jayne's heart flipped over and she thought she was going to be sick. It had taken eighteen years, but she'd finally found the first love that had slipped through her inexperienced fingers. *Speak* she willed herself, *say something amazing, something heartfelt and articulate. Show him what he's been missing for nearly two decades.* Opening her mouth to speak, to add to the magic of the moment, Jayne's first words were suddenly indecently smothered by an officious voice shouting, 'Jayne Brady, ready for your scrape and polish?'

Chapter 2

The next few seconds happened in a blur; Jayne's heart thumped loudly in her ears. Her thoughts whizzed through her mind faster than they ever had before and yet she instinctively rose out of her chair as her name was called. She'd never been one to defy authority, or sidestep an obligation; in fact her reliance on rules and propriety were a regular topic of ridicule from her sister. Jayne took three steps towards the nurse before she stopped abruptly in the middle of the room. What was she doing? She'd dreamed of this moment, well, not *this* moment exactly, she'd never considered that this was how it would happen. Semantics aside, it suddenly seemed ludicrous to her that she was prepared to pause it while she had her incisors whitened.

'Um. You know what? I think I'll reschedule. Er, if that's okay? If it's not, I'll come now, but I'd really rather not,' she heard herself say. Turning around to seek approval from Will and Rachel at her impulsiveness, she saw that they'd both stood up already and Will was holding her coat open for her to step into.

Will and Rachel had excitedly chosen the pub that the three of them were now walking briskly towards. Their speed had little to do with the unforgiving climate; they were propelled instead by their eagerness to allow almost two decades to melt into insignificance. Jayne kept pace with them, hearing their animated chatter, yet unable to add to it herself.

There wasn't a day in eighteen years that she hadn't fantasised about this moment; most mundane tasks had been tinged with a fleeting thought of where or what he was doing, she'd concocted the most creative and implausible scenarios where serendipity would thrust them together again, and now it was actually happening. On an icy pavement in a London suburb, against the tide of collar-up commuters, she was walking with Billy.

**

On the night she first met Billy, Jayne and Rachel were sitting in their kitchen, still in their school uniforms with the remnants of their microwave meals congealing on the plates in front of them. Rachel was engrossed in carving the words INXS into the back of her calculator with a compass while Jayne was studiously rewriting her essay using her sister's slightly more sloped handwriting, remembering not to dot her 'i's' like she would have done, but to draw a small bubble over each one instead.

Their mother, Crystal, was precariously balanced on the edge of the worktop hanging up a Native American dream-catcher in the window that she'd just bought in a gemstone shop in Totnes. 'I've got a new client coming round later for a reading, girls, so make yourself scarce.'

Of all of Crystal's money-making schemes over the years this was the one that Jayne hated the most, and yet sadly was the most lucrative, so Crystal had no intention of cancelling it. Simply by closing her eyes, leaning forward in her chair and saying the words, 'they are safe on the other side, and they love you,' she made forty quid a session.

'And?' Rachel had yawned, leaning back in her chair.

'And, this one might be my ticket out of this place, so don't be like you usually are.' Neither daughter had even flinched at their mother's choice of words, they'd heard much worse. 'It was bloody bad luck,' was how Crystal had always described her unplanned pregnancy. 'It was a night of passion under the stars, but I've been paying ever since!' was the title tune on the backing track of their childhood and it was usually accompanied by a Chardonnay-scented hiccup and a sharp inhale of a Lambert & Butler.

Apparently their father's name was Neil, aka Jupiter. That's as much as they'd ever managed to get out of their mother regarding the identity of their dad. To be fair to Crystal, it wasn't that she was deliberately withholding specifics from them, it was the only information she'd gleaned from him before she'd shed her sarong on Thailand's Koh Pha Ngan beach and celebrated the full moon with some intoxicated love-making. Neil left Paradise Bungalows the next day for a school-building project in India and Crystal moved on soon after to a rice farm in Bali.

She'd initially put her tiredness and weight gain down to the carb-heavy diet and intense manual labour, but five months into her pregnancy there was no mistaking what was happening inside her body. She flew home to have the girls and her free spirit evaporated a little more each day, leaving behind a bitterness that was impossible to shift.

Despite only knowing Neil for a matter of hours, and ignoring the fact that little of that was spent talking, Crystal still blamed Jayne's shortsightedness on this teenage lothario, along with her ability to put on a few waist inches by passing a wrapped chocolate bar. But over the years Jayne had learnt to channel her grandmother's mantra of 'deal best you can with the lot you've been dealt'. She reasoned that she should know, having had to help raise her eighteen-year-old daughter's dark-haired twins in a seaside town where being from Exeter was considered exotic.

By the time the doorbell went that evening, both girls would have forgotten about Crystal's grieving client had it not been for the overwhelming smell of sandalwood incense that engulfed the house, which apparently energised the spirits. 'It's what the clients expect,' Crystal had said the first time the girls coughed their way through the fug.

This client seemed to fill the doorway; his broad shoulders were slightly stooped, yet still blocked out whatever remnants of daylight were left in the reddening sky behind him. Crystal had been characteristically effusive in her welcome. The social niceties and wide smile that only made their appearance when in the company of vulnerable people with cash were flaunted with abandon.

This time was different, though. The girls had almost walked straight past the man's smart navy Volvo that was incongruent with the potholed driveway and forlorn wasteland of a front garden. As Jayne drew level with the driver's window she had glanced in and seen a teenage boy sitting low in the seat, shoulders hunched, his dark lanky hair obscuring his eyes. She'd tapped on the window, but he didn't respond. She'd knocked harder, hurting her knuckles, until he'd slowly raised his head, his eyes tired and lifeless.

He'd reluctantly leant across and wound down the window an inch. Rachel had nudged Jayne to move on, to see the inch as a deterrent, not an invitation; his whole demeanour had suggested that he just wanted to be left alone with his dark thoughts, a concept alien to Jayne, yet one that Rachel recognised and understood.

He'd answered her questions with expressionless shrugs and turned down the invite to join them on their walk into town with an almost imperceptible shake of the head. So

Jayne had no choice but to open the back door of the car and climb in. Which is where she spent the next half an hour. Talking to the back of his head.

She'd once tamed a baby badger by leaving milk and bread out every night, crouching still in the shadow of their dustbin until it gradually relented, delaying its retreat back behind the shed by a few more seconds every day. Cracking Billy was slightly harder, but even he had a breaking point. A few days later when his dad had booked a repeat reading, Billy eventually surrendered and agreed to join them on their early-evening walk into town.

'You go, Jayne,' Rachel had nudged her in the back towards the off-licence door.

'No! Why? You go!'

'I can't, that's the bloke that knew my ID was fake last time.' The sisters had then both turned and looked at Billy, their looks of expectation fading as they realised that he barely looked all of his fifteen years, let alone three years older. 'Billy, tell Jayne to get the cider,' Rachel had ordered.

'Um, Jayne, I think you should get the booze, you look really old.'

'Gee, thanks Bill, way to win new friends.'

'Um, I, er, just meant that with your, you know, natural assets . . .' He'd broken off to mime two mountains jutting out from his chest, 'and your height, you're the best choice.'

'Well, thank you for the impromptu game of charades just there, but I'm actually the same height as Rachel.'

'Yeah,' Rachel had interrupted, 'but your hair adds about five inches. For the love of all that's holy Jayne, get the frickin' booze, and remember, 11th October 1982, 1982, 1982.'

Having confidently secured the contraband the three teens had headed to the park to drink their stash, lament their luck in being allocated such crap parental role models and to lie back on the grass and gaze up at the light pollution. As the days had turned into weeks, and aided by cheap strong cider, they had graduated from grunts to words, from vague teasing chat to whispered, confiding thoughts – the type that only teenagers have the right to voice out loud.

They were an unlikely threesome back then. Jayne with her jolly optimism and round John Lennon-in-the-Yoko phase glasses; Rachel with her morose moodiness, clad in the current season's must-haves – a walking oxymoron if ever there was one. And Billy. He had been one of those boys whose width hadn't yet expanded in line with his height. He was already over six feet tall, but his body had looked as if it had been stretched. His jeans were perpetually falling down, not through any desire to be a frontrunner in the fashion stakes, purely through the lack of any discernible body shape. He wore glasses too, but his were thick-rimmed like Buddy Holly, and his hair flicked over his collar, due entirely to the fact that the person who used to drag him to the barbers was no longer around.

He'd been a helpless bystander to his mother's swift decline. In the space of three months his home had gone to one filled with tantalising odours of dinner and the sound of Italian folk songs from his mother's native Sicily, to one where only whispering was permitted and the only fragrance was disinfectant and disease. The doctor had said that cancer doesn't have a smell, but Billy said it did. Before she'd passed away his mum had written him lots of little notes, each one clearly labelled in her neat handwriting, which had started to show signs of shakiness.

For every milestone in his life there was a corresponding envelope and in a fit of grief after returning from the crematorium he'd ripped open all the ones right up until his fortieth. He'd barricaded himself in his bedroom, away from the black-clad relations eating heat-direct-from-the-freezer sausage rolls and the unrelenting sound of their disrespectful chatter. He'd kept hearing little flashes of laughter rise up the stairs, which had made him so angry he'd punched a hole in the partition wall, so he'd moved his poster of Faye from Steps over it so his dad wouldn't see and try to talk to him about his feelings.

He'd been lying on his back when he'd told Jayne and Rachel this, deliberately looking up at the cloudless sky and not at them so they wouldn't see a small tear slowly run down his cheek and pool in his ear. But Jayne did.

It was edging towards the end of the summer and the three of them had shunned their usual spot in the park for a little cove between Torquay and Paignton that only the Devonshire locals knew about. They'd bought some crisps and sweet dessert wine that they were drinking from the only plastic cups that the Co-op had in stock, ironically, considering the turn the conversation had taken, with colourful party balloons on them.

Billy had flipped over then so he could see them better. In doing so he had given Jayne a tantalising glimpse of his taut stomach, tanned from a summer mainly wearing just board shorts. Her pulse had quickened, although she hadn't at the time realised why.

'Now here's a question,' he'd said, 'Why do you both call your mum Crystal and not Mum?'

Jayne quickly glanced at Rachel to see which one of them was going to respond first. The answer would be the same regardless of which sister spoke, but Jayne knew her version would be less peppered with expletives. Rachel's eyes were cast down, concentrating on her finger tracing patterns in the sand. 'Ironically, her name is actually Catherine,' Jayne said. 'But she changed it to Crystal when she was a teenager. Catherine the Clairvoyant doesn't really have the same ring to it, does it?' Jayne paused. 'But when we were really young, we were on this beach actually–'

'On the rare occasion she took us anywhere,' Rachel had interjected.

'Yes, on the handful of times we were allowed out of the cellar – Jesus, Rach, it wasn't that bad! Anyway, we were here, about six or seven years old and there was this bloke she fancied–'

'Sensing a pattern yet, Billy?' added Rachel, picking up clumps of sand and letting the small grains cascade gently between her fingers.

Jayne carried on, 'and one of us shouted 'Mum', and she went ape and said that from then on we had to call her Crystal and to say that she was our sister, and our real parents had died in a fire.'

'Jesus.' Jayne still remembered how Billy's eyes had grown wide with disbelief and how the cloak of pity that he'd worn around him ever since they'd known him then extended to include his two new friends too.

That summer was one of Jayne's favourite memories of adolescence. Actually, if she was completely honest, it was her favourite hands-down. She didn't have many happy recollections to choose from, so you could argue that it was all relative, but even taking that into the equation, the summer they had met Billy was a game-changer. She and Rachel had always avoided any outside interference from anyone else; they'd never explicitly talked about why they didn't try to integrate themselves with anyone else at school, or on their road, but they both knew why. Crystal's inability to relate to children was even more pronounced, if that was possible, if she didn't share some DNA with them.

Billy's detour into their lives was a timely reminder that there was life outside of their twindom. But as the cooler evenings started to seep in, Billy's dad was offered a job with his brother's brick-laying business in Slough.

Billy had ridden around on his bike the morning of the big move, despite them having said goodbye the evening before. 'I got this for you,' he'd mumbled, blushing. He'd held out a red and green friendship bracelet. 'I thought you might like it. Or not. You don't have to wear it. Bye.' He'd turned to go, swinging one leg over his battered BMX.

'Wait!' She'd shouted, 'Um, thanks Bill, it's really nice. I um, actually got you a book – it's only second-hand, but you once said that you liked Terry Pratchett and this is his new one. Wait here.' Jayne had run upstairs to get it from underneath her bed. It had been there for nearly three weeks, still wrapped in the rough, recycled paper bag it came in. She hadn't known how to cross over into the realm of present-giving-for-no-reason without it seeming odd, so she had carefully stowed it until she had figured out a way to give it to him without simultaneously combusting in morti-fied embarrassment. She'd bounded back down the stairs, flushed. 'Here,' she'd said, thrusting it into his hands.

'Thanks, Jayne, this is great. I'll start it in the car now. Um, say bye to Rachel too, and, um, well. Bye.'

He'd looked as though he was going to start peddling and then thought better of it; then he'd quickly leaned over and crushed his mouth onto hers. His tongue had darted frantically into her mouth, then out again, and then he was off, wobbling furiously down the cul-de-sac.

**

23

They'd suddenly stopped walking and were standing outside a restaurant. Jayne didn't need to look at its name or see the menu to know that it was Italian. Rows of Chianti bottles with wicker bases and eruptions of hard candle wax lined the windows, and you could glimpse the ubiquitous red-and-white-checked tablecloths beyond. Jayne tuned back into what Billy, *Will*, and Rachel were discussing. It seemed as though they'd decided that a celebratory drink deserved an upgrade to dinner.

'This suit?' asked Will, gesturing to the restaurant. In that moment he could have bought a can of dog food and three plastic spoons and she'd have nodded just as eagerly as she found herself doing now.

Chapter 3

It may have been the warmth of the room or more likely the potency of the house wine, but Jayne found herself starting to relax. Having been initially shocked into silence, she was making up for it now, gabbling and prompting, asking and touching. She couldn't stop touching him, actually couldn't stop herself. She was peppering every question by gratuitously resting her hand on his forearm, which he, in turn, instinctively flexed a little each time it happened.

Rachel was sitting back in her chair smiling. It had taken her four years to persuade Jayne to cut his friendship bracelet off her wrist, by which time it was all matted and the once-vibrant red and green had faded to a grimy sort of grey. 'Darling girl, it's time,' she'd said, approaching her sister with her nail clippers as they'd sat in Jayne's room in her hall of residence.

Wearing his friendship bracelet had become a sort of talisman, a constant reminder that someone once thought that she was okay enough to buy a bracelet for. But Rachel was right; the chances of getting anyone else to ever kiss her were greatly reduced while she sported a grubby shackle around her wrist, so it went in the bin. Although, somewhat predictably, it didn't stay there long; Jayne had waited for her sister to leave and then unearthed it under the two chicken-and-mushroom pot noodles they'd had for their dinner and popped it in her drawer.

Jayne had never been one of those girls whose sense of self worth depended on how many boys flirted with her. In fact, she'd be the first to admit that she wouldn't have a clue if someone was actually flirting with her anyway – then or now. A wink probably indicated an eyelash gone rogue, a smile was no doubt meant for the person standing behind her and cheesy one-liners just elicited a quiet contempt from her, not giggles. In the months, then years, after Billy left, all the other sixth-formers were busy padding out their bras at the same time as their UCAS forms. Jayne, meanwhile, began burying herself in books, while glancing at her decorated wrist each time she turned a page.

Now that Jayne had the power of sight, and hindsight, she could see the shell of fifteen-year-old Billy was encased in a more mature, infinitely more stylish, and devastatingly attractive package. Even as a teenager he'd had an effortless soulful look that achieved that rare quality of never looking contrived. Back then, he'd never been so desperate for peer approval that he'd made a conscious decision to fit in, he just managed to. He listened to the Rolling Stones because he genuinely liked their songs, not because it embodied any sort of retro cool. He was the opposite of many of the kids at school, who swaggered about with a giant red tongue emblazoned on their t-shirts, while not being able to name five of their songs in a pop quiz. He still gave off that air now; nothing about him seemed put on or unnatural. He laughed because he found something funny and smiled because he felt like smiling.

Jayne was making no effort to conceal her excitement; she'd even wriggled to the edge of her seat, sitting as far forward as she could without gravity making the chair tip. 'I can't believe this! Okay, start with how you got here,' she said, taking a bite of her garlic bread.

'Bus. Number 33.'

'No, you arse, why are you in London? What do you do here? Do you live here?'

Smiling at Jayne's impatience, he said, 'Yes I do, I moved here after catering college and then—'

'You're a chef! You always said you wanted to be – well done! Wow! That's awesome!'

'He's a chef, Jayne, not a nuclear physicist, let the poor man speak,' Rachel rolled her eyes at her sister, 'Sheesh!'

'Sorry, please continue.'

'Thank you,' he bowed his head in mock reverence. 'So anyway, after college, I came up here to work in a kitchen in a hotel, which was really hard work but I stuck at it for about three years because even though the head chef was a nightmare, he was also amazing. But then I realised that I was in London and I should be enjoying it rather than being stuck in a sweaty kitchen pan-searing scallops all night every night, so I went to work in a riverfront café in Richmond, which was cool, very trendy, and stayed there for another three or four years and then last year I opened up my own deli.' He paused, looking from one sister to the other, 'What about you guys? Rachel, is Vivienne Westwood threatened by your genius yet?'

'Sadly not,' Rachel ventured as she dipped a breadstick in balsamic, 'but I did go down the design route, kind of. I work for an interior-design firm, we do bars and restaurants. But not ones like this. More glass and metal and uncomfortable bar stools. Places where city types go to spend huge amounts of money on martinis.'

'She's underselling herself,' said Jayne, 'you should see some of the places she does, they're amazing – the one at the top of the Midas Tower was incredible.' Jayne turned briefly to her sister, 'It was a bit dark, though. It was really difficult to read while I waited for you.'

'Jayne, you are the only loser who would actually bring a book to a bar, so no offence, but that comment doesn't count.'

'A-hem.' Will reached into his jacket pocket and held his book aloft for Rachel to see.

'Oh. Okay, you two are the only losers.'

Will and Jayne shared a conspiratory smile, and then he

said, 'So Jayne, what do you do, apart from sneak in unap-proved, yet indisputably genius, books to classrooms?'

'I teach English and drama.' She couldn't help but sound a little apologetic at her career choice – here he was fulfilling a dream he'd had since he was fifteen, as was Rachel, kind of, and she spent her days specialising in riot control at a rowdy comprehensive. She clearly recalled sitting on the harbour wall in Brixham eating chips with Billy, announcing that she was either going to be an actress, a criminologist or a marine biologist. As a teenager you had all these fanciful ambitions that it never occurred to you weren't realistic.

Mrs Slade, the careers advisor, once went around the room asking each child in turn what they wanted to do in life. Claire Bishop, who now showed people to their tables at The Inn on The Green, home of the two-meals-for-a-tenner menu, was adamant that she was going to work for NASA, and if you'd have told a fifteen-year-old Paul Ackroyd that he would forgo a future in politics for a spot on the fast-track graduate training scheme at Morrisons' he'd have punched you in the face. Although, the fear of the act of violence returning to haunt him when he reached the hallowed door of Number Ten might have stopped him.

'But teaching's cool,' Will said, 'is it fun?'

'You know what, it actually really is. I did drama at uni, and for a while wanted to go into acting, and so I did a couple of crappy plays that no one went to apart from friends of the actors who were in them—'

'That's not true, you were really good!' Rachel interrupted. 'Especially that one where you were an old Italian widow – what was that called?'

'I was a Romany gypsy, and no, I wasn't, but thank you.' Jayne tipped her wine glass at her sister in a silent toast, 'and so then I set up a drama club for kids who otherwise would be stabbing each other in the neck with sharpened pencils, and loved it, so then did a teaching course and here I am, ten years later, deputy head of English and Drama at what *The Globe* once called 'The worst school in Britain'.'

'And is it?'

'No, not really, it's in a bad area, and the exam results aren't great, but apart from your usual handful of sociopaths that I should probably tip the police off about now to save time later, the kids are fab, and I love it.'

'That's really good,' Will leant back in his chair, 'I'm so pleased both of you found things you really like, and managed to get the hell away from Cruella. Sorry, am I allowed to call her that?'

'That's being kind, and not leaving Paignton was never an option!' spat Rachel. 'Can you imagine, if we hadn't got out when we did, Jayne would be working in one of those amusement arcades that only have 2p machines that move back and forwards and I'd be on the game.'

'At least you'd make money from sleeping with lots of men,' Jayne jibed, 'at the moment, you're doing it for free.'

Rachel pinched her sister's arm while pretending to pointedly ignore her comment. Focusing her attention solely on Will, she said, 'I haven't been back to Devon since leaving home at eighteen. Jayne goes back a bit more than me.'

'What about your grandparents, though? You guys were quite close to them weren't you?'

'Sadly Pops died a few years ago, but Granny's still fabulous,' Jayne smiled, 'We get her up to London a few times a year – she stays in town and we go for afternoon tea at the Savoy and to Sadler's Wells to see the ballet. Basically she keeps us cultured in our otherwise heathen existences. But what about you? How long did you live in Slough?'

'Ah, Slough. You know how in the credits for *The Office* it shows that big grey 1970s building on a busy roundabout? Well, that's the best bit of it. I'm not kidding. Dad still lives there with his new wife, Trish, but I was hatching an escape plan pretty much as soon as we arrived there.'

'So where do you live now?'

'Richmond, above the deli.'

'I love Richmond!' Jayne gushed, 'So you've been a couple of miles away from us all this time.'

'Indeed.' Will's eyes twinkled, 'I can't believe you guys are here – this is awesome.' The three of them sat in an easy silence, the kind that only happens when you're with people who know each other really well, and even though almost two decades had passed since their last moment of amiable peace, it didn't appear to matter at all.

They were still reminiscing and laughing long after their

plates of tiramisu and coffees had been finished. The waiters started upending chairs on all the empty tables around them. The message couldn't have been less overt had the staff all come out in their pyjamas.

'I think that's our cue. Subtle, aren't they?' Rachel said, thanking Will as he gallantly helped her back into her faux fur.

'So, do you live near here? I can walk you back if you like?'

Jayne quickly replied, 'that would be great,' trying to sound as nonchalant as a bottle and a half of thirteen per cent wine would allow, at the exact moment Rachel replied, 'No thanks, we'll be fine.' Sensing the eagerness, bordering on desperation, in her sister's voice, Rachel then countered, 'I mean, if it's not too much trouble . . .'

Jayne knew she'd said it before, and no doubt would do again, but as the three of them linked arms and started weaving drunkenly towards the door, she made a telepathic pledge to work really hard to stop all wars and be the catalyst for bringing about world peace if God could just manage to make Will fall in love with her. Again.

Chapter 4

She felt a bit guilty about asking Him for an escape route out of singledom when there were refugees and victims of human trafficking and lepers in the world. Were there still lepers in the world? Jayne drunkenly wondered as they reached the Thai takeaway they lived above. Rachel started fumbling with her keys in the lock when Will leaned forward and said quietly in Jayne's ear, 'I'd really like to see you again.'

Deliberately misunderstanding, to protect herself from looking stupid Jayne replied, 'That would be great, I'll check with Rachel when's good for her and let you know.' Rachel's back stayed resolutely facing them, even though she'd already turned the key in the lock.

Will, slightly chastened, swayed from foot to foot, 'Um, obviously I want to hang out with both of you sometime, but I actually meant just you. By yourself. With me.'

'Oh. Cool. Um, yes, that would be fine. I mean great. That would be wonderful. I'm free tomorrow.' She checked her watch and saw that it was after midnight, 'I mean today, tonight. Oh Jesus, does that make me sound really desperate? I mean I usually do have a really packed rock'n'roll schedule, but as luck would have it I've just had a cancellation,' she grinned sheepishly. 'And now I'm talking too much. You can retract your invitation at any time and I absolutely will not be offended.'

He smiled and ducked his head so his lips brushed her cheek 'Tonight sounds awesome. There's a little wine bar in Richmond called Magnum's, do you know it? How about we meet there at eight?'

Will was barely out of earshot when Rachel spun round on the doorstep screaming. 'O.M.G. He asked you out! You're going on a date with him! This is beyond brilliant!' Her eyes suddenly grew wide in horror, 'Oh God. You have absolutely nothing to wear. If only we were the same size, that new DVF shirtdress I bought last week would be perfect. Right. I'm meant to be doing Zumba with Marco but I'll tell him we're spending the day finding you something gorgeous, he'll understand.' She started typing furiously on her phone, 'I'll tell him to meet us at Selfridges at ten.'

'Ten? A.m.? On a Saturday? Seriously Rachel, I've got clothes, it's not as though I walk around with nothing on all day every day, I'll dig something out.'

'Dig something out? Please tell me you didn't just say that you would 'dig something out' for possibly the most important date you've ever had or ever likely to have? Jesus, Jayne, can you start taking this seriously?'

It had always been the same. When they were little Rachel used to lay out Jayne's clothes for her each morning to take away the risk of her making a huge sartorial error. Even Rachel's school uniform had been customised to the point of bearing little resemblance to its original incarnation. Her skirt had given two fingers to the school regulation of knee-length and she'd even cut her tie in half all the way down before carefully hemming it. Jayne had commented at the time that she'd looked like a country-and-western singer, but like Rachel had swiftly retorted, 'It's called fashion, Jayne. You wouldn't understand.' Which was true. It wasn't that she didn't care how she looked, but she'd always placed function above form in life, and warmth and comfort received greater prioritisation than colour or shape.

Jayne sighed. Resistance was futile. 'Fine, if it's so important to you to take me shopping and do a Gok, then okay, I will allow you and Marco to guide me through the maze of Selfridges, but if either of you make any attempt to manhandle me into dresses or make any reference to my 'bangers', I'm walking out and you can get another hobby.'

'Deal.' Her phone pinged. *I'm there like a bear. Mxx*

Dear Lord, what had she let herself in for? Thankfully Jayne had had a lifetime of dealing with Rachel, and Marco was the exact replica of her, right down to their shared love of the naked male anatomy. They'd felt a gravitational pull towards each other during design college somewhere between the module on concealing air-conditioning vents and the importance of layering textures in your soft furnishings. Back then he was called Mark, before the run-of-the-mill 'k' was dropped in favour of the most exotic 'co'.

Learning the art of making friends at the age of nineteen was a new one for both of the sisters but Rachel, with her chemically straightened afro cut into an angular black bob, heavily rimmed kohl eyes and a scowl that said, 'what the hell do *you* want?' permanently inked on her face, found it harder.

Jayne had tried to get her to smile encouragingly or even just tone down the stare that said: 'I could kill you with one sarcastic put-down'. Rachel had howled with mirth when Jayne suggested that 'a stranger was just a friend she hadn't met yet', which made her silently vow to stop reading the slogans on t-shirts and memorising them for future repetition. Rachel wasn't being deliberately rude or obtuse, though, the truth was she was just fiercely independent. Their upbringing had turned Jayne into an apologetic people-pleaser and given Rachel an almost impenetrable body armour.

Jayne had also spent most of her university life with her nose touching her textbooks, but for her it was borne partly out of love for her subject and more than she would ever admit because it was the first time she wasn't in the same class as Rachel. They'd never had to experience that moment where you walk into a new classroom and have to do the dreaded scan to see where the empty places were and who looked the least-offensive person to sit by, because they'd always been greeted by the other one with one hand in the air waving and the other firmly planted on the seat next to them, mouthing 'saved' at anyone that dared to attempt to sit down.

Everyone always assumed that being a twin meant that you had this invisible bubble sealed around you that repelled and reflected any outside interference, and this was sort of true, it does take a very special kind of person to see a crack and squeeze into it, and boy, was Mark/co persistent. When Rachel called her sister excitedly on her way home one day in her second term to say that she'd met this guy called Mark and they were going to see one of his friends play in a band that night at a random bar in Clapham, Jayne couldn't have been more surprised. Nice surprised. Not a little bit jealous in the least. Nope, not her. Good on Rachel. And Mark. She had hoped they were very happy together.

Thankfully this level of 'nicely surprised' soon gave way to 'actually nicely surprised' because Marco became the confidante that Rachel always wanted Jayne to be. It meant that she turned to him to discuss the guest editorship of the latest issue of *Wallpaper* and whether perspex platforms were going to make a comeback. Jayne had very little to contribute on either of these topics, so Marco being around actually worked in everyone's favour.

*

How Jayne escaped relatively unscathed from the morning's shopping she had no idea – in fact she was pretty certain Rachel and Marco would still be standing outside the changing room suggesting that if she leant forward, she could squeeze into the bodycon dress a little easier, had she not called time on the whole charade at about three. Jayne had got so bored she'd even resorted to taking armfuls of clothes into the cubicle with her, locking the door and then sitting in the corner playing solitaire on her mobile pretending to change, while her personal shoppers shouted out encouraging comments and questions, such as 'what does the teal one look like?' To which she'd replied things like, 'what's teal?' while putting a three of clubs on top of a four of hearts.

They'd finally all decided that skinny jeans were not made for her – Jayne knew this after trying one pair on; why she had to try on a further three pairs was beyond her, 'They're different brands, so different cuts,' was Marco's reasoning, but she thought the clue was in the name. But the outfit that finally raised a smile from Rachel, jazz hands from Marco and an 'Hallelujah' from Jayne was a long maxi dress with a swirly paisley print in oranges and reds, which, according to Rachel, was very 'retro-chic' which was, apparently, a good thing.

That evening she teamed her new purchase with her failsafe denim jacket that had been a faithful staple of her wardrobe for a decade, big hoop earrings and, miracles of miracles, hair that seemed to instinctively know that it had to behave itself, and she was ready to go.

'You look lush, Jayne, really lush.' Rachel stood to give her a hug and Marco gave her a big thumbs-up from the sofa, where he was lounging, throwing cashews into his open mouth. 'If you're not coming home tonight, text me.'

'Shut up, like that's going to happen. It's not even a *date* date. Just two friends talking about old times. Together. In a friendly, platonic, keeping-clothes-on kind of way.'

'Oh okay. I'll come too then, shall I?' Rachel said mischievously.

'Don't you bloody dare. See you later!'

He was already sitting at the bar when Jayne walked in, and spotting her loitering at the door, gave a little salute. Oh God, he was gorgeous. She had a flashback to the restaurant last night, even once she had the gift of 20/20 vision, she'd been so overwhelmed with the reality of who he was she hadn't fully comprehended quite how absolutely beautiful he was. The gaunt, lanky features of fifteen-year-old Billy had mellowed and softened, and thankfully his dark straggly mullet had since been ceremoniously lopped off. Even his childlike nickname had morphed into a more mature moniker that suited his new broad shoulders and strong silhouette. The ridiculously blue eyes that had once been hidden behind a centimetre-thick piece of glass were now dancing. He stood up as Jayne approached him

– gentlemanly too, she thought – and he towered over her, which, as she was just shy of six foot herself, almost never happened.

'Hey you.'

'Hey.'

There was a semi-awkward moment where they both weighed up how to add an element of tactility to the greeting. Kiss, hug, both? Both it was. Excellent.

'So we don't see each other in eighteen years and then twice in twenty-four hours?' He helped her shrug off her coat and hang it on the back of her chair. He even waited until she sat down to perch back up on the stool himself. 'I ordered a bottle of Prosecco to celebrate. I know it's essentially poor man's fizz, but I thought this moment warranted something sparkly, and I am, lamentably, a poor man.'

Jayne grinned to put him at ease, and also to give her mouth something to do, 'bubbles are bubbles to me, and that sounds super.' Super? *Super?* Jesus, Jayne, why not just order lashings and lashings of ginger ale and be done with it.

After returning the bottle to the ice bucket on the bar he turned and held out a glass for her. 'Here you go, Madam.'

'Cheers, here's to . . . erm . . . old friends?'

'Old friends. And new beginnings.' They tapped glasses, 'Um, did that sound as cheesy as I think it did?'

Thankful that the first laugh of the night was aimed at his awkwardness and not hers, she giggled, 'yes, a little bit, but I know what you mean.' She could see his neck and cheeks colouring a little – if she didn't know better she would say that he was nervous, which was ridiculous, he couldn't be. That would be like Heidi Klum in awe at meeting Meatloaf. Rachel said she did this too much, exaggerate her flaws for comedic effect, and she knew she was right. Obviously she didn't actually resemble Meatloaf, that would be incredibly unfortunate, but she was also fairly realistic that neither, sadly, would she ever be mistaken for a close, or even distant, relative of Ms Klum's. Except perhaps in one of her annual over-the-top Halloween costumes. See? I did it again, Jayne thought.

'So,' Will said finally, taking a Dutch courage sip, 'How were the last nineteen hours since I last saw you?' Jayne started regaling him with the highlights of her day spent with the fashion police and soon they were both laughing, which proved to be quite difficult while balancing precariously on a barstool that was about half the width of her behind.

Thankfully, before too long a couple vacated the battered leather Chesterfield that was nestled at the end of the bar, so they could continue their inane banter in more comfort. They sat alongside each other, both turned inwards, he stretched his arm along the back of the sofa and Jayne kept getting whiffs of a heady combination of expensive aftershave that almost masked his coconut shampoo, and his natural masculine muskiness that made her want to run her tongue all over his face. She didn't, though. Not yet.

He told her all about his day in the deli over a sharing platter of fried seafood, giving her enlightened observations on all the regulars that came in for a chat and a slab of stinky Italian cheese. It seemed to Jayne as if he'd built up a proper little community around his shop; she had no doubt that the quality of his produce was outstanding, but she was also absolutely certain that the Bugaboo Brigade found other reasons for choosing his establishment as their regular low-fat latte haunt – less to do with what was on the counter and more to do with what was behind it. He seemed totally oblivious to his own personal merits, though, just delighted that his carefully sourced prosciutto was garnering such a following. Bless him.

'There's this old dude called Bob the Boat because he lives on a canal barge,'

'And his name is Bob?' Jayne helpfully interjected.

'Exactamondo. And by all accounts he was this proper Romeo back in the day, with a little black book of women that was not very little. He's hilarious. He's over eighty and is always entertaining different 'companions' on his barge – so he comes in for exotic ingredients for aphrodisiac canapés, dirty sod.'

'Good on him.'

'That's what I thought.' Will raised his glass, 'Here's to Bob the Boat, and all who allow him to sail in them.'

'Eugh! That's gross! You're gross.'

He paused for a moment, studying his glass before looking sideways at Jayne. He reached over to tuck a stray curl behind her ear and said quietly, 'And you're beautiful. I thought it then, and I think it now.'

They half-walked, half-ran, doing a funny sort of power walk that Jayne had only ever seen lycra-bottomed mums with pushchairs and wrist weights doing along the towpath. Quickly weaving in and out of people meandering slowly along the pavement, Jayne didn't know who was pulling whom along, they both seemed equally eager to reach their destination.

As soon as the door to his flat slammed behind them they'd collapsed on the stairs, ripping at each other's jackets, buttons and belts. His fingers were in her hair, then tilting her chin so his lips could run around her neck, his teeth gently biting her earlobes. Her mouth desperately searched out his and their lips locked as they fumbled out of their clothes. With their tongues still heatedly circling each others' Will kicked off his shoes so he could wriggle out of his jeans, while Jayne reached behind her and unlocked her bra. Will gasped and pushed her breasts together. He buried his face in between them and they both laughed.

'We could actually go upstairs?' He murmured into her chest.

'No, let's stay here. I've never made love on the stairs before.'

'Are we about to make love ?'

'It certainly looks that way. Now stop talking.'

Chapter 5

Jayne backed away and looked suspiciously at the beige-green sludge that Will was offering to her on an outstretched spoon. 'Try this.'

'What is it?' she said gingerly, edging a little closer, but still not fully entering into the spirit of the game.

'Elderflower and pear chutney. I don't know if I've got the right amount of juniper berries in it or not. What do you think?'

Cautiously she allowed the tip of the spoon to touch her lips, 'Oh my days, Will, that's amazing,' she opened her mouth wide so he could put the whole spoon in. 'You need to do something about the aesthetics, though, because it looks like snot.'

'Thanks for that, sweetheart, beautifully put. I might put that on the label as its tagline – *Looks like phlegm but tastes delicious.*'

'There's something to be said for honesty in advertising. Can I have another spoonful?' she said leaning in.

'No. You're procrastinating, go to parents' evening.'

'Don't make me,' she whined, laying her head on his shoulder. 'I can't cope with the angry stage mums no doubt already forming a line to abuse me for not picking their kids for the main parts in the play. Can't I stay here and eat chutney all evening with you? *Please?*'

He kissed her on the top of her head, momentarily flattening the wild black ringlets that fizzed out at right angles in every direction. He gave her bottom a playful swat. 'Go. Go and be charming, be beguiling, and lie through your teeth as to why their cherished offspring didn't make the cut. I, meanwhile, am going to attempt to master a pumpkin, orange and chilli marmalade. I may save you some if you're good.' He started humming the same jaunty tune he always did when he was concocting culinary brilliance. 'Call me if you're done by ten and I'll come and join you in the pub.'

Despite her procrastinations, which she reasoned were completely understandable – who wouldn't want to spend their evening perched on a kitchen stool being spoon-fed tenderly invented recipes from the love of their life – Jayne actually quite enjoyed parents' evenings. Admittedly nothing really prepared her for one parent a couple of years ago sticking their iPhone into her face saying 'Can you say again for the tape how Mia can improve her comprehension skills?' Or the dad who kept rolling his eyes and making quack-quack movements with his hands whenever his wife was talking – she could tell he was a real keeper.

The hubbub of noise emanating from the hall could be heard from the adjacent staff room, which was packed with every member from each faculty. Jayne nodded, waved and smiled her way through the throng to the kettle, where Abi stood waiting for her, two mugs of extra-strong Nescafé in her hands. She handed Jayne the one saying 'Keep Calm, It's Almost Summer'. They'd joined the school at the same time almost ten years ago, both of them fresh from finishing their PGCEs, sporting wide Bambi-eyes and proudly clutching their meticulously filled-in and highlighted lesson plans with noticeably shaking hands. Fast-forward a decade and the hopefulness that they had then was still there, despite an unhealthy dose of hard-earned cynicism trying its best to erode it.

Abi blew across the top of her coffee and said, 'So what's it to be this time?'

'I was thinking about that on the way over here. I think Queen.'

'As in your son is one?'

Jayne laughed and spilt a bit of coffee on her shirt, 'Oh no! Quick give me a tissue!' She arranged her scarf over the damp patch of brown and shrugged, 'That'll do. Right, what's mine?' They'd devised this game to get them through the early years of parents' evenings to keep the terror at bay and it had become a rather un-PC ritual they did every term now.

'Eiffel Tower.'

'Bugger off. I can't just drop in the words Eiffel Tower when I'm talking about year eight English. Make it an easier one.

'Okay . . . what about ice skating?'

'Wow, you're on fire tonight. Okay, fine. Ice skating.'

They took their seats at adjacent tables in the hall and, despite the parents all having booked their allotted ten minutes with each teacher, there was already a jostling crowd gathering in front of both of them.

A few parents in, Jayne remembered the task in hand. 'Right then, okay, well, Sophie did very well on the Anne Frank project, some very insightful creative writing on the diary excerpts, which gained her a B+, which was excellent.'

'Why didn't she get an A?'

'Well, I like to think that grading projects is like judging an ice-skating competition,' Jayne heard a muffled snort from the next table, 'every technical aspect has its own mark and there are floating marks for added flair and flourishes, so in that respect, B+ was the end result. So all in all, very good effort.'

Bidding a weary farewell to the last parents, the two teachers sat back in their chairs, mentally exhausted. 'Jeez, how many different ways can you cover up the fact that you haven't got the faintest idea who their child is?'

Abi's acerbic comments delivered with her singsong Irish accent made Jayne laugh every time. The first time they'd met was the interview day for the new intake of NQTs. Abi had run into the crowded classroom late, the door slamming behind her, punctuating her arrival, her dishevelled hair piled high on her head with a colourful scarf wrapped around it. She'd hurried to the empty seat next to Jayne and after a time whispered, 'I'm going for the art job – please tell me you're not or I can't be your friend.'

'You're safe, and so is our friendship,' Jayne whispered, 'I'm English.'

'That's unfortunate, but you shouldn't be too hard on yourself,' she had muttered back, without a hint of sarcasm.

Jayne had tried hard to suppress a giggle and failed. 'Is something funny?' barked the deputy head who was in the middle of her surprisingly unwelcoming welcome speech. Abi had surreptitiously winked at Jayne after they'd shaken their heads in unison and Jayne knew that wasn't the last time this barmy woman from County Mayo would get her in trouble.

In the summer holiday after their terrifying first year had ended, she'd taken Jayne back to Ireland to decompress for a few weeks. Her family were from this gorgeous little town on the banks of the River Carrowbeg called Westport that was bathed in the shadow of the Croagh Patrick Mountain. It was so beautiful that a big-shot Hollywood director visiting Ireland to discover his ancestry had decreed it was the perfect setting for his upcoming rom-com, which even before the first scene was filmed was already being hailed as the hit of the following summer.

Abi had told Jayne on the ferry over that the whole town, 'nay, the whole county, was excited beyond belief to have this happen, then a week into filming they realised it was the biggest load of ball-ache that ever was.' But on the flip-side, her parents, who were born and bred in Mayo, had rented out their two spare rooms to movie extras and had made enough to finally leave Ireland for the first time and go on a cruise around the Greek Islands. 'Every cloud, Abigail, is sewn with a lining of silver thread,' her mother had poetically said at the time.

It was the perfect way to unwind after three terms of permanent heart palpitations. They had spent their days sleeping, eating breakfasts cooked by the mother Jayne wished she'd had and drinking unfancy coffee on the river-front promenade. Their evenings invariably ended up with them seven sheets to the wind singing in the lively Matt Malloy's in the town centre. Everyone knew Abi, welcoming her back to the town with a hearty wave or heartfelt hug, and as a friend of hers – albeit an English one – Jayne wasn't denied the odd embrace either.

'It would have been so fabulous to grow up here, where everyone looks out for one another,' Jayne had said wistfully one afternoon as they sat on a bench overlooking the river, eating little pots of ice cream, that had flecks of real vanilla seeds in it, none of your supermarket own-brand impersonal white tub for the County Mayo folks.

'Aye, it's alright when you're being good, but as soon as you decide you want a bit of fun, your mam knows about it before you've even done anything.' As brilliantly timed evidence, the butcher from the shop opposite stood in his doorway and shouted across the road, 'Abigail Sheeran, can ye tell ya mammy we've got some lovely steaks in for your da's supper?'

Abi had raised her hand and nodded her assent, before turning to Jayne and muttering, 'Exactly how many days until we bugger off back to London's wonderful anonymity, where nobody cares what the hell you're having for your dinner?'

Jayne had leaned her head back on the bench, closed her eyes and allowed the warm afternoon sun to bathe her face, 'Seriously, enjoy it, if we'd have gone to my mum's we'd be sitting in the dark with the curtains closed to avoid either the landlord collecting rent or cajoled into joining a séance or something.'

Jayne smiled at the memory of that summer as she watched Abi gather up her papers on her desk and stuff them into her large straw bag.

'Why are you grinning like an idiot?' Abi said accusingly, looking up.

'Nothing, nothing at all. Right, are we going for a drink?'

Jayne paused, 'Will said he might join us . . .'

'What? How's he going to do that if he's not real?' Abi was convinced that Will was a figment of Jayne's imagination, carefully crafted so she didn't have to go on any more soul-murdering blind dates with men that she described as 'perfect apart from [insert interchangeable disgusting trait here]'.

Jayne didn't know why she'd delayed introducing Will to any of her friends, and both him and they were starting to question her motives. She supposed the truth was, because she'd never really had a boyfriend before, she had no idea how to share him. Rachel imagined that it all stemmed back to the two of them pitching themselves against the world, and with Will, Jayne had fallen into the same default setting. She didn't quite know exactly how being part of a couple could transfer to being part of a couple in a crowd of people.

It had been six months and so far she'd sidestepped the inevitable introductions, but he'd recently brought up the subject of them moving in together – albeit carefully shrouded in a discussion about 'unnecessary outgoings'. He'd even casually mentioned that he'd been thinking that a three bedroom flat was too big for a man on his own . . . he might have to bring in two lodgers . . . oh hang on . . . He'd delivered this speech in a nonchalantly informal non-rehearsed way, that smacked completely of someone who had very much rehearsed it, very formally, in front of a mirror.

Jayne hadn't really answered yet, just giving nonchalant nods and saying that she'd talk to Rachel, whilst inside she was screaming 'Hell to the Yes!'

'I thought I told you Abi, he's real, but just invisible.'

'Aye, so you did. So the only way we'll know he's there is if he pees on the floor and we see a puddle?'

'Exactly. So you're very lucky you're not wearing your expensive LK Bennett heels this evening as they'd be absolutely ruined by my boyfriend's wee.' Jayne tried to dodge the register of parents' names that Abi had deftly rolled up and was aiming at her best friend's head. 'Come on then, the Pitcher & Piano?'

Soaking from the rain outside, Abi and Jayne both stood in the doorway of the pub, shaking themselves like wet Labradors, when Abi looked up and whispered, 'Jesus, Mary and Joseph, Jayne, three o'clock.'

Jayne was bent over the welcome mat scrunching her hair up, 'What?' she shouted.

Abi started talking out of the corner of her mouth. 'Look at your three o'clock, he's like Colin Farrell mixed with David Gandy, and oh Jesus, he's waving. Jayne, I love you with all my heart, I do, but if he asks to buy me a drink, you have to bugger off quickly.'

Jayne straightened up and looked to where Abi was staring. 'Stop perving, you moron, that's Will.'

There was already an opened bottle of wine and three glasses on the table and he stood up as they walked over,

'Hey baby,' he leant over and kissed Jayne on the lips, then turned and put out his hand and said with his eyes twinkling mischievously, 'You must be Abi. I was starting to think that you were pretend. Either that, or Jayne was having an affair every time she said she was going out with you.'

Abi pumped his hand up and down and grinned, 'It was the latter, I'm afraid, but I managed to persuade her to give the other fella up and to give you a chance.'

The women started to regale Will with the highlights of the evening, and one bottle turned into two, which turned into three. And then he excused himself and headed to the loos. As soon as he was barely out of earshot, Abi spun round, 'You're kidding me? Now I know why you've hidden him away. Jeez, Jayne, I'm speechless, what an awesome guy. Marry him. Marry him now, and have babies that look like supermodels, but healthier versions. Oh my God, he's amazing, and so funny, and lovely, and he's totally besotted with you, he can't take his eyes off you.' She shook her head, 'Wow, I'm speechless.'

'So you keep saying, which is odd considering the amount you're talking. Oi, enough with the hitting!'

'Girls, girls, take it outside,' Will said with a smile as he moved the table a bit so he could squeeze back onto his bench. 'You're meant to be respectable members of society, moulding our young, inspiring youthful minds.'

'That is exactly what we're supposed to do, Will, you're

right,' Abi nodded, 'but instead I spend most of my time washing paint off walls and placating tearful life models because my very immature A-level class think it's okay to laugh and point and shout out, 'you've got a tiny wiener.' Little bastards. Anyway, Jayne tells me you run your own deli? That's got to be fun?'

'Yeah, I really love it,' he replied, picking up a Budweiser beer mat and flipping it idly between his fingers, 'I was a chef and didn't really get much of a chance to experiment much and make what I wanted to make, so this way I can potter around in our kitchen and thankfully people seem to like it and want to buy it, although I don't know if I'll ever get rich selling five-quid pots of chutney.'

Even though most people would think that his devastating dimples were reason enough for Jayne's infatuation, this was the side of Will that she loved – his modesty and complete lack of arrogance. He even seemed completely oblivious to the second-takes he commanded wherever he went, but she always spotted them and then basked in the envious staring that happened every time he kissed her or held her hand.

Rachel had asked her quite a few times if it bothered her, the reaction he got from women. The first time Rachel had seen it for herself was in a dry-cleaners, of all places – not that they were in the habit of accompanying him to do his laundry, that would be weird – but they were walking down Richmond High Street to get a coffee and he popped into the dry-cleaners to pick up a few shirts and came out all chuffed when the fawning woman behind the counter waived his bill. He couldn't understand why, thinking that it must be 'free-cleaning Friday' or something ridiculous like that, and then Rachel, ever the diplomat, said, 'it's because she thinks you're smoking.'

'Smoking what?' he'd even asked naively, before he had realised what she meant and blushed furiously. He'd ironed his shirts himself ever since.

'Do you do catering as well?' Abi leant in, her chin on her palm, pretending to be interested in the finer points of deli-management.

'Nah, I did think about it, but it's just me at the moment and that would mean taking someone else on, and I can't do that until it makes more money, which ironically, I can't do until I take someone else on, so I'm a little bit buggered either way. Jayne suggested hosting a couple of book clubs a week, and that's become really popular, so I do the catering for those, but that's just plates of nibbles really.'

'We also put a little stand in the deli recently with second-hand books on, where you leave one and take one, so it's sort of like an informal lending library,' Jayne added, 'It just encourages people to spend a bit longer in the shop and have something to eat with their coffee.'

'Except the only people to really use it are us and that homeless bloke that sits outside the station who comes in every week to get a book for free.'

'Richard?' Jayne replied, 'He does love his science fiction. Bless him.'

'But in answer to your question, I do sell hampers and stuff for Christmas, you know with some handmade biscuits, cheeses and chutneys, they're always a nice little earner, and I was thinking about doing Valentine's hampers, so you can pick up a little basket of stuff, with maybe a bottle of bubbly in it too and go straight to the river or the park for a picnic.'

'Awww, that's lovely – is that what you're going to do for me?' Jayne asked.

'No, darling, that's what you're going to do for me.'

'Dammit,' Jayne thumped the table sighing melodramatically, 'I've just put a deposit on a troop of singing dwarves who paint themselves blue and pretend to be smurfs. Do you not want that? I wish you'd said, it cost me a fortune.'

'No, that sounds much better than a crappy romantic picnic, champagne is so last year anyway, whereas dwarves never go out of fashion.' He put his arm around Jayne's neck and pulled her close to him before planting a kiss on her forehead.

Jayne grinned as Abi gave a low whistle and said, 'Wow, you two really are made for each other. You're both bonkers.'

Chapter 6

Rachel held her hair-straighteners in mid-air, steam curling softly upwards. 'He wants us to move in with him?' She paused. 'Both of us?'

'Yes, as lodgers. Sort of. He's got two spare rooms and is a bit short of cash, and thought we might prefer to live in Richmond rather than Twickenham – the commute's shorter for both of us and the deli's downstairs so we'd always have food, and he can cook for us, so no more nasty kebabs, and I stay round there most of the time anyway, and I don't want you to be lonely here by yourself, and . . . and . . . I sort of love him. Sort of.'

Rachel started running her GHDs through the length of her bob again, and then smiled at their reflections in the mirror. 'That sounds bloody lovely. Say yes.'

Two weeks later the sisters sat in the middle of their living room with a screw-top bottle of wine, surveying the emptiness that surrounded them. They'd spent most of the day painstakingly peeling blu-tac off the walls where a map of the world and some Jack Vetriano prints had once been. Their drawers and cupboards had been squashed into brown boxes labelled STUFF R and STUFF J and yet neither of them was in any hurry to lock the door for the last time.

This flat had been the place of their dreams once; the refuge that they'd talked about since their early teens. It was more than just a place to live for them; it was a symbol of their success. Whenever Jayne had passed a new shop with the signage being hoisted up outside, she'd always pictured the hope of the new owners, the moment when they would gather their family and friends outside on the day of opening and proudly unveil the shop front, switching on the lights to delighted ahhs and oohs, to backslapping and chinks of plastic glasses and short speeches about dreams being fulfilled and new beginnings. This poky flat above a take-away was that place for the Brady twins. On the day they moved in, they'd sat in exactly the same position on the floor, surrounded by very similar boxes, with another screw-top bottle of wine, elatedly rejoicing their escape from a future of no potential.

Moving to Will's home was a mere postcode upgrade for Rachel, but for Jayne it was huge. Much like those faith-filled shopkeepers who only had a vague plan and blind optimism to help them sleep at night, she mentally ricocheted between gung-ho whooping at her good fortune and rocking back and forth, head in hands, wondering whether she was making a monumental mistake.

It wasn't that she doubted Will in any way – she knew he was pretty darn perfect from that first cider-swilling afternoon in the park when they were fifteen, but she couldn't help feeling that things like this didn't happen to people like her. Surely it would only be a matter of time before the bubble burst, or the other shoe dropped, or some equally baffling phrase that describes the moment it all goes wrong.

But while Jayne waited for that to happen, they had some shopping to do. And that's how the three new housemates found themselves in Ikea on a Friday night negotiating over how many tea lights is too many and what they were going to put in the hundreds of box photo frames that were stacked in the trolley. Family photos were overruled by all of them on the reasoning of not wanting to be reminded of their genetic origins – through shame and the desire to forget them for the girls, while Will was content keeping his own photos in his memory box under his bed. He didn't need to walk past pictures of his parents in the hallway every day to know they were with him. So the consensus was to leave much of the décor up to Rachel, who was describing a jigsaw effect she wanted to create by painting a huge abstract, and cutting it up into rectangles that fitted into each individual frame, 'art that reminds us to look at the big picture,' she'd said, or something like that.

'And a peace lily, we definitely need one of them.' Will said as he wedged a rather sorry-looking plant into the gap between a new toilet brush and a set of six wooden hangers.

'How the mighty have fallen.' Rachel yawned, automatically picking up a white wicker basket and tossing it in. 'It's Friday night, people. Friday night. I hope this isn't an indicator of what life with you will be like, Will, because, truth be told, I don't think I can cope with this level of hedonism.'

'I wanted to warn you quite how close to the edge I live, but neither of you would have believed me.' Will put his hand on top of Jayne's as she steered the trolley past the woks. 'And if you both behave, I may well treat you to a £3 plate of Swedish meatballs.'

Later that night Will and Jayne were sprawled on his old leather sofa – which was now beautifully adorned with vibrant throws – and Rachel was slumped in a newly acquired Fatboy beanbag when Jayne judged the moment to be right to casually mention that she was heading down to Devon to see their granny the following Saturday and would anyone like to join her. By anyone she meant both of them. By would they *like* to join her, she meant they *would* join her. From the stunned silence that ensued you would have thought she'd said, 'so I was thinking of draping myself in a Union Jack and going camping in the mountainous region between Pakistan and Afghanistan – is anyone keen on tagging along?'

Will purposely didn't move his eyes from the television, he had very little inclination to revisit the place where his last days with his mum were played out. 'Um . . . next weekend? Saturday's my busiest day in the shop, um . . . sorry, sweetheart, you know I'd love to otherwise.'

'It's okay, I thought of that and Abi said she wouldn't mind holding the fort for the day.'

'Oh. Well the pricing system's quite complicated and the till is a bastard to work if you don't know how.' He shrugged apologetically, 'Sorry, darling.'

'She's coming round on Wednesday after work so you can show her how it all works. Next excuse?' Jayne turned to Rachel, 'Oi, sharer of the womb, you're very quiet over there.'

'Why the hell do you want to go back down there again? Weren't you only there a few weeks ago?'

'It was nearly a year ago and Granny sounded a bit quiet on the phone earlier, so I just thought us all going down would cheer her up, and she always asks what you're up to, and she hasn't met Will yet, and I thought it might be nice.'

'Nice? Don't get me wrong, Granny's a sweetheart, but I Skype her every week. I don't feel the need to physically be breathing the same air as her to fully bond.'

'So I'm going alone, then.' Jayne looked from her boyfriend to her sister, 'By myself. Unaccompanied. Flying solo. Bereft of company. Deserted. Abandoned–'

'Oh for the love of all that's holy, I'll come if that will shut you up!' Rachel growled. 'Will, you're coming too. No arguments. If I've got to do this, you're not getting out of it.'

'Won't it take ages to get down there?' Will asked.

'Three hours or so, or we could stay over somewhere – make a weekend of it?' Jayne said.

Rachel and Will both chimed a resounding, 'No!' completely in sync.

Despite Jayne putting on re-runs of *Doc Martin* to get them all in the mood for a spot of South West fun and games, a bleak depression had descended over the spruced-up lounge, which even the fourteen new Summer Fruits-scented candles couldn't disguise.

Today in Talk Devon we are discussing the frightening topic of a new wave of seagulls that are plaguing the seafronts of South Devon, and having a devastating effect on the profits of beachfront ice-cream sellers. We have Keith on the line from Salcombe. Keith, are you there . . .?

Will idly flicked the volume down on the radio.

'What are you doing?' Jayne yelped, reaching for the dial, 'I want to hear about the killer gulls.'

'You can talk the girl out of Devon, but you can't take Devon out of the girl,' laughed Will. 'It's great, though, a whole phone-in for debating ice cream-loving birds. I would say it's a slow-news day, but I guess this is headline-making stuff down here.'

'Don't come over all townie on us Will Scarlet, you were a Devon boy for a while too, don't forget.'

As the car took the exit at Newton Abbot and began the

all-too-familiar descent along the coastal road towards Pine Grove Residential Home for the Elderly, it was as though someone had pressed the mute button – the mood in the car changed from jovial and jocular to silent and reflective. Rachel and Jayne were staring out of the windows, taking in the familiar sights that they'd grown up with – the sea to their right, the numerous B&Bs to their left, with comedy names like Dunromin and ambitious ones like Water's Edge.

Small shabby hotels with paint peeling and no-smoking stickers in the windows along with AA rosettes from the 1980s and sad sun-faded signs that permanently said 'vacancies' flashed past. Boards outside advertised en-suites and colour TVs, the height of decadence once, and still perhaps a source of misplaced pride for the host. Occasionally you'd get a better class of bed and breakfast, one that deigned to call itself a 'boutique hotel'. These had wi-fi and individually decorated rooms, which were sometimes even themed, because apparently there are people who want to pay money to come to the English Riviera and stay in a suite called *Out of Africa*. 'Cheaper than Kenya and not as far,' one sign read.

Growing up in a seaside town was a strange experience, Jayne thought. Your town is almost like a timeshare – wholly yours for the crappy part of the year and handed over to coach-trippers as soon as the sun shines. They always felt slightly superior to the grockles – as they called them then – watching them squealing while paddling their pasty white legs in the sea or queuing up for overpriced aniseed balls and fizzy cola bottles in the pick-n-mix at The Pavilion in Torquay. Getting their children's faces captured in pastels by the resident artist sitting on the steps, who worked in Lidl during the winter months. It's funny how a holidaymaker's experience of the town you've lived all your life in is so different to your reality. Not once in eighteen years did Jayne buy a pick-n-mix bag of sweets, or get her portrait done.

Pine Grove was an imposing, lavender-clad manor house that had once been a beautiful private home before the owners realised in the 1990s that they had wildly underestimated the upkeep costs of such a grand property and sold it to some eager-eyed developers for bulging pots of cash. Home now to twenty of the area's most affluent pensioners, it was considered The Place to end your days. Morbidly, much excitement was felt among families on the waiting list whenever news of a resident's demise hit the grapevine.

Helen Brady, the twins' grandmother, was the daughter of a wealthy fishing family that owned twenty of the area's trawlers. After her father's death in the Second World War, her new husband, Tom, took over the business. He'd been one of the 'lucky' ones, making that coveted return journey from France, albeit not as complete, physically or mentally, as he had been when he'd left just days after their wedding. He'd suffered the indignity of having tiny shards of shrapnel embed themselves in his thigh and groin, making him, at the age of twenty, in all likelihood infertile. Helen had borne the news with characteristic fortitude. Twenty years later, just as she was coming to terms with early signs of the menopause, the family doctor had told her the news that she was, in fact, expecting a baby.

Helen and Tom had enjoyed a privileged life in Torquay, living in a large villa that boasted expansive views across the whole of Tor Bay. But even though Helen had never intimated such a thing – she wouldn't – her granddaughters knew that it must have come as something of a shock when her eighteen-year-old daughter interrupted her quiet idyll by introducing a pair of screaming babies into the equation.

Thankfully their grandparents had stoically risen to the challenge of being the only dependable constant in their drama-filled world. Ever ready to practise spellings, subtly prise off stained uniforms to quietly launder them, listen to their pre-pubescent witterings and whimsy and shoulder their teenage angst with good grace and the benefit of experience and learned lessons. Rachel and Jayne had loved standing on the bench at the end of their garden, hair thick with sea salt being whipped around their shining faces, passing their grandfather's heavy leather binoculars back and forth between them, excitedly spotting dolphins and feeding the gulls that dipped and swooped over the cliff.

As she had got older and, sadly, alone, Helen had become more introspective, pensively reflecting on the childhood the twins could have enjoyed had she and Tom insisted on raising them, and not given Catherine – Crystal – the benefit of the doubt, again, and again. But hindsight was a wonderful, and quietly destructive, thing.

'Darlings!' Her warm, plummy tones greeted the trio as soon as they walked out into the gardens, where she was sitting watching some of the other inmates, guests, how would you describe them? Jayne wondered, enjoy a sedate game of croquet. 'And this must be the handsome Will I've been hearing so much about.' She started to rise out of her chair, knuckles whitening on the arms, when Rachel and Jayne rushed to push her back down.

'Granny, sit down.' Rachel eloquently ordered.

Helen let a little laugh escape, 'Yes, Sir. How was the trip darlings, was it okay? You must be famished, let me ask them to get a tray of something together.' She started looking around for one of the staff and raised her veined hand slightly to attract their attention as they sat down on the bench alongside her. 'I'm so thrilled you came all this way from London. I'm very honoured! Now Will, Jayne and Rachel have told me that you are something of an entrepreneur?'

He smiled and dipped his head slightly, 'I'm afraid you've been duped, Mrs Brady.'

'Please, call me Helen,' she interrupted.

'Helen. I've got a very small Italian delicatessen in Richmond selling hams and cheese, that sort of thing, hardly *Dragons Den* material.'

'And he makes the most delicious chutneys, Granny. We've

actually brought you a hamper of things – we'll get it out of the car in a minute.'

'How wonderful! You needn't have brought me anything, though; just seeing you down here is such a joy. Now, tell me, Rachel, have you finished that restaurant you were doing at the airport? The drawings you showed me on Skype looked marvellous. What a wonderful way to start your holiday, having supper in a place like that, have you seen it Jayne? Ask to see her sketches, it looks fabulous.'

The rest of the afternoon passed amiably. Helen proved with every sentence that her memory was as sharp as it had ever been; in fact she had no reason to be in a residential home apart from it being an antidote to her loneliness. One of the things Helen had found most difficult to accept about old age was the sad truth that her best days were behind her. She had spent her whole life assuming that tomorrow would be better than today. That this time next year what she was striving for in this moment would be fulfilled and the ambitious prophecies that kept her awake at night would materialise. That one day she would eat dinner from a street cart in Seoul and see the Northern Lights. She would watch Tosca in the Sydney Opera House and hop on a tram on San Francisco's California Street. Yet, as she attended the funerals of her parents, her siblings, her husband, she began to reach the startlingly bleak conclusion that she'd had her time. For someone like Helen, whose eyes still danced, this was a horrible realisation.

Jayne was tuned into every nuance of her grandmother's interaction with Will, silently willing her to love him. She knew this was unnecessary; the mutual adoration society had been launched the minute they met.

Helen had actually remembered meeting him back when he was fifteen. Jayne and Rachel had brought him up to visit her and Tom and camp in their back garden one warm July evening. Will had been given a tent by one of his dad's friends and even if the three teens had put their pitiful money together they couldn't stretch to paying the exorbitant peak-season ground rent at one of the hundreds of campsites littering Torbay's coastline, so they pitched it in Helen and Tom's garden. Helen had even bought them a small disposable barbecue for them to cook some sausages and marshmallows on, while looking endearingly at her granddaughters' newfound maturity. Nothing says 'I'm a grown-up' more than turning raw food into edible food over a naked flame. Jayne had completely forgotten about this memory until Helen brought it up.

'It was so funny, your grandpa kept watch on and off during the night from an upstairs window and was incensed when he saw you, Will, crawling out of the tent and spending a penny on his petunias.'

Will's hand shot to his mouth, blushing redder than Jayne had ever seen him, as he stammered, 'I can only offer my heartfelt apologies, Mrs Brady, Helen, what can I say? I was fifteen, stupid and had a very weak bladder.'

'Oh, no need to apologise, it's made me smile quite a number of times since, thinking about it. Now look, as much as I love having you here, it's nearly tea time and you need to push off if you're going to be in London before dark.' Helen had this thing about getting to places 'before dark'. It might have been the Blitz mentality of nightfall being quite literal. She added quietly, 'Now, have you seen your mother lately?'

'No. And we're not going to now, either.' Rachel replied before Jayne could interject with a more diplomatic response.

'I think you should stop in. She's a little . . . different recently.'

'Different how?' Jayne asked at the exact-same moment Rachel said, 'Whatever.'

'Just pop in for ten minutes. It's on your way back to the motorway anyway. For an old lady?' They all gave her hugs, and she squeezed Will's hand, 'Marvellous to meet you, you seem every bit as fine as Jayne said. Now look after my girls, they're rather special.'

'I know, and I will. Lovely to meet you Mrs. . . . Helen.'

Ten minutes later the Ford Focus they'd borrowed from Will's friends Duncan and Erica for the day was swerving along the coast again, its windows down, with them all laughing about Helen's fabulous eccentricities when Rachel shrieked, 'Hell no! We're not going to Crystal's, Jayne. I said I'd only come if we just went to Gran's; I'm not going to Crystal's. Stop the car. Will, stop the goddamn car!'

They swerved into a bus stop and Rachel started clawing at the handle, desperately trying to open the child-locked door. Jayne swivelled around in her seat and said, in what she hoped was a soothing tone, 'Rachel, she's our mother, just say hi and then we'll go. Seriously, two minutes tops. In and out. We're almost there, anyway. We can't come all this way and not even have a cup of tea with her.'

'Well, I'm not coming in,' Rachel replied sullenly, crossing her arms and pouting, 'I'm staying in the car.'

As they pulled up onto the driveway, a stunned silence filled the car as they each took in the beautiful freshly cut lawn, completely devoid of overgrown yellowing weeds and thistles. Planted borders lay where previously only discarded fag butts had been and gently cascading flowers in hanging baskets framed the newly painted front door. They parked behind a shiny silver Mercedes with a disabled badge in its window. 'Has she moved, do you think?' Will asked finally.

'She must have done. I'll just go and see.' As Jayne got out of the car, she reasoned that it wouldn't be entirely out of character for Crystal to have legged it without telling anyone. When they were five she dropped them off at Helen's for the night with their teddy bears and Strawberry Shortcake pyjamas and picked them up four months later with a tan and a smattering of Spanish by way of explanation as to her whereabouts for a whole season.

Jayne walked up the driveway and surreptitiously peered

in through the kitchen window as she passed it. It had been less than a year since she'd last popped in for a quick coffee with her mother, on her last visit to Helen, and nothing had changed then, but this time everything seemed different. Gone were the crusty dishes that perpetually lived in the sink, and a pristine white Shaker-style kitchen had replaced their grubby cream-and-brown one. A recycling bucket lay next to the front door; in it were empty Granola boxes and plastic smoothie bottles, evidence of a different class of consumer to the cheap wine-swigging previous owner. She rang the bell and turned back to the car, where Will and Rachel were leaning forward in their seats staring and shook her head and shrugged, as if to say, 'your guess is as good as mine'.

The door was opened by an elderly man, probably in his early eighties, slightly stooped but otherwise sprightly, 'Hello, hello! How can I help you, young lady?'

'I'm really sorry to bother you, but my mother used to live here, until recently, and I just wondered if you knew where she went, or if you have a forwarding address for her?'

'Oh my, are you Jayne or Rachel?' he boomed cheerfully.

'Um, Jayne?'

'Your mother is going to be delighted to see you back in one piece!' He went to the bottom of the stairs and shouted up, 'Come down, Jayne is here!' Turning back to where Jayne stood uncertain and more than a little stunned, he enthusiastically beckoned, ushering her into the living room. 'Come in, come in.'

She had no idea what was going on, who this man was, or why this house sort of looked like her old one, but after a *60 Minute Makeover*. Behind the reproduction Victorian fireplace was a wall covered in a beautiful cornflower-blue-and-cream wallpaper, the type that depicts French scenes – she could never remember the name of it, toile something she thought, Rachel would know – depicting historic country life, delicate sketches of peasants shovelling hay into carts and flocks of geese about to take flight. When she and Rachel lived there with Crystal a broken three-bar electric fire was surrounded by a nasty 1970s brickwork fireplace, Jayne couldn't even remember what colour the lounge walls were, a sort of nicotine shade, she imagined.

'When did you land?' he asked affably.

'Um . . . land?'

'Yes! Is this a short trip back to the UK, or are you back for longer? I don't suppose you can say too much about it, eh?' He tapped the side of his nose, 'Mum's the word, sorry, no more questions, I don't want you to have to kill me!' he chuckled.

'Darling! How wonderful to see you! I can't believe it!' Crystal swept into the living room, but, much like the surroundings, she'd been the recipient of a drastic transformation. Her bleached platinum hair had been replaced by a sleek dark-blonde feathery cut, her make-up was still substantial but looked like it had at least been put on with a selection of task-appropriate brushes rather than a garden trowel. She was wearing some sort of emerald silk kaftan that shimmered slightly as the light caught it and made a faint rustle as she walked. As she enveloped Jayne in a big hug, possibly her very first from her, she was shrouded in a cloud of Issey Miyake. *What the hell?* On Jayne's last visit a year ago she'd opened the door a couple of inches, which was as much as the chain would allow, dressed in a stained dressing gown, her hair comically sticking out as if in mid-electrocution, eyes bleary and breath honking of stale cigarettes and last night's bar bill.

Jayne peered at her, disbelieving, 'Crystal?'

'Oh hush, darling, you know I hate it when you call me that!' She squeezed her shoulders just a tiny bit too hard, 'This is such a wonderful surprise. Now, darling, sit down and tell your mummy everything!' *Mummy?* Jayne looked back at the old man, who was rocking back on his heels, hands in his cardigan pockets, smiling at what looked, for all intents and purposes, like a touching mother-daughter reunion. For a split second Jayne thought that she was either being secretly filmed by a Saturday-night TV show and Ant and Dec were going to spring out from behind one of the new linen drapes that were dusting the floor, or she'd stumbled into some kind of parallel universe. Crystal tapped the sofa seat next to her, 'Come on, Jayney, and don't leave anything out!'

'Um . . . Rachel and my boyfriend, Will, are in the car . . . I should go and fetch them.'

Crystal clapped her hands together in delight, 'Oh my goodness, my Rachy's here too! And you have a boyfriend? You never said!' Jayne didn't quite know during which make-believe conversation she was meant to have relayed this information, seeing as they hadn't spoken since her last visit, but decided to play along to whatever was going on in her mother's head.

'Um, yes, Will, sorry about not mentioning it before, I . . . er . . . wanted it to be a surprise. I'll, um, go get them in, then, shall I?'

'The more the merrier!' Crystal and the old man chorused.

During her deliberately slow walk to the car she tried to understand what had just gone on before she tried to artic-ulate it to the two people who knew her best in the world. And what she came up with was: 'Mum's gone loop the loop, you better come in.'

Rachel's arms crossed defiantly, 'I've already told you, I'm not setting foot in that house.'

'Believe me, Rach, you're going to want to see this. I think she's got some sort of dementia, and there's this old guy, who might be her carer or something, and the house looks like it belongs in *Country Living*. I don't know what's going on, but you have to come in.'

'Dementia?' Will slammed his door, 'does she recognise you?'

'Yes, but she wants me to call her Mummy and sit on the sofa and, you know, *talk* to her.'

'Is she pissed?'

'No, that's the weird thing, she seems completely sober. It's like she's got a wholesome twin we never knew about and they've swapped lives.'

'Okay, okay, this I have to see.' Rachel begrudgingly got out of the car and all three of them trooped into the house.

'Rachel!' A flash of emerald and a swoosh of silk and suddenly Crystal was hugging a stiffened Rachel, whose arms remained resolutely at her side, one of Crystal's arms then loosened, drawing Jayne into the embrace too. 'My babies, my babies are back!'

Rachel mouthed 'What the fuck?' over their mother's head, and Jayne gave a little shrug back. Will was loitering by the door taking in the whole scene; he told them afterwards that he was trying to work out how to take his phone out with no one noticing and start filming the scene in case they needed to use it as evidence to have her sectioned.

Briefly breaking away from her daughters when she spotted Will, Crystal visibly straightened and purred seductively, 'and who is this?'

In an act that can only be described as pure territorialism, in fact, Jayne couldn't have been more blatant had she peed in a circle around him, she darted to his side, grabbed his hand and said, 'Crystal, er, Mum, this is Will, my, er, boyfriend.'

Crystal looked at him, then at Jayne, then back at him in sheer disbelief, her mouth slightly ajar, eyes narrowed, if she had the ability to raise one eyebrow, this would have been the moment that skill would have been used for. 'Well you're not the only one to bag yourself a hunk,' she slowly walked over to the fireplace and slipped her arm around the old man's waist, who seemed to be leaning against the mantel for support, and said, 'Darlings, I want you to meet someone rather special to me, my gorgeous Stanley.' They then kissed in the way only old people can, Stanley with his dry, wrinkled lips pursed together, eyes closed, their mother taking this show of affection to an entirely unnecessary level by putting her hand on his chino-clad bottom.

'Jesus Christ, Crystal. You'll give the old man a heart attack,' muttered Rachel with a disgusted sigh.

'I think that's the point,' Will whispered and flinched as Jayne poked him in the ribs.

'So, who's for tea?' Stanley asked brightly, clapping his hands together.

Before his words had even finished forming, Rachel snapped back, 'We can't stay.'

'I think we can manage a quick cuppa,' Jayne widened her eyes at Rachel and Will before following Stanley into the kitchen to help. She still hadn't got a hold of the situation unfolding. There was this arthritic pensioner who Jayne charitably thought seemed very nice, there was her mother, who'd quite clearly been possessed, and this house that resembled the one where they grew up only by the number on the front door. Stanley clattered some Denby cups and saucers onto a tray.

Growing up, all their crockery had the emblem of Little Chef on their bases, which had been slipped into Crystal's bag when she'd done her first and only shift there. Remnants of those six hours she'd spent employed had been scattered liberally around the house – including salt-and-pepper shakers, a clock, batteries and an extension lead. She would have taken the electrical appliances that had been attached to the lead as well had she brought a bigger bag to work that day. 'Rookie error' she'd described it at the time.

Jayne filled up the kettle and started making inane comments about how nice the garden was looking, and was Stanley a keen horticulturist – the type of questions that old people love, but you never thought when you were younger would actually ever come out of your mouth.

'I do enjoy going round the garden centre, I must admit, choosing what should be planted, although the days when I can bend down, fingers sifting soil, have long gone, I'm afraid. But Crystal's found this young chap who's ever so nice, to come round a few times a week and tend to it when I'm out. He's a bit slow on the old weeding front. Sometimes when he's been here for an hour or so I don't really know what he's done, but Crystal tells me he's been ever so busy, so I don't really like to probe.'

79

He raised his voice over the noise of the boiling kettle. 'I've been so lucky finding Crystal.'

'Um, how did you two meet again?'

'Well, she found me, actually, my wife had just passed – we'd been together for fifty-two years – and a little article came out in the *Torbay Gazette* about Beryl. She was once the Mayoress, you see, so they wrote this lovely piece about her and Crystal wrote to me after that, giving her condolences and passing on a message that Beryl had for me from the other side. She's terribly gifted, your mother, and we struck up a friendship. She's like a breath of fresh air to me, so loving, and she could see that I was rambling around in that big old house by myself, seeing Beryl in every room, so when she suggested selling it and moving here with her and using the money to make our own little palace, I thought, what a lucky chap I am!'

Jayne opened the large American-style double-door fridge under the pretext of getting the milk out, but she took the opportunity while her back was turned to close her eyes and take a deep, steadying breath without him seeing. As she closed the fridge door a photograph that was tacked to the front of it with magnets caught her eye. It was a picture of two female soldiers in camouflage gear, grinning through their war paint at the lens, long rifles and cumbersome backpacks slung on their shoulders. 'Are these your grandchildren, Stanley?' Jayne asked, thinking it best to try to show the old man any ill will they had was not aimed in his direction. She admired his sentimentality and patriotism, proudly displaying his granddaughters.

He chuckled, 'That camouflage paint certainly does a good job if you can't even recognise yourself! That's the photo of you and Rachel you sent your Mum from Iraq. She didn't want to put it up, though, official secrets act or something, she said, but like I said to her, Crystal dear, I think Al Qaeda have better things to do than keep an eye on houses in Paignton for clues, I think we'll be okay! Do any of you take sugar?'

Jayne was stunned; she'd clearly underestimated the depths to which her mother could sink to. 'Um, yes. Please, one for Will and me. Rachel will just have black. Um, Stanley, what else did my mum say about our, um, time in, er, Iraq?'

'Oh don't worry about me, my love, all your secrets are safe with me.' He mimed zipping up his mouth, locking it at the corner and slipping the imaginary key into his breast pocket. 'What you girls are doing for our little country, it's admirable. I was a year too young to fight the Germans, more's the pity, and so I have nothing but awe for you two.' His eyes started to look a little watery, 'We're just both thrilled that you came today. I know that you only get leave every few years, which is why you couldn't make our wedding, so this is a really lovely surprise.'

Wedding? 'We're really big on surprises in our family.' Jayne flashed him a smile that hovered between sympathy and commiseration. 'Shall I carry the tray in? It looks heavy.'

As they walked into the living room the atmosphere was dripping with vitriol. Unpleasantries had obviously been exchanged and the three of them were sitting in stony silence. Will and Rachel, who shared a sofa, were staring at the floor in front of them, while Crystal was flicking the screen on a jewelled iPhone that she tossed under a cushion before flashing Stanley and Jayne a wide smile that ended at the corners of her lips. Will stood up and Jayne thought he was going to take the tray from her, but instead he said, 'You know what, Jayne, I don't think we've got time for tea, I think we better hit the road.'

Rachel rapidly jumped to her feet, 'Absolutely, come on, Jayne.' They both bundled her out of the door, leaving a bewildered Stanley standing in the middle of the lounge holding a teapot and Crystal idly lounging, Cleopatra-style, on her chaise longue, giving a cursory wave to their departing backs.

'What the hell was that all about?' Jayne snapped angrily as soon as they reached the newly crazy-paved driveway, 'that was so rude – Stanley had made tea.'

'Darling, seriously, it's much better for us to go now.' Will slammed the passenger door on Jayne as soon as she'd sat down. 'Your mother's not right in the head, and I wanted us to go before she upset you.'

'Why, what did she say?' Jayne caught Will flashing warning eyes at Rachel in the rear-view mirror.

'Nothing in particular, she was just a bit off.'

'She's been a bit off all our lives – that's no reason to just up and leave! I think we should go back in there to apologise!'

'Jayne, listen to Will, and Will start the sodding engine.'

'Guys, what's going on? What did she say?' Jayne turned around in her seat to look at her sister as the car reversed down the driveway at top speed, 'Jesus, Rach, I can take it, I'm a big girl, what did she say?'

Rachel sighed and Jayne was sure she detected a note of uncharacteristic embarrassment in her voice, 'She asked Will how much you were paying him to pretend to be your boyfriend.'

'What?'

'She thought I was a gigolo,' Will added, rolling his eyes to emphasise the lunacy of this suggestion.

'That's not entirely idiotic – if I pimped you out we could seriously earn a fortune. None of this teaching and chutney-making, we could make big bucks.'

'Jayne, you don't get it. She was serious. She said that there's no way that you could pull someone like Will, so you must have hired him to impress her. She started naming figures that you'd paid him.'

'It doesn't matter,' Will snapped, and reached over to put his hand on Jayne's thigh, 'she was probably high on something, Jayne, take no notice. You're gorgeous and fabulous and worth ten of me.'

'But she needs to know what Crystal said. You don't need to protect her, Will.'

'Rachel's right, it's okay.' Jayne shrugged. His reticence was sweet, but unnecessary as far as her mother was concerned. She wouldn't be surprised at anything Crystal had to say. Her mother's lack of diplomacy and social niceties didn't surprise her at all, but Crystal had probably merely said what most people were thinking. She'd seen the double-takes of people in the street whenever they walked by holding hands; that moment that lasted a split second too long between her saying, 'let me introduce my boyfriend' and the polite but baffled responses.

Even when she was introduced to Will's best friends, Duncan and Erica, for the first time, they'd failed to conceal their split-second surprise that she wasn't a petite blonde with a tiny waist. As the wine started flowing that night in Ping Pong in Soho, Jayne had soon reverted to a tried-and-tested method of winning people over by sticking chopsticks in her upper lip and pretending to be a walrus, doing one heck of a Aretha Franklin impression and dancing like a robot. Admittedly doing all three of her party tricks on the same night was neither big nor clever; it meant their next meeting was inevitably duller, but at least the ice had been broken.

'It's fine,' Jayne told Will and Rachel, who were both taking Crystal's meanness far more seriously than she was pretending to, 'I just feel sorry for her poor new husband.'

'Her what?!' Rachel spluttered.

'Her husband. The hunky Stanley. Who, by the way, is actually a lovely bloke.'

Will looked in his side mirror before indicating, 'Looks like Crystal's taken her old trick of getting money out of widowers to an entirely new level by actually marrying this one. My dad had a lucky escape.'

'Jesus. And I suppose he's the bank behind the new house and flash car?'

'Yep. And, get this, she'd told him that me and you, Rach, are some sort of MI6 undercover agents in Iraq, which is why we never visit! She's even pinned a photo of a pair of randoms onto the fridge, pretending it's us.'

'What, that she'd found on the internet or something?'

'She must have done. That's why I didn't want to leave. I wanted to poke around a bit more.'

'We should tell him the truth,' Will said, pulling out onto the roundabout, 'I'd want to know if I'd married a con artist.' Jayne visibly recoiled a little at hearing Crystal described like that. She wasn't necessarily in denial about Crystal's ability to get money through dubious means, but taking advantage of Stanley was a new low. He obviously just needed a sympathetic smile and a reason to get dressed in the morning. How long, Jayne wondered, until the poor man realised that his wife's smile was as fake as her sympathy?

Jayne leant her head against her window, watching the small droplets of rain racing across it, each in their own lane, like a staggered relay. Her breath made a misty patch on the glass that receded as she inhaled, and grew with each sigh. Crystal had always played the doe-eyed victim for whom life had a distinctly citrus twang, but there was no real reason for it as far as Jayne could see. She'd had two parents who adored her and funded her year away to 'find herself', and, yes, it must have been a bit of a spanner in the works to find yourself drinking potent Indonesian rice wine under the stars one day and the next be back in Paignton pregnant with twins, but it was hardly the immaculate conception. During their entire childhood she'd jumped from one job to another, disappearing for months at a time, blindly following whatever man or whim had potential. She would describe herself as a 'lost soul'; her daughters saw it rather differently.

She tuned back into the debate Rachel and Will were having, about how to break the news to Stanley without prompting a premature reunion between him and his late wife.

'Stanley seemed so happy, though,' Jayne interrupted, 'we don't want to ruin his life.'

'I think Crystal's probably going to do a good enough job of that on her own,' muttered Rachel, 'it's just whether we let him enjoy it while it lasts or step in before it all goes horribly wrong.'

'I'm pretty sure she's banging their gardener as well,' Jayne murmured into the window.

'You were in the kitchen with the man for about seventeen seconds, how can you know all this!'

'I have a way of making people talk. I learnt it at spy school.' Jayne exhaled loudly and leant her head back on the headrest, 'I don't know, guys; the whole thing is completely messed up. I mean, fancy making up such outlandish lies about us. We're her children!'

'Why are you so surprised? She's been doing it since we were born. Remember when Granny gave us tickets to the pantomime in Exeter and she made you sit in a wheelchair so we got upgraded to the front of the stalls? Or whenever there were people in front of us at Tesco or the dentists, or wherever, she'd tell them in that whisper that people only usually reserve for the words 'cancer' or 'lesbian' that one of us had 'special needs' and it's only a matter of time before we kick off and so can we go in front of them? Taking advantage of every situation is as natural to her as drinking white wine is to us. Speaking of which, God do I need a drink. Wake me up when we get near London, I need to put my make-up on before we get home as I'm going straight out.'

'So are we not turning round? We haven't got onto the motorway yet. We could still go back and speak to Stanley?' Will asked.

Rachel gave a non-committal shrug, as though anything their mother did was of no relevance to her. Jayne felt torn. On the one hand she didn't want to be part of the deception, but also, a little part of her was hopeful that perhaps Stanley might be good for Crystal, that maybe the stability of being married to him might actually change her. 'No, keep going,' she said. 'I'll speak to Granny about it and see what she says.'

They travelled along the motorway in silence for almost twenty minutes before Will stroked the side of Jayne's leg with the tip of his finger and asked tenderly, 'Are you sure you're okay?'

'Yes of course. You forget, like Rachel said, we've had a whole lifetime of this.' She shrugged her shoulders, 'I don't know, I guess I just always hope that one day she will be like that for real. This whole 'tell mummy everything' routine. It would just be nice, I guess, if she actually *did* want to know everything. But we both know that will never happen.'

'Well at least your granny seemed chuffed to see you.'

'Crazy old bird. I hope I'm like that one day.'

'You already are, darling. You already are.'

Chapter 7

Abi had told Clive, the life model for her art class, that his services were no longer required. She'd never fired anyone before, but assumed it couldn't be that different to putting a full stop at the end of a sexual liaison, so had practised the 'it's not you, it's them' speech until it played on a loop in her head. He'd only had the job for four weeks but already his previous jaunty gait had been downgraded to a disheartened shuffle, his once-proud shoulders were now stooped, and she swore that during the last class she could actually see his body hair turning grey as the minutes slowly ticked by. As it turned out, never before had a man been so relieved to be sacked. The weekly taunts directed at his manhood made the seven pounds an hour seem ten times too cheap and Abi didn't want to be the reason for his spiral into self-loathing depression. So it wasn't entirely altruistic when she offered her students up as unpaid graphic-design artists. She needed a new module for them and Will needed flyers for a new venture he'd been brainstorming.

Will had mentioned it to Jayne for the first time a month or so ago. They'd started taking a rug and picnic basket down to the Green in the early evenings and lying on their backs staring at the swirling shapes the clouds were making in the pink sky, pointing out rooster heads and octopuses, or octopi as she'd lovingly corrected him. It was reminiscent of the summer of 2000, where everything seemed possible and probable. Dreams were intentions, not fantasies.

Will had started tentatively outlining a plan he had been mulling over to supplement the limited income the deli was making. He had realised that even if he sold every jar of roasted peppers, every bottle of chilli-infused oil and every last sliver of decadently creamy, oozing goat's cheese, the profit hit its ceiling somewhere around the 'alright, but not great' mark.

Jayne could tell how excited he was with his idea by the earnest notes that had crept into his speech. He had tried to disguise his boyish eagerness by cloaking it in a mature and well-thought-out strategy. It was clear that his plan to start running cooking classes from the deli after closing had gone beyond the 'what if' stage and was firmly implanted in the 'when and how' phase.

'So I thought that if I chose simple Italian classics each week, and showed people how easy it is to make them at home – like how to make your pesto and pizza dough–'

'And tiramisu, don't forget tiramisu,' Jayne interrupted,

'Definitely tiramisu. I'll make extra that lesson, just for you.'

'Well in that case, you'll have my unending support and unconditional love forever.'

'But will it work, do you think?'

She had found it endearing, his craving to seek her counsel and pursuing her approval. She knew that all he wanted her to do was to stroke his head and tell him in the same soothing tones that you find on a hypnotherapy tape that he was a strong, confident man, capable of global domination of the delicatessen industry. He needed her to say, 'Yes, darling, jolly good idea.' So she did.

'I think that's a fab plan, baby, you'd be great at teaching, and unlike my charming delinquents, your students will actually *want* to be there.'

'What if nobody comes?'

'That's not going to happen – it's going to be awesome and you'll be turning people away.'

'How do you do that?' Jayne had experienced a jolt of déjà vu as he flipped over onto his stomach so he could see her better, his white t-shirt rising slightly above his studded belt, giving a hint of his muscular lower back.

'Do what?'

'Know what I needed to hear and then say it.'

'Because I know you, and it happens to be true.'

He leaned closer until his lips brushed hers. 'Thank you.'

'Don't be daft. That's what we do. Anyway, tell me what sort of things you're planning on teaching?'

He had stretched out and put his head on his interlocked hands, looking sideways at Jayne, 'I've put together three eight-week lesson plans with recipes using natural, fresh ingredients, sort of low-maintenance dinner with friends.'

'Oh, you mean an organic kitchen supper?' They had both sniggered at Jayne's sarcastic reference to how a recent customer had described her upcoming informal dinner party to Will – a term that hadn't been rolled out since cousin George got Julian, Dick and Anne in a spot of bother. Will had even scrawled *organic kitchen supper* on a notepad next to the till after the customer left so he wouldn't forget to relay it to Jayne later, that's how much it had amused him.

'Yes, I thought what the world needs more is organic kitchen suppers,' he laughed. 'But it's not the food bit that's bothering me. You know me, I'm at my happiest pottering around a kitchen throwing herbs in a pot.'

'And on the floor.'

'Touché. And on the floor. But I don't know how to spread the word. I really can't afford an ad in the paper, and I'm not sure just having a notice up in the window is going to grab people's attention enough.'

'We should get some flyers designed and hand them out around Richmond,' she'd suggested, picking the white petals off daisies and watching them flutter down, trying hard not to repeat 'he loves you, he loves you not' in her head, but finding it impossible not to.

*

On reflection, Jayne wasn't sure that it was entirely ethical for her to ask Abi to make Will's new commercial venture her students' Spring-term project, but apparently they had embraced the task with unbridled gusto. These were Abi's words not hers as Jayne knew the kids in question only too well. She imagined the only things they did both unbridled and with gusto happened behind the public library in the nine minutes between last orders and their dads picking them up in battered Nissan Sunnys. But Abi swore that after getting over their initial disappointment that the assignment had nothing to do with the weekly viewing of a stranger's gonads they were really chuffed that the winning design would actually be used and people would actually see it.

'Wow, Chinese child-labour lords have nothing on you!' Will exclaimed when he saw the large pile of designs Abi was getting out of her bag. She'd come round early before the deli opened and spread them all out on one of the café's tables. The smell of freshly ground Kenyan coffee lingered in the air and the first batch of croissants and muffins were slowly baking, emitting delicious notes of cinnamon and toasted almond.

'I quite like this one,' Abi said, pointing to a garish graffiti design, where the words 'GRUBS' UP' were spray-painted on. 'It's edgy and urban.'

'Um, I'm not entirely sure that that's the feel I was going for . . .' Will said diplomatically, shuffling through the other papers.

'And it's got appalling punctuation. Apostrophe abuse at its worst. Who did it?' Jayne asked, adding a dramatic shudder, to emphasise her disgust, both at her pupil's ignorance and her own apparent inability to impart vital grammar rules.

'You can take the English teacher out of the classroom . . .' Will mumbled.

Abi flipped the design over and looked at the childish scrawl on the back, 'Michelle Whittaker.'

Jayne grimaced. 'Of course. I'm not telling her, though, I value my face.' She held a page up to show Will, 'What do you think of this one?' It was classic monochrome, with italic scrolls around the edges.

'Nice, but a bit posh, and I'm not sure that I'd describe a beginner's guide to chutney-making and bread-baking as a Culinary Masterclass . . .'

'You're doing yourself a disservice – it's food, therefore culinary, and it's a class. But I take your point, perhaps a little bit too country manor-house wedding circa 1900.'

'Now, this one I like,' Will held a simple white card aloft. It had a simple pencil sketch of the outside of the deli, with its striped canopy, a few metallic bistro chairs and tables outside and an understated, but inviting window display of exotic olive oils in a pyramid. The words *Taste, Enjoy, Savour* floated above the drawing, while in the bottom-left corner the words *Learn the basics of beautiful flavours at Scarlet's School of Food.*

'Scarlet's School of Food?' Jayne imitated his voice, 'It's a beginner's guide to bread-baking.'

'Does it make me sound like I'm a bit up myself? I don't want people to think I'm a wanker.'

'I'm only kidding – no, I think it's perfect.' Jane smiled.

'Yes, it's exactly what I'm after,' retorted Will, 'it's got a lovely feel about it, like it's the deli-equivalent of *Cheers*. Minus the grumpy postman; no space for misery in here.'

'Cliff? He was a national treasure, wash your mouth out,' Abi jibed.

'Abi, you're the national treasure,' he flapped the design at her and kissed her cheek, 'Thank you so much, this is The Chosen One. Now I've just got to make 300 copies of it.'

'Where are you going to put the flyers?' she asked.

'My beautiful girlfriend over here,' he did a ta-da with his hands at Jayne, as though she was a magician's assistant, which she responded to by putting her hand on her hip and fluttering her eyelashes, 'has kindly agreed to stand outside the deli all day today and hand them out to everyone passing who doesn't look weird.'

'I did remind him that it's one of the busiest weekends of the summer, which means I may be keeping more leaflets than I give out.'

'I'm not meeting Dirk until about eleven, so can help you for a couple of hours, if you like?' Abi offered, gathering up the rest of the designs and shuffling them into an orderly pile before stuffing them back into her straw-basket bag.

'Who's Dirk? And why does he have a name like the lead character in a 1970s cop show?' Will asked, wincing as he burnt his finger on the side of the muffin tray he'd just taken out of the oven.

'My new man. His real name is Derek, but everyone calls him Dirk,' she replied defensively.

'When you split up we can call him Dirk-the-Jerk,' Will shouted over the din of the coffee beans grinding.

Jayne tried not to laugh, she'd been hearing rather a lot about Dirk in every break-time for the last few weeks, so felt as if she knew the advertising account manager from Lewisham rather intimately. Too intimately. At least Rachel kept the minutiae of her eclectic sex life shrouded in a healthy veil of unhealthy secrecy, whereas Abi was only too ready and willing to divulge the length, and quite often the breadth, of each and every encounter.

It was nice to see her so smitten, though, Jayne thought, she'd flipped from one bad bloke to another in the ten years she'd known her, almost like a game of draughts – leaping from one to another, hoping to reach the end. She was at that blissful beginning stage now; she could see it in her eyes, which wistfully glazed over when she was talking. Jayne knew that even now, over a year into her relationship with Will, she was still like that, when every simple thing she did every day reminded her of him. Picking up a jar of paté in the supermarket, *Will makes his own paté.* Putting her shoes on, *Will has lovely feet, big too.* Buying a single-journey tube ticket, *Will has an Oyster card; I saw it in his wallet.* Putting a spoonful of sugar in her tea at work, *Will grinds his own coffee beans. Fairtrade, that's very important.* Shooing a stray cat away from her front door, *Will once owned a rabbit called Debbie, as in Harry.*

'You're not listening to me. What are you thinking about, you've got a weird-ass grin on your face. Are you drunk?' Abi peered into Jayne's face, so close she could smell the chocolate on her breath from the warm muffin she'd just inhaled.

'Sorry, miles away. Right, Will, we'll take these over the road to the copy shop and get them printed – 300 did you say?'

'Yep. You're both superstars, can you flick the sign to open as you leave?' he yelled from behind the counter, where he was carving some Parma ham into tiny bits to put on taster trays. In order to get around the horrible truth that a nause-ating, yet fairly substantial, percentage of the population omit to wash their hands after visiting the bathroom, he'd stabbed cocktail sticks into each sliver. If anyone was getting NoroVirus, it wasn't going to be from his shop.

'So what convinced him to do these classes finally?' Abi asked Jayne later as they smiled enticingly, thrusting their leaflets at a group of yummy mummies navigating the narrow pavement with their designer prams.

'Our rent?' Jayne replied flippantly. 'No, of course it's a little financially motivated, these premises are stupidly expensive, but also, he just loves what he does. I really hope it takes off; he's so excited. He's planned out the whole eight-week course of what to make each week. I'd be so gutted for him if no one's interested.'

'Well, we'll just have to do our very best, then, won't we?' Abi smiled mischievously as she unbuttoned another button on her already low-cut shirt.

'I'm not sure that perverts are his target market, Abs.'

'Hey, you want numbers, I'll get numbers.'

Jayne liked to think that it was her wide smile, approach-able demeanour and impeccable sales technique that made forty-two people call and book lessons in the coming week, but she was pretty sure that Abi's ample bosom played a part, not to mention the fact that it was Will taking the classes. 'Who's running the cookery school?' a few women had asked. When she pointed inside the shop, they paid up front. She couldn't blame them; she would have done too. Just keep your hands to yourselves ladies, she thought.

Chapter 8

Three months later and the cookery school was a huge success, but then Jayne had known that it would be. Will had an infectious enthusiasm for food that made you want to squash a kumquat and mix it with dandelion leaves, just to see what it would taste like. He'd even taken on a wonderfully chirpy gent called Bernard to help out part time in the deli so he could concentrate more of his time on menu-planning and prep for the different classes.

Bernard (never Bernie, as they had found out about sixteen seconds into his first shift) had taken early retirement from his senior-management job at an oil company the year before. Six months later he found himself with a pension that would make ninety-eight per cent of the population blush and a feeling of nagging unfulfillment with the prospect of spending the next thirty years watching *Cash In The Attic* and re-runs of *Fantasy Homes by the Sea* that were filmed three property booms previously. His descent from sharp suits to comfy drawstring trousers was rapid and potentially terminal, until he spotted the small, neat handwritten card Will had pasted to the deli window. The moment Bernard donned a crisp white apron and started dicing up small cubes of Parmesan to hand around as tasty samples, he became alive again. He was how Jayne imagined Will to be twenty years down the line: unnervingly charming, but with a frisson of barely tamed naughtiness lurking close to the groomed and gently greying surface.

Jayne's timetable didn't allow for much time off during the week, as deputy head of department the diminished hours in the classroom were replaced by unending hours of admin and strategy and Ofsted prep and reports, and staff-training, and lots of things that didn't resemble teaching at all. But on Tuesdays she finished mid-afternoon and after her weekly Skype to Helen, it had become something of a cherished ritual to sit on a stool at the far end of the counter chatting lazily to Will and Bernard until the commuters stopped pouring out of the tube station opposite or the chiller cabinet emptied, whichever happened first. They chatted about everything from the size of Putin's ego to the appeal of Monty Python; the Japanese obsession with Hello Kitty to why Brussels sprouts are essentially little cabbages but taste so vile. They paused their easy banter only to refill their mugs or to exchange cheerful pleasantries with a customer.

Watching Will sprightly discuss the merits of pimento-stuffed olives versus their Parmesan-filled counterparts with an elderly lady wearing a transparent pac-a-mac, Jayne remembered a bollocking she'd given him a few weeks into their relationship. She had sat in the exact seat she was currently perched on, watching him hastily spoon some chargrilled peppers into a pot for a customer, while clutching his mobile between his chin and his shoulder. His voice had risen to that terse volume one notch under a proper yell, but above the level comfortable for witnesses. He'd taken the woman's money, thrust her change back across the counter together with her bag, all without interrupting his angry tirade about a late delivery.

'You weren't a very nice character in that lady's story today,' she had said that evening as she handed him a beer and emptied half a bag of pretzels into a bowl, before putting them on the breakfast bar between them.

'A what in her what?'

She had ignored his bemused raised eyebrow that mocked her and continued, 'You know, everyone has a different story of their day – of their lives – with people like their parents, sisters, brothers, husbands, wives, children, all playing the principal roles, and then during the course of a day, you have minor bit-part extras coming into their story, affecting it in some way. That customer today that you ignored while shouting to your cheese man has cast you as a bit of a dick.'

'But I'm not. I was just angry about the cheese.'

'I know that, but that's only because you've got a bigger

part in my story. I've had the pleasure of watching you in different situations, for longer acts, but you only had one scene with that lady and in it you were a dick.'

He'd taken a small sip of beer and while a large part of him must have thought, and not for the first time, that his new girlfriend was nuts, he did look a little bit chastened.

'So what can I do to change my part from a baddy to a hero?'

'You can't. Not in her story, anyway. You'll be forever cast as a dick'

'What am I in yours?'

'An enthusiastic and talented lover with some dickishness, which I'm doing my best to iron out.'

Jayne smiled as she remembered how Will had spent the rest of that evening showing her exactly how enthusiastic and talented he was.

But this afternoon was a rare treat to have Will's company as well. As their evenings had now been commandeered by eager food-lovers, and the odd disillusioned house wife just wanting to enjoy Will's perfect cheekbones at close quarters, Tuesday afternoons had become rather more precious.

They were experiencing the mid-afternoon lull before the after-school rush descended with harassed mums dragging their reluctant offspring in to pick up some slices of home-made sundried-tomato quiche for dinner, or a sweet treat to reward a history project well done. 'How many people,'

Jayne pondered out loud, 'try to pass Will's cooking off as their own, do you reckon?'

'I'd say four out of five,' Bernard replied, handing her a vanilla latte, made just the way she liked it with skimmed milk to counteract the two shots of vanilla syrup. 'Just think about it, on Fridays and Saturdays most of the customers are picking up things for dinner parties they're hosting, and I'm not just talking ingredients, I'm talking whole pies or cheesecakes. We're in the throwing-money-at-the-situation-to-make-life-easier era.'

'Well, the more money they put in that till certainly makes my life easier!' Will quipped, hearing the tail end of the conversation as he staggered in through the back door carrying a precariously balanced pile of crates crammed with fresh vegetables. He now taught four nights a week and all day on Saturday, but rather than making him tumble into bed each night world-weary, he skipped into the flat each night, brimming with stories, laughter and general merriment. 'Can you help me out preparing the salads, Bernard? I just want to do a little bit of prep so I'm not rushing later.'

'Of course, Chef, no problem.' That was another endearing trait of Bernard's, thought Jayne. He insisted on calling Will Chef, purely out of respect and reverence to his employer's background and culinary skills and without a hint of irony. At first, through embarrassment, Will tried to sidestep this new moniker and yet soon realised that any resistance was futile. Discernible only to Jayne, he seemed to stand a little straighter and gave an almost unnoticeable flicker of a smile whenever Bernard addressed him like that.

'What's the topic tonight, Chef?'

'Tonight's class is called 'Appetising Appetisers – Not a Melon Ball in Sight'. You can thank Jayne for the comedy subtitle; she thinks my original names were too dull.'

'Which they were,' Jayne mumbled into her latte.

'Which they were.' Will repeated, smiling at her. 'Now, guys, since I have you both here, I need your honest advice on something one of the people in my class said last night,' Will started ripping the cellophane off an arugula lettuce and tearing off its outer leaves. 'There's this woman who has missed a couple of lessons due to her child being ill, or something, and she asked if she could have a catch-up session. Then another bloke in the class said the same thing as he has to go on a business trip next week, but doesn't want to miss learning about seafood, which is the next class. Now I physically don't have time to do extra lessons for those that miss them, but equally I don't want them to be pissed off that I'm not doing more to help them learn what they've missed when they've paid for the whole term. Bernard, can you pass me that colander? Thank you. So then the man, Philip, suggests me doing a little video of the dish I'm teaching that week and posting it on YouTube, and everyone who signs up for the class subscribes to that channel so you never miss anything.'

He ran the colander full of cherry tomatoes under the tap and shook them out before wiping his hands on the cloth that was tucked into Bernard's apron string. 'Then Jackie piped up that the video would really help her recreate some of the dishes from the class at home, because she can do it in the class, then as soon as she gets home she's forgotten it, so watching me explain it again would really help. And everyone seemed to agree. So I then asked my other classes if they felt the same way, and almost everyone said yes.'

'I think it's a great idea,' Jayne said encouragingly, 'and it would be so easy to do.'

'Are you sure, though? It's not a bit 'look at me, I'm making a video of myself'?'

'It's entirely 'look at me, I'm making a video of myself' but in the name of helping your students, not shameless self-promotion.' Jayne scooped up the last remnants of froth from the bottom of her mug with her finger and sucked it.

'Which makes everything alright?'

'For what it's worth Chef I think it's a great idea too. And jolly good fun to put together I would imagine.' Bernard added. 'Do let me know if you want me to steady the tripod or hold one of those big light-reflecting circular things, or, oh I've always wanted to do this, snap the clapperboard shut and shout 'Action'!'

'Whoa!' Will held his hand up to stop Bernard mid-flow,

'I would imagine it's going to be less Universal Studios and more Shaky-Hand Productions.'

'I think shaky-hand productions are banned from YouTube, that's an entirely different sort of website.'

Will playfully pushed his bottom into Jayne's hip. 'No need for your smutty comments, Brady. And, actually, now you mention it, while we've got the video camera out, we could always put it to some other use . . .'

Bernard coughed quietly and started busying himself cleaning the already spotless tables while they laughed amiably at his embarrassed expense.

Chapter 9

The rain was just strong enough for Will to hear it softly patter against the window as he lay motionless, trying not to think about how a light drizzle would be really good for his newly planted lettuces and berries, because that would make him middle aged and he wasn't yet. He turned his body really slowly so he could face Jayne without waking her. He watched her soft pink lips gently part with each breath and tenderly observed how her deep-black ringlets bucked and fizzed all over the pillow. She was the most exotic woman he'd ever seen, and he'd seen a few.

He must have been about twenty-two or three when he first realised that maybe he wasn't destined to always be the lanky nerd he'd been during his teens. Sharing a house with three other lads at university curtailed any notion of vanity he might have developed had he been around fawning girls or, indeed, reflective surfaces more. He knew he wasn't ugly, and he'd be lying if he said that he wasn't vaguely aware that occasionally women looked at him longer than was entirely appropriate. It wasn't until after graduation, when he had started working in kitchens that he became uncomfortably conscious of the waitresses' giggles and coy hair-twisting as they loitered around his workstation when the head chef wasn't looking.

Belinda followed Amanda, who preceded Caroline and Daisy – an alphabet of flattering yet unfulfilling lays – paraded around anonymous bars and birthday parties, with an arm tightly and territorially linked through his, characterised most of the next decade. He'd had an epiphany around his twenty-eighth birthday, a few months after starting the deli. He'd woken up naked on a Saturday morning next to a very pretty girl called Camilla, who he'd been dating for a few months, lying in the exact-same bed and position as he was in now, staring at this girl sleep and suddenly realised that she didn't know a damn thing about him. The night before, she'd been hinting about wanting to meet his parents and he realised that he hadn't even told her that his mum had died. That's how little they had conversed.

Gazing at Jayne now, watching her make-up-free face shine in the half-light, her eyes softly closed, he felt this overwhelming tingle inside, almost like the start of an orgasm or a drunken head-rush. The duvet had fallen away slightly so he could see the curve of her breast; she really did have the most amazing figure. So many of the girls he'd dated had grimaced at non-existent inches on their slender bodies, shuffling leaves around a plate. As a chef, cooking for someone counting every calorie was only marginally better than preparing a dish for a lactose-intolerant vegan coeliac. Their first meal together as adults in that Italian restaurant she'd ordered lasagne with garlic bread, followed by tiramisu. He'd known then that he'd be happy with this woman for the rest of his life. He loved her beyond anything he had ever known before.

She had met him at his most vulnerable, when all his hooded tops had sleeves damp with hastily wiped-away tears and a vocabulary filled with bravado. She'd made him a better person then and still did now, delicately encouraging him, always using 'we' instead of 'you', and weaving his dreams into her own. She had a knack of always seeing the best in people, even people like Crystal who didn't deserve her second, third or fortieth chances. Since their visit to Devon, Rachel and he had tried to convince Jayne to call Stanley to enlighten him about his wife, but Jayne refused to. 'Everyone deserves some happiness,' she'd said. The world would certainly be a better place if everyone thought like Jayne. *His* Jayne. With an almost imperceptible smile etched on his face, he started dozing again.

Is leaning on the counter a little bit twattish? he wondered. He straightened up and put his right hand, which had never bothered him before but that now felt like a weird swinging appendage, on his hip. Too camp. Leaning it is. He ran his tongue over his teeth for the tenth time and smiled a toothy grin. Too desperate. Lips closed. Too creepy.

'Have you got Tourette's?' Jayne asked from behind the camera, blowing her hair out of her face as she battled to adjust the height of the tripod.

'I don't know what to do with my hand. Or my face.'

'If you want more hits, then stick it in your pants.' Rachel said, swinging round and round on her bar stool. Will wished that she wasn't there to witness his filming failure, where his on-screen career was doomed to last less than seven seconds. He knew that falling in love with a twin meant you were essentially going with two people, but only sleeping with one of them, unless you were Hugh Hefner or Charlie Sheen, but in situations like this he wished he'd put a bolt on the outside of Rachel's door.

'I'm serious!' He flapped his hand around in the air, 'Look, I don't know where to put it!'

'Will, you've lived with that hand for thirty-one years, it's not a new thing.' A click and the war with the tripod was won, 'Okay baby, ready when you are.'

Will ran his hand through his hair, cracked his neck from shoulder to shoulder and took a deep breath. This was crazy, he thought. Jayne had already agreed that if it was rubbish they'd have a good laugh and destroy the tape, so why was he so nervous? The red light on the camera blinked at him, taunting him.

'Will.'

'I know, I know, I'm just getting ready.' He puffed out his cheeks and slowly exhaled. 'Hi there, I'm Will Scarlet, and this is the first of eight short films showing you how to make every mealtime an occasion to remember – from fluffy, fabulous pancakes and honey-soaked granola to bring that special someone in bed, to easy, yet impressive, dinner-party fayre to share with friends. I hope you enjoy the series as we embark on this fabulous culinary adventure together.'

For the next twenty minutes he chopped, he stirred and he flirted; he baked, he flipped and he smouldered. Occasionally looking up to the camera to grin lopsidedly, roll his eyes as he spilled something, or to give a few words of gentle explanation as to what he was doing. He finally slipped the pile of buttery pancakes onto a plate and spooned over the glistening berry compote. Finishing the decadent stack with a sensually squeezed trickle of maple syrup he looked up from beneath his eyelashes and tried to gauge the sisters' reactions. They both stared back at him in silence, open-mouthed. The red light still glared at him, slightly less menacingly now that he'd managed to do the intro without vomiting, but still intimidating none the less.

'What? Say something!'

'Wow.' Rachel had stopped spinning around and just stared at him. He could feel his neck starting to colour, which is where the angry pink blotches always started before they seeped upwards to his cheeks, a cruel reminder telling him maliciously that he was a shopkeeper not a film star. What was he thinking? Pure arrogance that's what it was. Why would anyone want to see a video of him anyway? Jayne was still mute, one hand resting on the camera, her eyes wide and unblinking. Jesus, was he that bad? Without saying anything, Jayne slowly walked to the other side of the breakfast bar, leant over to where he was standing, cupped either side of his face in her hands and gave him a long, lingering kiss.

They filmed four more episodes that afternoon and uploaded them that evening after Jayne had painstakingly faded Jack Johnson's 'Banana Pancakes', Van Morrison's 'Days Like This' and Caro Emerald's 'Liquid Lunch' around his words. Will emailed the URL link to all his students; Jayne sat on the floor of their living room with a bottle of cold Corona by her side and pasted the links onto all three of their Facebook pages.

'Remind me why the world needs to see me make a prat of myself?' Will asked.

'It's not the whole world, Will, it's our friends, and it's a good way to drum up business. And for the record, you're a very handsome prat.'

As soft snores replaced their low moans and whispered words of sentimentality, Jayne nestling into the crook of his arm, his leg overlapping hers, the uploaded videos were watched and shared; posted and savoured, re-watched and re-tweeted.

Film me and post it on YouTube, he said. Let's upload it onto the internet, she said. And then let's stand back and watch our world come crashing down around us.

Chapter 10

The Week Their World Changed . . .

Monday

*E*ach *Charlie and Lola episode is eleven minutes and thirty-three seconds, which Sara reckoned was just enough time to regain a modicum of her sanity by having a sneaky glass of rosé wine and a flick through Facebook while the baby slept. She used to feel a sharp stabbing of guilt every time she resorted to a few sips of the potent pink stuff before the kids were in bed, but she had bypassed self-reproach a long time ago and was now firmly in the 'whatever gets you through the day' camp. Scrolling through her feed she saw that her sister had posted up a new album of her perfect brood all lined up in front of some dinosaur remains at the Natural History Museum. Sophie and Oliver were even holding hands. The only time Sara's own children had skin-to-skin contact with each other was to attempt murder. Maybe if she took them to museums instead of relying on*

CBeebies for their entertainment they'd morph into their cousins. She might try that. One day.

The rest of the updates were of the 'Well I didn't expect that!' and 'Only 4 sleeps!!' variety that tried desperately to elicit responses of enquiry, but just served to annoy her. If you have something to say, say it. Further on down the page, posted yesterday was a status update from Jayne Brady. She hadn't seen Jayne since they worked together on Saturdays at a second-hand bookshop when they were teenagers. She was a fun girl, always laughing, but quite podgy, she remembered, mind you, she was tall enough to carry it off. When they were studying the BFG at school one of the boys had shouted out that it was about Jayne. Everyone laughed, and Jayne had been absent for a few days after that. Funny, she'd forgotten about that until now.

It was rare to see Jayne active on Facebook, she was actually quite surprised when Jayne had accepted her as a friend a few months ago as it had been over fifteen years since they'd seen each other. Jayne had one of those profiles that had maximum privacy on it, so she couldn't snoop through albums or anything, although it didn't look like she'd made any anyway. Her profile picture was a fairly innocuous photo of half of her face in a shadow, so you could barely make out her features, but she looked happy, if a bit tubby still.

Jayne Brady
20 hours. West London, United Kingdom
Don't know what to have for dinner? Check out Will Scarlet's new series of delicious recipes to accompany his cooking school – and remember to buy all the ingredients at his deli in Richmond!
http://www.youtube.com/watch?v=IpbDHxCV28B

She must be in PR or something and this is one of her clients, Sara thought, as she glanced up at the clock. Four minutes of peace left. She clicked the link.

**

Tuesday

The baby's tiny rosebud lips pulsed with each sip of her mother's milk as Caroline tried to get used to the unfamiliar sensation of breastfeeding. The angry red throb of the bedside clock taunted her with the fact that it was only an hour and a half since the last feed had ended. Her husband was cosily ensconced under his duvet, dreaming in the spare room next door. She knew he had an early meeting, like he did most mornings. Like she used to. She picked up her Kindle to try to stay awake until the baby had finished; she'd heard stories about babies rolling off their dozing mothers and falling to the floor and didn't want to be the next example calmly used as a precautionary tale at an ante-natal class. The night-light wasn't bright enough to see the screen and she'd decided against buying the one with the backlit screen, as it was thirty pounds more. Sighing, she picked up her phone and turned on her 3G. It buzzed immediately. All the mums from her NCT class had set up a WhatsApp group and most nights a few of them were awake and lonely in the half-dark at the same time. There was a certain solace in knowing that at this exact moment, spread across a city, or a country, other new mums were also propped up in bed, one pillow bent in half, supporting an arm that supported a little head, a half-drunk glass of water on the bedside table, a stack of well-thumbed baby manuals next to the bed where a supportive husband should be.

Sara Blackwell
Girls, just saw this video on my friend's fbook – you HAVE to see it! Every woman HAS to see it!
http://www.youtube.com/watch?v=IpbDHxCV28B

12:17

Watching it re-awakened something in Caroline's large maternity pants that she hadn't felt for many months – in fact, after her difficult forceps delivery she'd woefully suspected she would never experience again.

She watched it three times, the volume on one bar above mute, less for her newborn's sake and more to hide her furtive perving from the man she'd agreed to forsake all others for. Imagine being presented with that in bed every morning. And the pancakes looked good too. Sara was right; they needed to spread the cheer. With her one free hand she logged into her Mumsnet account.

'Girls, phones away now, please.' Jayne barked at the gaggle of giggling sixth-formers crowded around Nicola Blake's iPhone. She dropped her bag onto the floor next to the desk and wriggled out of her coat for the fourth time that morning. It was so annoying, it used to be that the teachers stayed put in their toasty classrooms and the kids tramped all over the school to each new lesson, but then the head unwisely decreed that it was a much more productive use of everyone's time for the students to stay warm and cosy in their classrooms while the teachers scuttled along corridors, between buildings and up and down the stairs, every forty-five minutes. The only upside to this was the potential for weight loss, Jayne thought, but then the extra exercise has seen a proportional increase in her appetite too, thus so far a lose-lose situation. Taking a swig of tepid coffee from her thermos, she repeated. 'Nicola, I've asked you to put that away, or you can come and get it from me at the end of the day.'

'Sorry, Miss. I was just showing them a new film of this sexy chef bloke.'

'Does it have anything to do with E.M. Forster and his *Passage to India*? No? Then my class is neither the time nor the place for it. Now last session we discussed the different representations of religion in the text: Christianity, Islam and Hinduism, but this lesson we're going to look at the unity of all the living things in the novel and why this is a strong recurrent theme. Seriously, Nicola, bring me the phone. I did warn you. Come to the staffroom at 3.30 and you can get it back then.'

Forty minutes later, when the bell went and every inch of the whiteboard was filled with scribbled words and arrows linking all the main themes and quotes, Jayne shrugged her coat back on and gave her students a cheery wave before setting off across the quad for her next lesson. As she trudged, head down, as if butting the bitter November wind away, the words 'sexy chef bloke' popped into her head. She shook her head as if this would make the thought fly out of her ears. It couldn't be. They'd only uploaded the videos two days ago, and it was only meant to be to help Will's students catch up with missed lessons and be a little bit of extra marketing for the deli, not for hormone-ravaged seventeen-year-olds to salivate over. It must be something else they were talking about.

The only two seats in the staffroom were next to Gary Brown, one of the games teachers. Oh well, Jayne thought with a barely disguised shudder, better next to than opposite. He had this unfortunate habit of wearing loose shorts, a few inches above being publicly decent, and anyone sitting across from him could often inadvertently glimpse the mouse escaping his house.

'Shift up, Gaz, there's a good lad.' Abi plonked herself in between them with a theatrical sigh and a crinkled nose.

'So how's Dirk?' Jayne asked.

'Wonderful. Well, really great. Good. He's fine. Everything's fine. Well, if I'm honest, he's starting to get on my nerves a bit. He's got this whole 'Cor Blimey Guv'nor' thing going on, when he knows and I know that he grew up in a detached house in Buckinghamshire. He's one shiny suit away from being a parody of himself, except he'd think parody was a funny parrot.'

Jayne laughed, 'So remind me why you're with him?'

'I know, I know, I'm shallow and I'm bored and the sex is amazing. A-mazing.' She fished out her tea bag and dripped little tea droplets across the patchy threadbare carpet tiles to the bin next to the sofa.

'Well, you've given it a good shot – three months isn't it?'

'Five. If you count the first two months when we weren't exclusive.'

'You were, he wasn't.'

'Well, yes, technically he was the only one who wasn't being exclusive.'

'I guess if you have a gift you have to share it.' Jayne said, making no attempt to veil her sarcasm.

'Funny, that's almost to the word what he said.'

'Well, if you can tear yourself away from Dirk and his limited talents for an evening, Will has a class tonight and I really want to see that new Cameron Diaz romcom film – it's on at 7.45, do you fancy it?'

'Aw, sorry honey, I've got plans tonight; one of Ma's neighbour's nephews is new in London and she volunteered my services as tour guide. I'm meeting him at five, so if I can ditch him earlier, I'll give you a buzz.'

They both paused to sip their tea and momentarily tuned in to the conversation two young teachers were loudly having in the seats behind them.

'Then he does this stirring thing with his hand, while he looks up at you and smiles, but not like a full-on smile with teeth, a sort of flirty lip curl.'

'Was that the one with the bruschetta? I loved it when he licked some balsamic off his finger.'

'You would, you dirty mare. Does Craig know?'

'As if–'

Abi grinned and looked back at Jayne, whose eyes had widened in disbelief, and she was leaning her head back to hear more. 'What's wrong?' she mouthed. Jayne shook her head and reached into the deep pocket of her coat, which was haphazardly folded by her feet. She took out Nicola's iPhone and tapped the screen to life. Frozen in time was the last face she saw each night and the one she woke up to every morning.

Will could feel his phone vibrating in his pocket and smiled when he saw Jayne's face flash up. It was a photo that he'd taken of her in Richmond Park one crisp sunny day, when her scarf was pulled up over her mouth and you could sense her wide grin beneath it only through the shape of her eyes. Her hair was in its usual frenzied disarray and her cheeks blushed with the cold. 'Afternoon, light of my life, my one true love and reason for being.'

'Will, the weirdest things are happening here, I've heard two different groups of people talking about you and your videos. The first were some sixth-formers, and then some teachers. People are watching them, like *real* people, not just our friends and your students.'

'I know!' He cradled the phone under his chin as he motioned for Bernard to take over serving his customer, lest he be the bad guy in someone's story again. 'The phone has not stopped ringing; I've had to make a waiting list for the courses. I might even think about hiring some more people to help out, because the shop's been rammed all day, we're completely out of most of the fresh stuff, I've had to double tomorrow's orders already. It's madness!'

'But don't you think it's weird that people we don't know are watching you and talking about you? I mean, these are my students and colleagues.'

'Are they giving you gyp?'

'No, not at all, no one apart from Abi and a few of the others know that you're my boyfriend, so it's not that. It's just a bit cringy that women I know are perving over you.'

'Perving, eh?' Will couldn't help being amused at Jayne's uncharacteristic jealousy, 'was it my bulging biceps or my eyes that are as azure as the ocean?'

He could sense her rolling her eyes as she replied sarcastically, 'I think it was maybe your modesty.'

**

Wednesday

Samantha wasn't yet at the stage of desperation whereby she'd ring a celebrity at random and ask if they were homosexual, when invariably they'd shout 'No!' and fling down the phone, so she could then file the story under the headline 'XXX Denies Being Gay' but she was close. She'd put in calls to all of the guerilla photographers to see if anyone of note was snapped going in or coming out of Mahiki, Nobu or the Wellington Club. Heck, she'd even settle for The Harvester tonight, but it seemed that with the excesses of Christmas just around the corner all celebs, major and minor, had undertaken a mass retreat back behind their front doors, even the cast of TOWIE, which was unheard of.

She'd written up just eleven pieces today, all way below the Lifestyle Editor's expectations, more poop than scoop. The highlights being a Big Brother reject frolicking in the Dubai surf; a boy from Rochdale who found an eyelash in his Petit Filou and pictures of Kate Moss and her daughter ambling along Covent Garden's Neal Street arm in arm, but as Kate Moss is one of the celebrities who would sue the arse off anyone who printed her daughter's face, it was a non-story. It's a supermodel nearing the end of her career walking next to a big blur. Hold the front page. Even the British weather, which could normally be relied on for a couple of top stories had let her down – heat waves equalled overweight D-listers and their muffin tops; flooding provoked awkward politicians to buy wellies and wade into people's houses looking concerned, and snow prompted a whole swathe of amateur photographers to send in their blanketed landscapes, which was a ready-made photo gallery begging to be posted, but sadly you didn't get any prizes for overcast greyness.

She pressed the button for Cappuccino Without Sugar on the ageing Douwe Egberts coffee machine in the staff pantry and waited for the little brown cup to emerge. This had been her dream job. Out of everyone on her journalism course at the University of East Anglia, she'd been the only one to land a staff writing job on a national after only three months as an unpaid intern. Some of

*her friends were still working for free on regional maga-
zines, busy making unwanted phone calls and running
all over the country, paying for their own bus tickets,
seeking out stories, only to hand the byline onto someone
else once the legwork had been done.*

*But she got her own name in print every day – well,
not in print, on screen, but on one of the world's most-
visited news websites, with 114 million daily visitors. She
still couldn't really get her head around those figures, but
with upwards of 500 new stories being posted every day,
if she wasn't filing an article at least every seventeen
minutes, she'd very quickly find her tiny desk filled by
someone who thought they could. Her eyes glanced
upwards to the huge clock that dominated the newsroom.
15:34 – the West Coast of America was just waking up,
demanding to be entertained by mindless transatlantic
gossip during their protein shakes and herbal teas. She
took a sip of her coffee and logged onto Mumsnet Talk
to see what was bothering harassed mothers today –
usually there were a few vitriolic threads going that she
could base a short opinion piece on. She clicked on Most
Active and the top thread Breakfast In Bed? Yes Please!
was posted fifteen hours ago and the comments already
ran on for twenty-two pages. Bingo.*

Wearing a dressing gown you'd once 'borrowed' from an
airport Hilton with your head still wrapped in a towel was

not a good look to be sporting ten minutes before your guests are about to arrive, Jayne reasoned. But with Will still in the kitchen faffing about piping perfect swirls of a smoked salmon-and-cream-cheese concoction onto home-made blinis and Rachel knee-deep in almost identical-looking dresses, Jayne had no choice but to be the one to light the tea lights and put on the Rat Pack compilation CD to create the right ambience for a dinner party. Hearing the doorbell ring, she hotfooted it across the landing to the intercom and shouted, 'Come on up, it's open!'

The match was burned down almost to its tip, perilously close to singeing her fingernails when she heard footsteps coming up the stairs, 'I'm so sorry, I'm literally on the last candle, and . . . done!' Jayne swung round with a grin that instantly vanished when she saw a short, mousey young woman who she didn't know standing in the doorway, 'Oh, my goodness, who are you? Sorry, I mean, um, hello, who are you?' She self-consciously held the dressing gown tighter around her chest as the opening strains of Sammy Davis Jr's 'The Lady is a Tramp' ironically began belting out from the speakers.

Samantha gingerly held out a card and Jayne took it, glancing at it just long enough to see the unmistakable logo of *The Globe* in the top right-hand corner.

'Is Will Scarlet around?' Samantha asked nervously, looking around her, deliberately noting every aspect of the living room to add a bit of – pun intended – flavour to the story. The bookcases were crammed with old Penguin classics, their distinguishable orange and white spines lined up. On the lower shelves lay a stack of coffee-table books like the ubiquitous *1001 Movies/ Places to Visit/ Books to Read Before you Die* and *Earth From the Air* – the gift you give when you don't know what else to give. A rather striking pair of white Eames Eiffel chairs flanked the fireplace and the unmistakable aroma of vanilla tea lights mixed with cooking smells. She'd expect nothing less from the man she was planning to call Britain's Tastiest Dish.

Hearing voices, Will bounded into the lounge, wiping his hands on the comedy apron of Michelangelo's naked David that Rachel had given him last Christmas. He stopped as soon as he realised that a stranger was amongst them. 'Um, hello there,' he offered politely, extending his hand. Samantha pressed another business card into his palm. His eyebrow raised when he saw the logo, 'How can we help you, Samantha?'

'I am writing a story about your rapid rise to fame and I live nearby so thought I'd just pop in on the off-chance that we could sit down and I could ask you a few questions to add some original quotes into the story?'

'Fame? I don't know what you mean. And what sort of story?' Will asked warily, his brow slightly furrowed. Jayne still stood mute, self-consciously still in her flannel robe.

'Your videos on YouTube are some of the most watched. You've had over three million hits. Of course people are going to want to know about the man behind the breakfast bar.' Jayne could tell that this Samantha woman was trying out her provisional subheading for size. *The man behind the breakfast bar* . . . a little bit too Delmonte for her own tastes. Hang on a second, did she just say three million? The penny must have dropped with Will at exactly the same time, because he then croaked, 'did you say three million hits?'

'Over. Around three point four, did you not know?' Samantha enquired incredulously. 'Your video has gone completely viral. Has no other journalist been in touch yet? Oh my God, I can't believe I'm going to break this story!' Her eyes flashed with excitement and her voice had gone up an octave. 'It's my first big break! I normally just write about people from Essex walking down streets, I can't believe I'm going to be the first one to interview you! Oh my God, this is so exciting! I knew coming to see you would be better than phoning. At first I thought that it would be a bit stalkerish, and then I just thought, no Sam, you're a proper journalist now, what would Kate Adie do?'

For a split second Jayne locked eyes with Will and recognised the familiar twinkle as he looked back at the young hack and said, 'you are completely right, Sam, is it? Kate Adie would have got on the District Line and gone to that delicatessen and, by Jove, she'd have got that story.'

Jayne left them sitting side by side on the sofa, Samantha's phone sandwiched between them, recording their conversation. She excused herself under the premise of 'making herself decent' and sprinted down the corridor to Rachel's room. The door slammed behind her and she leant her full weight against it, as though expecting it to be ram-raided. 'You are not going to believe who's in the lounge!' Rachel was standing in front of her full-length mirror, her toned body clad in matching maroon bra and knickers.

'Oh Jesus, have they already started to arrive? I'm having a serious wardrobe malfunction.'

'Rachel,' Jayne hissed, 'there's a journalist in the lounge! Talking to Will! He's had nearly three and a half million hits on YouTube. Three and a half MILLION!'

'What, since Sunday? But today's Wednesday. Three and a half million people have watched Will, *our Will*, cook food and now a reporter is interviewing him?' She was speaking deliberately slowly, as if talking quickly might hamper her understanding of the situation.

'Yes. In there,' Jayne nodded towards the wall, 'now.'

'So what are we still doing in here?'

The sisters ran between their two bedrooms, putting on and taking off clothes, applying make-up and scrunching hair mousse as though they were in a cartoon that had been speeded up. The doorbell rang and Jayne jumped in front of Rachel, putting her hand over her sister's milliseconds before she pressed the button that opened the front door at the bottom of the stairs. 'You don't know who it is. Ask first.'

'It's either Marco, Duncan or Abi.'

'That's what I thought before, and then Kate Adie's enthusiastic apprentice strolled in. Seriously, ask who it is.'

Half an hour later, an ecstatic Samantha had been dispatched, clutching her phone with forty-six precious minutes of sound-bites that she was convinced were going to catapult her straight into the editor's corner office.

Two tables from the deli that Bernard had helped Will carry upstairs earlier were now pushed together and artistically draped in a white tablecloth at one end of the living room. A haphazard array of chairs loaned from each room in their flat clustered around it – Jayne perched on the stool from her dressing table, while Abi swayed on a wheeled office chair. Rachel sat a head or so above everyone else on a bar stool, Duncan and Erica were the proud tenants of the Eames chairs and Will, Dirk and Marco sat on three uncomfortable, but practical, metallic chairs from downstairs. Every inch of empty space on the table was taken up with platters of carved Spanish meats, little bowls of stuffed olives and peppers, big plates of torn buffalo mozzarella interspersed with fat slices of glistening red tomatoes. Chunks of homemade olive focaccia and Parmesan ciabatta crowded into baskets at either end, and tall bottles of different oils and vinegars replaced the traditional floral display that Hosts from Dinner Parties Past would have favoured.

'So, then what did she say?' Duncan asked, his mouth full of bread.

'She asked about where I grew up, and when I started cooking, and then asked about my favourite food–'

'What did you say?' interrupted Abi.

'Torquay and Slough, when I was six, toad in the hole.'

'Honk honk!' guffawed Dirk. 'Toad in the hole. Geddit?' he repeated to six pairs of reproachful eyes and one angry girlfriend, who shook her head disapprovingly and placed one finger to her mouth in a silent shush, like you would to a small child.

'You were talking for ages. What else did you talk about?' Rachel asked.

Will emptied the rest of the bottle into Jayne and Erica's glasses, before reaching behind him to get another bottle from the wine rack. 'I don't know really, nothing deep and meaningful. I think it was her first interview, so no real probing.' At the phrase 'real probing' Dirk opened his mouth again, caught Abi's glare and remained petulantly silent.

'Three million. For a cookery show. I can't believe it. I thought that the flash mob we did of Beyonce's 'Single Ladies' in the food court of Westfield was going to go majorly viral, but we got less than 300 hits. What is wrong with people?' Marco grumpily speared a big forkful of undressed rocket into his mouth. He didn't know what was worse, hearing this news, or being on a no-carb, no-alcohol diet when he heard this news.

'Well, I think it's fabulous,' Erica said, to no one in

particular, 'about time something other than pets and sex was popular on YouTube.'

'I think sex has a little something to do with Will's success . . .' Marco replied cattily.

'What do you mean?' Will asked innocently, 'I even took off my Michelangelo apron.'

'Do you really think that you'd have got three-and-a-half million hits if you looked like me?' Duncan amiably spread his arms out, revealing an impressive beer belly, which was admittedly in its early stages but still showed distinct promise of growth. His rugby-playing youth had resulted in a crooked nose and one ear that was a tad cabbage-like. 'Mate, let's be honest, people upload how-to-cook videos all day every day, but people who look like you, don't.'

'People who look like me? You mean a bit crinkly around the edges, a few grey hairs?'

'Yes, that's exactly what he meant. Jeez!' scolded Rachel, 'But I think Marco's right, I'd wager that ninety-five per cent of the people watching that video are women looking for a bit of a thrill, and the other five per cent just want to learn how to make good pancakes.'

'What about the gays, Rachel?' Marco asked, affecting a nose-in-the-air outrage, 'Most of my friends have seen it, and loved it.'

'Not sure how I feel about that,' Will said, his nose crinkling a little, then spotting Marco's 'oh no you didn't just say that' glare, added 'obviously, I love gay men and would be delighted if they loved me too'.

Duncan thumped the table, 'And there, Miss Journalist, is your main quote for your article. Such a pity she's left already!'

'You must realise that you are exceptionally good-looking,' said Erica with a slight hiccup, 'and I can say this as one of your oldest and dearest friends, who is married to one of your best friends, so I am saying this as a neutral party, with no motive to shag you. But at university, everyone wanted to. Even me at one point.'

'Good God woman, pull yourself together,' everyone laughed at Duncan's mock outrage. 'Two kids together and then you drop the bombshell that you once wanted to bonk my best mate.'

Erica's eyes had taken on that glassy quality that is usually accompanied by either vomiting or shameless self-indulgent monologues, fortunately, or unfortunately, in Erica's case, it was the latter. 'I just mean,' she added, swaying a little, 'that Will has always been very, very beautiful. I don't know whether it's because his eyes seem to bore into your soul when you're speaking to him, or the way his hair flops about, just being shiny, and, well, floppy. I think it's also because he's really tall. Not giant tall – that would be a bit strange – but just good tall.'

Jayne could tell that Will was getting embarrassed at the turn the conversation had taken, he was twirling the stem of his wine glass between his thumb and finger, staring down at the way the wine ebbed and flowed against the glass. A small smile played on his lips, but it was his uncomfortable smile, created out of politeness not mirth.

'Darling, I think it's fabulous and very well deserved,' Jayne said, starting to pile the empty plates up.

'I think it's weird,' he replied.

'It is a bit weird, but it'll all be forgotten soon, so ergo . . .'

'Ergo . . . what?' Will repeated, smiling at his girlfriend's pigeon Latin.

'Ergo . . . just enjoy your five minutes.' She reached over and ruffled his hair, 'Because you're going to be ousted off the top spot by a dancing cat any minute now . . .'

**

Thursday

Darren was late into work again. Wednesday night being the new Thursday night that was the new Friday night meant that at that moment across London first-jobbers just like him were preferring to suffer their hangovers on the penultimate day of the working week rather than let it ruin a perfectly good Friday or Saturday. He ran up the escalator with his boss's soy low-fat latte, wishing, in his haste, he'd picked up a cardboard holder to dilute the tingling scalding that had now numbed his left hand. He could feel the beginnings of sweat patches seeping into the synthetic cotton of his light-purple shirt, which had come in a pack of three from Next.

'You're late,' observed the botox-frozen receptionist, who last week was called Olga but was now called something else, Amanda maybe? Flinging his coat and bag in the vague direction of his workstation, he ran into the frosted glass box that was his boss's office.

'Afternoon, Darren.' Michaela held out her manicured hand for the Costa cup. 'I need you to get a guy called Will Scarlet on the phone. He's going to need an agent to stop him saying anything stupid, so before every agent in town finishes their pre-work Pilates I want him to sign with us.'

Darren scrabbled around in his pockets for the little notebook and pen he usually had on him, ready for when Michaela barked a name or instruction at him, but every pocket was empty. Bugger bugger, buggering bugger. 'Um, okay, Will Scarlet, um, who's he?'

'Look him up on YouTube, GlobeOnline, Buzzfeed, HuffPost or any number of blogs he's now trending on and maybe, just maybe, use the initiative you promised me you had in your interview. Now go.'

Samantha's article had gone live late Wednesday night, squeezed between an article on the new wave of oligarchs invading London and a photo gallery of the finalists of

Strictly Come Dancing leaving their dress rehearsals in their tracksuits. As a piece of investigative journalism it wasn't going to win any awards, but what it lacked in eloquent maturity it made up for in its sensationalism. Using descriptions that Jayne thought belonged more in a Barbara Cartland novel than a national tabloid – 'his dangerous blue eyes' and 'long, adept fingers' being just two examples of many that had made her roll her eyes.

Samantha's neutrality was severely lacking. It was clear from the first paragraph that she had fallen deeply in lust with her subject, and judging from the notorious comments section at the end of the article, so had the majority of the readers. Of course, there was the usual, and expected, smattering of 'Poofter, and the pancakes look rank' remarks, but these were firmly red-arrowed as soon as they were posted. Being Will's biggest fan, she wasn't surprised by the seemingly global outpouring of appreciation – there were even comments from Australia, Malaysia and Mexico amongst the ones from Milton Keynes and Wrexham. He had that winning combination of natural flirty charm, insane bone structure and he could obviously cook – what was not to love? And Rachel was right, most of his newly acquired fan base did seem to be women wanting to escape their daily drudgery with a little bit of harmless titillation disguised as a desire to reinvent family mealtimes.

'Hey guys, sorry I'm late, I had to help Bernard in the shop,' Jayne explained breathlessly as she arrived in the pub,

'Will had retreated upstairs to escape his legion of fans, so I had to step in to help, and Friday evening is always manic with people getting stuff for the weekend.'

'No problema, Chica. Here, get this down you.' Abi handed her a large glass of white wine that looked more like a small bucket. 'And how is the delectable Bernard? Give him my love next time you see him, won't you?'

'I will, and his head may very well explode when I do. You know he has a crush on you, poor guy.'

'Will you two behave!' Rachel interrupted, 'he's about twice her age!'

'He's eighteen years older than me, a mere drop in the age-gap ocean.' Abi flicked an imaginary piece of fluff off her shoulder, 'Anyway, keep your knickers on. I'm joking. I'm still hanging in there with Dirk, who, incidentally, gets a little bit more annoying by the day.'

'He is a little bit of a, um,' Jayne struggled to find the right adjective that meant loser, but didn't sound so bad.

'He's a knob.' Rachel stated with characteristic frankness.

'Ouch.' Abi pretended to be affronted, but then nodded in agreement. 'Actually, no arguments here.'

'Do you know what? Even though I thought the three-generation gap thing was a little gross at first, I can actually see you with Bernard.'

'Oh Rachel, are you softening in your old age?'

'Not a chance. But even though he's fifty-odd, he's hardly Stanley is he?'

'Stanley?' Abi asked.

'Our mother's husband. Don't you remember, I told you about him?' Jayne said. 'He's an octogenarian and wears cardigans.'

'And smells of cupboards.'

'Speaking of old people, I heard Mrs Stokes describe your man Will as a 'bit of a fox' earlier today.' Abi said laughing. Mrs Stokes was something of an institution; they all had to attend a party for her last year as she celebrated forty years of teaching at the school. Jayne used the word 'celebrate' in its loosest term. Despite reaching a decade there herself, she thought forty years' walking the same corridors, using the same parking space every day for 365 times forty (minus school holidays) was a lot, whatever it came to. The head even pushed the boat out and hired a windowless room above the Fox and Hounds, rather than handing round the usual supermarket-bought cake and cheap sweet wine in plastic tumblers in the staffroom whenever there was a staff celebration.

'Who's Mrs Stokes?' Rachel questioned, taking a big slurp of her gin and slim.

'Home economics teacher.' Jayne answered. Her brow furrowed, 'And how would she know who Will was anyway? She makes quotation marks in the air whenever she says the word 'Internet' so I can't really imagine her spending her evenings surfing YouTube.'

'Once you're on *The Globe* everyone knows who you are.'

139

'Honestly, it's been a crazy couple of days, neither of us ever expected so many people to have read the article. Will popped down to post his Dad's birthday card this morning and he was gone an hour and a half, with different people wanting to meet him and shake his hand – one woman even asked him to sign the back of a grocery receipt!'

'It is really bizarre,' agreed Rachel, 'I mean, this time last week he was just an ordinary bloke who sells smelly cheese and smoked meats and now he's signing his name for people in the street. It's *Will,* for God's sake, not David Beckham.'

'How's he taking it?' Abi asked, while motioning for the barman to bring another round over. You normally had to order at the bar in this pub but Abi and Louis, the barman, had once enjoyed an episode a couple of years ago one night after closing time involving semi-nakedness. His gratitude for said episode had resulted in a lifetime of table service.

'He's being, well, Will about it all. Utterly bemused, a little bit pleased and rather intimidated by all the attention. Do you know, he's been inundated with calls all day by publicists asking to represent him!'

'Represent him doing what?' Rachel said incredulously, 'He makes food taste nice, and it seems like the deli has all the publicity it needs now.'

'Well, they seem to think that he could branch out into TV and do some cooking spots as a guest chef, or something. He's meeting one woman, Miranda, Michaela something now, actually.'

'In the evening?'

'Well she lives in Richmond too and said she wanted to meet him before the weekend, so they're having a drink.'

'Together. On a Thursday night.' Abi shook her head, 'well you're a braver woman than me.'

'What do you mean? This is Will we're talking about.'

'Exactly! Will with his dangerous eyes and long, talented fingers.'

'Adept. The journalist called them long, *adept* fingers. As in adept at chopping stuff up.'

'That's not what most of the women reading the story interpreted it as, that's all I'm saying.'

'Jingle Bells, Jingle Bells, Jingle all the way, La la la, I can't hear you.' Jayne was saved from her embarrassment by the literal bell of her phone chiming.

Hey Baby, home now, it went well – will tell all when you get back, Heart you Wxx

She smiled at his use of their longstanding in-joke. When they'd first got together, they'd both shuffled around the 'L word', despite both knowing that serendipity had decreed that they would never be single again. Saying 'I love you' out loud seemed too hackneyed, too clichéd. That was the stuff of greeting cards, the phrase that filled post-coital silences when the endorphins had put a stop to anything more original being thought of.

They had been sitting on the living-room floor in Duncan and Erica's scruffy Victorian house in Putney. Oscar, their eldest child, was showing Jayne the mechanics of his WWI trench that he'd crafted out of papier mâché and she was making his day with her effusive encouragement. As Oscar had momentarily bent down to fasten a helmet made from a pistachio shell onto a little soldier, Will whispered *I heart you* into her ear. 'It means the word we're not saying, but it's ours,' he'd explained later after they'd indulged in some very unhackneyed and unclichéd lovemaking. 'Heart you too,' she'd murmured happily in reply.

After they'd all said goodbye and Abi had made Louis' day by standing at the pub window and giving him a coy little wave with just her fingers, the twins started walking home with their arms linked together. 'So how are you *really* feeling about all this?' Rachel started.

'What do you mean?'

'I mean, this is me now, and how are you *really* feeling about all this?'

'I'm just so happy that he's finally getting the recognition he deserves, he works so hard, doing these crazy hours and now he can get more people working in the deli and maybe another teacher for the classes and he can start building the business that he's always wanted to.'

'Very commendable answer. If there was a prize for supportive girlfriend of the year, you would get it. Now how are you *really* feeling about it?'

Jayne smiled and hugged Rachel's arm closer to her, 'Just what I said! Stop digging around for feelings I don't have!

Of course I'm a little amused by all these women commenting on my boyfriend's face—'

'And fingers, don't forget the fingers,' Rachel interjected.

'Yes, and his fingers,' Jayne rolled her eyes. 'But, if anything, it makes me feel all smug and superior that I'm the one that gets to wake up next to that face every day. And his fingers,' Jayne added cheekily, narrowly avoiding crashing into a shop window as her sister barged into her side.

'We're home! Where's my international superstar?' Jayne cried loudly as they tramped up the stairs to the flat.

'He's in here, disguised as a bloke that owns a deli,' Will called back. The sisters fell into the living room and collapsed on the sofa opposite to where Will was lounging on a faux-fur beanbag – the latest addition to the home, courtesy of one of Rachel's clients who had over-ordered on a hotel project. 'Perks of the job,' she'd shrugged when Jayne had enquired whether that could be classed as stealing.

'So? How did it go? What was she like?'

'Well, and efficient.'

'Will!'

He smiled, 'Sorry, yes, it was good. She was this uber city-type, with a power suit and monogrammed MacBook Air. You could tell that she's the type to have a personal trainer at 5am and a personal shopper on speed dial.'

'I hate her already,' said Jayne.

'But she seems to really know her stuff. She set up the

agency herself with one of her friends after working for one of the top PR firms, and all her clients followed her to her new company, so she's doing well for herself.'

'Enough about Ms Shoulder Pads, what did she say about you?' asked Rachel impatiently.

He started fiddling with the zip on the side of the beanbag, 'She said that I should be on TV, and that if I sign with her she'll start putting some feelers out for me to do guest cooking spots – she was even talking about book deals, ad campaigns, she had this whole strategy worked out.'

'So what did you say? Did you agree to do it?

Will looked up at Jayne, 'Of course I didn't. I wanted to talk to you first to see what you think I should do.'

'I think you should call her back and say yes.'

He sat up, or at least as much as you can when you're on a beanbag. 'Are you sure? It means that our lives might get a little crazier for a while. I mean, we could just stop this now and concentrate on expanding the business – all this extra attention has meant the sales have gone through the roof. I mean, you saw the queues in the shop today, I've already had to double most of the orders, and with all the people on the waiting list for classes now I could teach for twenty-four hours a day every day. Maybe we should just stick at that. What if I do a TV thing and completely dry up, or burn something, or set the kitchen on fire, and then I'm a complete laughing stock? Yes, I'll just stick with the deli. Maybe I could even save up for some bigger premises or open another one nearby. What do you think?'

Jayne was smiling patiently during this impassioned monologue and waited for him to stop deliberating and procrastinating before she gently said, 'Will, call this woman back and tell her to start putting her plan into action. You're always going to have the deli and the classes, but how often do ordinary people like us get the chance to do something exciting like this?' She picked the house phone out of its stand on the side table next to her and held it out to him, 'Call her'.

**

Friday

'We've got Gavin Walsh, and—'

'Is he still alive?'

'Of course he's still alive. He does that game show The Firm or something.'

'Okay, who else?'

'Steve Hennessey – you know, the mechanic in Emmerdale?'

'Okay, has he been in anything else recently?'

'A few things . . . can't remember the names now—'

'Right. Who else?'

'*Um, that's it at the moment.*'

'*That's crap.*'

'*They're household names.*'

'*Simon, I thought one of them was dead and the other one looks as though he should be. Where's the exciting new talent? Where's the sexy young starlet who's going to give me an erection as soon as their tight little ass bounds onto the stage?*'

'*I'll find one.*'

'*Come and tell me who's going to be the third guest by lunchtime. And I mean it. I want fresh blood. I want our show to be named as the one that shot this person into the big time. Lunchtime.*'

'Hackett and Finch, good morning, please hold. Hackett and Finch good morning, please hold. Hackett and Finch, good morning, please hold. Thanks for holding, how can I help? Putting you though. Thanks for holding, how can I help? Sorry no unscheduled appointments until March. I know it's November. Please call back then. Hackett and Finch, good morning, please hold–'

Jayne and Will exchanged wide eyes as they listened to the receptionist earning every penny of her mediocre salary. 'I'm exhausted now, and we've only been here five minutes,' Will whispered.

'I know! I'm never going to moan about teaching again.' With the mention of teaching Jayne felt a fleeting pang of guilt at phoning in sick today. She knew what a nightmare it was organising cover for absent teachers at short notice. At least today wasn't a heavy teaching day, and the classes she did have were quite good ones; they'd be only too happy to do a bit of quiet reading or a spot of creative writing. Some of her other classes might well have made a substitute teacher cry at best, or want to change career at worst, but she felt that the sub was on safe ground today. And Will had really wanted her to come along to this first proper meeting at the agency.

It was one of those trendy offices that you assumed only existed in films or Uptown Manhattan. A backlit frosted-glass panel took over the whole of the wall behind the receptionist with *Think Big & Believe* artily scrawled in pink-neon loops on it. They were sitting on two of four black-leather armchairs, which Jayne recognised from one of Rachel's magazines – Moooi Smoke Chairs, she thought they were called, where no two were the same as they were set alight during manufacturing, so each one burned in an individual way. It's astonishing what people pay good money for.

'Will?' A heavily gelled early-twenty-something boy-man scuttled into the reception area, extending his hand as he ran. 'Darren, Ms Finch's PA. She's ready for you now.'

'This is Jayne,' said Will to the back of Darren's suit jacket as he scurried away.

'Good to meet you too,' muttered Jayne, blissfully ignorant

of the fact that this wouldn't be the last time that no one cared what her name was.

'Will, how are you this morning?' Michaela rose out of her seat, her figure framed by an extraordinary backdrop over the Thames.

'Good, good, this is Jayne, my partner.'

'Please—' she motioned to the hot-pink sofas at the other end of her office, 'Have a seat. Darren, three green teas.' Dutifully dismissed, Darren reverently backed out of the room.

'So, Jayne, what do you think of your boyfriend's sudden rise to prominence?' At the word 'boyfriend' Jayne was sure she detected a hint of derision, but she couldn't be sure. Leaving no pause for her reply, Michaela turned her upper body to squarely face Will and crossed her legs. Despite the fact the year had well and truly turned its back on autumn, her long legs were bare and tanned. Jayne self-consciously tugged at her maxi skirt, hoping it covered the thick woollen tights she'd opted to wear that morning – stupidly once again choosing function over form.

'I had a very interesting call from the booker on *Good Morning*; they are interested in you doing a little segment on the show next week. I said yes. They suggested something topical, perhaps to do with a Christmas breakfast – I said you'd need ten minutes, they said six, we agreed on eight. I said Tuesday, they said yes.' This time she did pause, obviously expecting a gushing retort, or perhaps even applause.

'Wow, *Good Morning*?' Will looked at Jayne with his mouth open, 'That's amazing! Thank you!'

Underneath her Botox, Michaela looked pleased. 'Excellent. They said it's only a one-off while you're still hot property, but wow them and you'll be invited back. Right, so that's the first thing, second thing, we need to think about your image. I love the whole tongue-in-cheek geek chic meets *Esquire* thing that you've got going on: it's very now, it's very in. V-neck t-shirts rather than round neck, though, that's crucial. God gave you that collarbone for a reason.'

As far as Jayne was aware, God gave him that collarbone to keep his shoulders joined to his chest, but what did she know, she wore woollen tights.

'I've booked you into see Fernando at eleven today in Covent Garden to tidy up your hair and to give you a shave, so by Tuesday you'll have just the right amount of stubble to look like you've just stumbled out of bed.'

'And that's a good thing?' Jayne cut in.

'I don't really like stubble,' Will admitted, 'It's itchy.'

Michaela gave them a look that straddled pity and contempt. 'Eleven. Also, it's good that you did that *Globe* interview, but any more impromptu reporters turning up at your door, send them my way, giving them nothing more than a smile. Thankfully you didn't say anything too ridiculous, or if you did the journalist was too stupid to turn it into copy, but from now on, keep schtum unless I tell you not to. We have to create your brand carefully, so no going off piste.' She stood up, indicating that the meeting had reached its conclusion. 'Any questions, Darren's phone is always on, so don't hesitate.'

A minute later and they were standing outside on the pavement a little shell-shocked.

'She seemed – nice.' Jayne eventually ventured.

'By nice do you mean absolutely terrifying?'

'Like the love child of a supermodel and a pit bull.'

'Jesus,' Will's colour was starting to return, 'What are we even doing here? We're not in Kansas any more, Toto.'

'Nope. We're going to Fernando's for a shave and a haircut. Maybe you can have a mani pedi as well while you're there. Wax your eyebrows or something.'

'Oh bugger off,' Will playfully wrapped both his arms around her as they started walking down the street. 'Anyway, what was that nerd comment about?'

'Oh I don't know, Mister-I-Often-Wear-Braces-Under-My-Blazer, I have no idea what she was talking about. And didn't you just buy a cardigan?'

'It's a sports jacket and braces are underrated in their coolness.'

'Of course they are. Right, we've got an hour before Fernando turns you into a metrosexual. Buy me a full-fat vanilla latte to get the taste of that God-awful green tea out of my mouth and I'll love you forever.'

Chapter 11

She'd been tasting slivers of that, teaspoons of this and whole chunks of the other since 7am and while the majority of it had been a pleasure and not a chore, she had to call time on it before the top button pinged off her jeans. Will, meanwhile, hadn't even raised his head from the worktop for over three hours, so was in danger of developing a hunchback rarely seen outside of Notre Dame. Every pinch of something new he added meant another taste test, followed by a hurried scrawl in the notebook next to him. The sink was piled high with pans, dishes and ramekins – Jayne didn't even know they owned rame-kins, but then, to be fair, she wasn't a regular visitor to their crockery cupboard, more an erstwhile tourist, who only arrived there by accident while searching for the biscuits.

She could tell that he was in heaven, as long as he put out of his mind the fact that he would be recreating this dish on live national television in three days' time, he was having a wonderful time tinkering about with the contents of the spice rack. This was how he spent most of his spare time anyway, just pottering about the kitchen wondering what tarragon and cinnamon tasted like mixed together. Not nice, apparently. Even when they went out for dinner he tried to guess every single ingredient in each dish, which sounded like it should be annoying, but she never found it so. She had tried to join in at first, but after getting pork and chicken confused in one of their early games, she felt that her input lacked credibility.

'Why don't you make those awesome cranberry muffins you made last Christmas? They were yummy.' It had been so sweet, it was their first Christmas together and he'd hidden his phone under his pillow so when the alarm vibrated it wouldn't wake her, then he'd piled a tray full of goodies, warm muffins, champagne – the real stuff, not the fizzy imitation of their first date – and a little stack of parcels neatly wrapped in brown paper and tied with raffia string and a little sprig of mistletoe and brought it into the bedroom, wearing nothing but a Santa hat and a smile.

'No, Jamie Oliver has cornered the market on breakfast muffins, Gordon Ramsay owns eggs and smoked salmon, so I'm thinking that I'm going to go with gingerbread and treacle butter. What do you think?'

'Sounds amazeballs. Can we wait a couple of hours until the next tasting session, though, I need to lie flat for a while.' He laughed as she jumped off the bar stool and pretended to waddle like a sumo wrestler out of the room, even turning sideways to walk through the door.

She was just at the part of the film where Colin Firth's manuscript has blown into the lake and the Portuguese girl has stripped off and is diving in to get it when the front door slammed and Rachel came bounding up the stairs.

'Jeez, you know it's Christmas when *Love Actually* gets dusted off.'

'You know it. And shush, I love this bit – come under here and watch it with me.' Jayne lifted up one side of the fleecy blanket and Rachel snuck under it. Jayne crinkled her nose. 'You smell of booze.'

'It was the Christmas party last night. I'm allowed to.'

'But it's 11am.'

'I haven't had a shower yet.'

'That's really skanky.'

'I know,' Rachel yawned, 'I'll go in a minute, just after Hugh Grant knocks on all the doors. I like that bit.'

'So who was the lucky man this time?'

'I stayed at Kyra's.'

'Really?' Jayne knew that this was a very unlikely story, consuming alcohol and sleeping alone never usually happened on the same night for Rachel.

Having such an unstable upbringing had affected the sisters in different ways – Jayne yearned for an aga, estate car and golden retriever, whereas Rachel was showing all the signs of having their mother's attention span when it came to romance. But of course Jayne would never say that to her.

She didn't actually know why Rachel wanted to sleep with so many men. In every other aspect of her life she was so self-assured and poised, and yet she seemed to need this added clarification from strangers as to her attractiveness, or maybe she was just reading too much into it, and it was merely to relieve a bit of boredom. She knew that watching box sets with her and Will every evening had a shelf life, and maybe indulging in one-night stands was a just a fun way to break the monotony of another season of *Mad Men*.

'Really.' Rachel replied. 'What? You can phone her and ask her if you like!'

'Steady on, I was only asking.'

'Sorry, I'm hung-over and stinky, and desperately need a shower and to brush my teeth, but now I never want to move from this blanket.'

'It's okay. And you're in luck, Will is preparing the best hangover cure ever at this exact moment – gingerbread and treacle something.'

'Is that what he's cooking for the show?'

'He thinks so. He's been trying different things out this morning, but that's the current favourite. He has to give them the recipe tomorrow morning so their cooks can make 'the one he made earlier'.'

'Hang on,' Rachel shifted position so she was facing her

sister, 'so when they take something out of the oven and say 'here's one I did earlier', they're lying?'

'Of course they are. You didn't think that the chef had been in the kitchen for hours making the same dish twice?'

'What about on *Blue Peter* when they did that thing with yoghurt pots?'

'Same thing. Didn't you notice how the one they were meant to have done earlier was always better than the one they were doing in real time? That's because it was a proper artist person doing the earlier one.'

'No. You're making this up. I'm going to ask Will. When I can be bothered to move.'

They both then sighed as a desperate Emma Thompson listened to Joni Mitchell after finding out that Alan Rickman had bought his secretary a necklace.

'Bastard.'

'Bastard.'

'Oh Jesus, is it *Love Actually* time again? Didn't you just watch this?' Will was balancing three plates as he backed into the living room, 'Here, try this. I don't know if the ratio of ginger and mixed spice is quite right. I put in nearly two tablespoons of ginger, but it might need more of a kick.'

Each plate had two slices of warm gingerbread cake on it, a dollop of treacle butter with tantalisingly small bits of honeycomb melting over the top of it.

'Oh. My. Gob, piff if amabing,' Jayne picked up a crumb from the sofa where it had fallen out of her mouth.

'Do you really think so? Is it good enough for TV, do you think?'

'Yes, absolutely, it's gorgeous. Now look, Jayne's starting a vicious rumour about the one chefs prepare earlier. Is it true that it's all a big con?'

Will put his hand up to stem Rachel talking. 'No comment. All questions now have to go through my agent.'

A blanket of remarkable calm had descended over the flat in the run-up to the show. Jayne knew that Will had been rehearsing his patter in front of the bathroom mirror because a) she'd heard him through the door and b) he'd left a small saucepan and a stopwatch next to his toothbrush. She'd offered to tape him rehearsing so he could watch it back to see it for himself, but he said that would make him more nervous if he could see what an idiot he probably looked. He was due to be on just after the regional news at 11.08, and they'd told all their friends to watch.

Rachel was in the sports bar over the road from her office with her colleague Kyra – they'd persuaded the manager to turn off re-runs of the Abu Dhabi Grand Prix and tune into *Good Morning*, which the handful of alcoholic racing enthusiasts weathered with surprisingly good humour.

Over at Pine Grove, Helen had commandeered the TV in the residents' morning room and was holding a coffee morning, with Will as the entertainment. Michaela and Darren were out on the studio floor, sandwiched behind the row of cameras and in front of a group of mesmerised A-level media studies students on a field trip. Duncan had taken the day off and was keeping Jayne company in the green room while Will was being walked through the set and having some foundation and bronzer put on his face, much to his best friend's mirth.

'Duncan, sit down, you're making me nervous,' Jayne said, chewing what was left of her nails.

'Sorry, this is just so exciting.' He bounced up and down on the blue sofa, 'Who do you reckon has sat in this exact seat?'

'Everyone – they even had David Cameron on a few weeks ago.'

'Never mind him, what about Kelly Brook?'

'Quite possibly.'

'Why's it called the green room and it's not green?'

'I think it dates back to theatres in olden times, or something, do you want a croissant?' Jayne walked across to the table where fresh pastries and big jugs of juice and water sat alongside coffee and tea. She thought she might actually throw up if she ate anything, but just sitting watching Will get his microphone clipped onto his new v-necked t-shirt via the big wall-mounted monitor was making her heart beat loudly in her chest, so she had to do something to stop herself staring at the screen.

All the way to the studio he'd been buzzing, like a little kid high on sugar and e-numbers, his fingers tapping rhythmically on his man bag, his mouth alternating between whistling and humming, but now, seeing him on the TV making the final check of the ingredients in front of him, he looked completely serene. Standing there, beautifully cool and coolly beautiful, mere seconds away from addressing the nation, Jayne realised this was exactly where he was supposed to be.

'Ten seconds to air, nine, eight . . .'

Will ran his tongue over his teeth again, he didn't know why. He hadn't eaten yet today so there's no way any stray spinach could have jumped up into his mouth without him noticing. The host, Clarissa, was standing so close to him, he could smell her perfume: a cloying floral scent he didn't recognise.

'Ready?' She flashed him a quick, genuine smile before replacing it with the fixed toothy beam familiar to the viewers. 'And welcome back! Today we have a real treat, a chef who's taken the Internet by storm with his short film series of delicious dishes, and he's here today to show us how to make an indulgent breakfast for Christmas morning. It's Will Scarlet. Hello and welcome, Will.'

'Hi Clarissa. Thank you for having me.' Smiling warmly, straight into the camera he said, 'And hello to everyone at home. Today I'm going to make some lovely soft gingerbread with a very decadent treacle butter. It's going to fill your house with those gorgeous festive aromas – ginger and cinnamon, as well as being a truly debauched start to the day, which if you can't have on Christmas Day, when can you?'

Picking up little bowls of butter, sugar, treacle and syrup he started tipping them all into a pan, 'You need your oven heated to 170 for this, so it's a good idea to do this breakfast just before you pop your turkey in, and remember to warn little people zooming about the house on their new roller skates that the oven's hot. Okay, so once this mixture has dissolved completely, sift together the flour and spices and in another bowl – one like this is perfect – whisk together the eggs and half a cup of buttermilk. Most grocery stores stock this in the dairy aisle – if you can't find it, don't worry, it's super-easy to make yourself: one cup of milk mixed with one spoon of white vinegar or lemon juice. Then you just need to fold the syrup mixture into the flour, and then the butter, pour it into a loaf tin and bake in the oven for about thirty minutes. Now Clarissa, I'm going to get you involved now. I'm hoping that you're a bit of a pro with a food processor?'

'I can press the on button if that's all that's needed?' she simpered, fluttering her eyelash extensions.

'Well, that's about the level of expertise you need for this, so that's excellent! Okay, just whizz together slightly crushed honeycomb, butter and treacle for a few seconds, not too long as you don't want to drown out the Christmas radio for too long do you? That's all part of the experience.'

'Speaking of Christmas music, what's your favourite festive song, Will?'

He put on some oven gloves and expertly removed the cake the crew did earlier from the oven. 'Well, it used to be The Pogues, until I really listened to the words and realised that after twenty years of singing it it's actually got very depressing lyrics, so my guilty Christmas favourite is actually Chris Rea's *Driving Home for Christmas*,' He looked up into the camera. 'But please don't judge me for that! But to be honest, in my house the Christmas CD goes on somewhere around mid-November, so even Cliff's 'Mistletoe and Wine' gets a fair amount of air time in my kitchen! Okay, and we're almost there – now just slice the bread into inch-thick slices and dollop a generous spoonful of this sumptuous butter on top, and look, you can see it starting to melt and ooze down the sides now – and there you have it, a stunningly simple but incredibly luxurious start to the festivities.'

'Will, thank you, it's been an absolute pleasure,'

'Thank you for having me. I've really enjoyed it, and happy Christmas.'

'To you too. We'll be back after this short break with some fabulous fashion for the over-forties, so stay tuned for some glam party looks that are sure to turn heads.'

As the red light went off on the three cameras in front of them the studio buzzed into action. Assistants ran onto the set setting up an impromptu catwalk and two harassed-looking women from the costume department started frantically dabbing at the front of Clarissa's shirt where a fleck of stray butter had landed. Clarissa's co-host, who had been sitting on the side during the cookery segment sauntered over holding out his fake-tanned hand, 'Hi Will, I'm Graham. You're a natural, that was great. Looks like I'm going to have competition with the ladies if you become a regular on the show!'

Clarissa smiled amidst the flurry of activity around her chest, and a make-up artist who was now unnecessarily topping up her blusher. 'Will, that was incredible. I think I may now be a little bit in love with you.' She laughed a little bit too loudly for a little bit too long.

'I really enjoyed it. Thank you for having me.'

'Thirty seconds to air, twenty nine . . .'

A clipboard-carrying assistant came onto the set to chivvy Will back to the green room, where Duncan and Jayne were hugging each other, bouncing around the room. Jayne flew at him as soon as he walked through the door, clasping him tight and covering him in kisses. 'Darling, you were amazing! Beyond amazing! Absolutely brilliant!'

'Mate, that was top. Really good,' Duncan pulled him in for a hug and some manly backslapping.

'Are you sure I didn't look like a pillock?'

'No, and I would tell you,' replied Duncan honestly.

'You were brilliant, baby, as though you do this all day every day.' Just then the door opened and Michaela glided in, followed by a grinning Darren, who was laden down with his rucksack and Michaela's own handbag and folders.

'Will, darling, you were sensational.' She gave him two enthusiastic air kisses, 'I've just had a quick chat with the executive producer and he wants to book you for two more segments in the run-up to Christmas, so next Tuesday and the one after that as well. He's calling me with more info after the show ends, so keep your phone with you this arvo and I'll revert then.' Two more air kisses, 'Sensational, darling. A superstar is born.' Jayne had never seen someone swoosh out of a room while wearing a trouser suit before, but apparently it could be done.

Will turned back to Jayne and swung her around, 'Two more shows! Did you hear that! He liked me! Oh my God, this is incredible!'

'Champagne! We need champagne!' Duncan boomed.

A jubilant Rachel, Kyra and Marco, who had told their bosses that designing bars necessitated an immediate field trip to one for 'research' soon joined the three of them. Erica had promised to come after dropping the boys at football practice and Abi was stuck elbow-deep in a papier mâché project with year eight until 2pm, but had demanded that a glass filled with bubbles be waiting for her upon her arrival.

Following Will's express orders, Bernard had put the closed sign on the deli's door and was currently arguing with Jayne over whose credit card should be used to cover another two bottles and some nibbles. She reluctantly let Bernard foot the bill for this round, on the basis of his harsh-but-fair reasoning that his monthly pension probably outweighed her annual teacher's salary.

'Here you go, guys,' she said, substituting a full bottle for the upended empty one in her sister's wine bucket.

'We were just saying how photogenic Will looked on camera,' Kyra smiled. Jayne had only met Kyra a few times before and only then in passing when she'd swung by the flat to pick Rachel up before one of their big nights out that invariably ended in Rachel's room not being slept in. She wouldn't necessarily have picked her out as a potential friend for her sister, not that she knew her well enough to say something like that. She was actually just basing her assumption on appearances, which she never normally did, but Kyra just grated on her slightly. Perhaps it was the fact that she was the same height as Jayne but weighed easily twenty kilos less, or the fact that her honey-coloured hair seemed to just cascade down her back, unlike her own, which frothed out in all directions. Jealousy is an ugly trait, she told herself, shaking her head and plastering on a big grin to go with her polite reply. If Rachel liked her, then so would she. It would just be easier to if she didn't look like Barbie's better-looking sister.

She glanced over at where Will was being fawned over by Marco, who had decided that green wasn't his colour after all, so had substituted envy for ecstasy. Will caught her eye and gave her a small wink. Even after nearly two years together he could still summon up the butterflies inside her with a well-timed smile meant only for her. She was beyond proud of him. All the way through the broadcast she had been transfixed, hands together as if in prayer, silently, telepathically urging him to succeed, to smile, not to forget what to say, not to blend his fingers instead of the butter.

On screen he'd looked like her Will, but also didn't at the same time. Gone were the faint worry lines that sometimes appeared in moments of his self-doubt, and the bright studio lights seemed to make his piercing blue eyes appear even brighter. A few of the salt-and-pepper strands of grey that had started to infiltrate his temples had been lovingly painted back to their original black by the effete Fernando, and even the stubble that they'd both rallied against made him look suave rather than just too lazy to pick up a razor.

Across the busy bar Will held his flashing phone aloft, mouthed 'Michaela' and gestured for Jayne to join him outside on the street to take the call. She grabbed their coats from under Rachel and Kyra, where they were perched majestically like two Cleopatras, and rushed after him.

'You're kidding me?' Will had already started talking when Jayne ran up behind him, wrapping his coat around his shoulders. He was still just wearing the white t-shirt that he'd filmed in and it was one of those sunny but deceptively sub-zero December days. 'That's crazy!' His voice had risen loud enough to garner a few glares from people hurrying past them on the busy street.

'What?' Jayne mouthed, unable to decipher his intonation as to whether it was good crazy or bad crazy. She really hoped Michaela wasn't calling to say that the show had changed their minds and that they didn't want him any more. He'd get over the disappointment, she was sure of that, but he was so excited about this new adventure and his confidence would take a bit of a beating if he was effectively a one-hit wonder.

'Okay, so that's Thursday at eleven, and then where is the show on Friday night? And then Saturday afternoon. What time is that? Can you email all that to me, I'm outside a bar now and don't have a pen . . . What do you mean? A bar . . . No, I'm on the street . . . I'm with my friends celebrating the show . . . Okay, okay, I'm going back inside now. Yes, okay, bye.' He pressed the end button and stared at Jayne in shock.

'What? Say something? That sounded good, didn't it? Was it good news? What did she say?'

'Uh, yes,' he started laughing, and ran a hand through his newly cropped hair. 'Uh, very good news. The producer wants me to do another slot on Thursday on *Good Morning*. Apparently they got loads of calls after the show and they want me to do all the cookery slots in the run-up to Christmas, so twice a week for the next three weeks, and they'll see about putting me on a contract in the New Year. Then I've also got a guest spot on a Channel Four talk show on Friday night – you know, the one that we saw when we were at my dad's – and then on Saturday afternoon I'm one of the guests on the lunchtime show on Radio 2.' He stopped, his right hand still in his hair, 'Jesus, Jayne. How is this happening?'

Jayne went up on her tiptoes and gently kissed his nose. 'You deserve it, baby. You work so hard and you're awesome and now everyone is going to know just how awesome.'

It was as though the kiss suddenly snapped Will back into the moment and he started shuffling Jayne backwards into the bar, being careful to avoid the throngs of single-minded Christmas shoppers and lost-looking tourists laden down with yellow Selfridges bags. 'Michaela flipped out when I said that we were standing on a pavement outside a bar, she said that she doesn't want to see drunk shots of me with a bar in the background, so let's go back inside.'

'You're not drunk. Well, not yet – wait 'til I order some jaeger bombs. Oooo, I should get a tray of shot glasses filled with water and then you can text her a video of you downing all of them. Then let's see her really flip out.'

'You are a wicked woman, Jayne Brady, and I love you, but this early in my career, I think I need her on my side, so let's save the histrionics for April Fool's Day, okay?'

'Every party needs a party pooper.'

'Heehee, you just said pooper,' mocked a voice that came from behind her.

'Alright, Dirk?' they both uttered as a cheap shiny suit slunk past them into the bar.

'Can you believe this?' Rachel slurred to Jayne, after a couple of women had peeled off from their office lunch and had asked Will for a picture with them.

'Not really,' Jayne admitted, 'it's incredible to think that two weeks ago we were sitting in the deli talking about doing a stock-take and now we're in a posh bar in Covent Garden celebrating the launch of his TV career.'

'No, I mean, can you believe there are women who want a photo of him.'

'Oi! That's my boyfriend you're talking about!'

'I know, but it's smelly old Billy, with his spotty face and greasy hair.'

'Rach, take a look. That Billy's well and truly gone. And anyway, he never had that many spots. Although, admittedly he may once have been a stranger to the shampoo bottle. But he's very hygienic now.'

'Will Scarlet, gorgeous and hygienic. What a combination,' Abi chimed in at the tail end of the conversation; despite arriving two hours after everyone else she had played catch-up with an impressive dexterity. 'Every mother's dream.'

'You're right there. Even our own mother has phoned. Eighteen months of silence, then her daughter's boyfriend's on the telly and suddenly she's come over all maternal, gushing over her 'talented family'.' Rachel said, rolling her eyes.

'I thought it was nice that she called.' Jayne said frowning.

Admittedly her mother's timing was a little suspect, calling only a few minutes after Will had gone off air. Jayne had tried to call her quite a few times in the months since the Devon trip, but she never picked up, nor returned her messages. She didn't want Rachel to be right, that Crystal's out-of-the-blue call was driven by a desire to share whatever limelight was going, rather than wanting to reconnect. Jayne shrugged. 'Whatever her motives, it shows she was thinking of us.'

'Of herself.'

'Of *us*. And Stanley even came on the phone wanting to pass on his congratulations.'

'Poor sod. How he's still alive I've got no idea.'

'What, you don't think your mum's trying to *poison* him?' Abi hissed incredulously, her straw dangling between her open lips.

'No, you moron, although I'm sure it's crossed her mind. I meant she's probably trying to shag him into an early grave.'

'Everyone has to go somehow. S'better than cancer,' Dirk cut in, slurring. 'Abi, gettus another drink, sbarman won't serve me.'

'Because you're being a nuisance. Just go home, Dirk.' Abi turned her body away from him slightly and shook her head apologetically at Jayne and Rachel. She hadn't wanted him to come at all, but he'd guessed they'd all be out celebrating and had called Abi relentlessly until she reluctantly told him where they were. Turns out his skin was a little thicker than she'd given him credit for because, short of yelling in his face 'you're a dick that nobody wants around,' he still persisted in inviting himself along to things.

'I think I'm going to have to stop sleeping with him, and then he might get the message,' Abi said with a sigh as soon as she'd returned from booting him into a taxi.

'Um, you think?'

The music in the brasserie had been turned up a notch to the level where Jayne had actually become aware that there was music playing. Their little group had shared the bar all afternoon with a few tables of suits who had made the transition from business lunch into the territory of 'well it's on expenses anyway, so let's order brandies', but they'd now been replaced with clusters of after-work revellers who had started to drift in. At the far end of the bar a band was starting to set up, tuning their instruments and their distinctly unmelodious twangs and ad hoc strumming coupled with nearly five hours of champagne-drinking had started to give Jayne a bit of a headache. Will snuck up behind her and snaked an arm around her waist, nuzzling into her neck. 'How's my favourite thing in all the world?' He was slightly slurring too and had the makings of a thousand-yard stare.

'I'm good, baby, but I think I might need to go home soon, but you stay out. I don't want to drag you away from your party.'

'Don't be silly. I'd much rather be with you,' he rested his chin on the top of her head as his arms wrapped around her. 'Shall we tell everyone we're going or just sneak out the bathroom window?'

'Crawling through a window sounds so much more fun, but I think they'll come after us. Quick hugs all round, then we're off. Deal?'

'Deal.'

After fifteen minutes of working their way around the group, sharing embraces that began as heartfelt shows of affection but turned into just holding each other up, Jayne and Will sat back in their taxi. They figured that if you can't treat yourself to a cab from central London to Zone 4 on the day you make your television debut, when can you? Their fingers were entwined, with their thumbs engrossed in their usual thumb-war battle to be on top of the other person's. 'How are you doing?' Jayne yawned, laying her head on his shoulder.

'I'm good. I'm, well, a bit numb, to be honest. This is all a bit mad, isn't it?'

'A little bit. But good mad. It's like looking through a window of a world not many people get to see.'

'I like that. It sounds very poetic.'

'You can use it if you like. It's now yours.'

He kissed her head. 'But I know what you mean, seeing the studio and the cameras and meeting the presenters, you just see the polished programme on screen and you don't realise that in every break they're flossing and having their noses brushed. And the lights were so hot on my face.'

'Were they? You couldn't tell. I remember watching a three-woman play on a tiny stage in a pub in Balham where the lights were so close to the stage one of the actress's wig got singed. So bear that in mind. No wigs on set.'

'Duly noted.'

They settled into a comfortable silence, leaning against each other, watching London whizz past them. All along the Thames the bare trees had been adorned with fairy lights that looked like stars caught safely in the branches. Christmas did something to this city, this huge city of anonymous, busy outsiders. For about six weeks of the year the whole place just seemed to take on an ethereal quality, a sort of mystical allure that sadly turned back into a pumpkin come January the second. As they stopped at some traffic lights they both watched a couple amble slowly along, stopping to hold the rail and watch a boat passing under a bridge. A night breeze blew their hair and the man reached down and picked up the end of his girlfriend's, or wife's, scarf and gently wound it around her neck again. Witnessing a moment of tenderness between strangers instinctively made Jayne and Will tighten their grip on each other's hand.

The tranquil solitude was rudely shattered by a gruff South London burr from behind the glass, 'You're that bloke, aren't you? The cook bloke.'

The cab driver was looking directly at Will in the rear-view mirror. Jayne could feel him shift uncomfortably in his seat, 'Um, yes?'

'Thought so. My missus made me watch your video on the internet. I got in loads of grief for giving her a hairdryer last Christmas, and now she wants me to make her bloody breakfast in bed this year. Thanks a chuffing lot.'

Chapter 12

Next to the bright-red toaster and matching kettle that they'd jubilantly bought in the John Lewis sale one rainy Sunday was the internet radio Rachel had given Will for his birthday last year. It was designed to look like an old 1950s radio, complete with proper dials and tuners, in a wooden casing. Much to Rachel's pseudo disgust it was currently belting out non-stop festive music, thanks to a Swiss radio station Jayne had found called *Radio Christmas* that only played Christmas tunes. It was astonishing, and brilliant, Jayne thought, that there was enough festive music out there to keep an entire radio station going for the whole month of December. For other years she'd relied on her trusty Christmas compilation CD that started off well but now had a scratch over Bing Crosby's 'Santa Claus is Coming to Town', so finding this radio station pretty much saved Christmas for her.

Thanks to Will's love of all things Christmas, and perhaps a little bit to annoy Rachel, their small kitchen above the deli had become something of a grotto. White fairy lights ran along the top of the cupboards, over the window blind and above the framed map of the world, while little fabric red-and-white- gingham hearts hung from each door handle. Downstairs in the deli, an endless snaking line of customers had been clamouring for hampers filled with festive treats every day for the last few weeks, so their oven permanently had batches of cinnamon this and nutmeg that baking in it, giving the whole building an enduring scent of Christmas.

Every afternoon from about four o clock, Bernard and the latest addition to the roster, a lovely matronly woman called Sylvia, had been handing out little paper cups of warm mulled wine to 'bring a little cheer to the dark afternoons,' so notes of hot merlot and sliced oranges also perpetually hung in the air. As if the business needed boosting any more, Jayne thought wryly, the deli had never been busier. The potential prospect of glimpsing the charismatic owner who had appeared on pretty much every chat show going over the last few weeks meant that half of London suddenly had a desperate and unquenchable need for feta-stuffed olives and jars of date and apple chutney.

The last month had been like being on an out-of-control carousel, which whirled round and round without stopping. The end of term was always a busy time, but previously she'd been able to trudge home armed with blank reports to studiously spend her evenings filling in, while Will would thoughtfully top up her glass of Baileys and laugh at her well-practised variations of 'your child is a Shakespeare-hating heathen.' But for the last few weeks they'd barely crossed paths, let alone limbs.

Michaela had proven to be something of a whirling dervish, certainly earning her status as the doyenne of the PR scene in London. She had every booker's number on speed dial and invitations to all the city's see-and-be-seen parties jostling for position on her metaphorical mantelpiece. Will was her new pet project and she'd have got him into the opening of an envelope if there was the slightest chance it might aid his swift ascent to stardom. Jayne tried recalling all the events he'd been to so far this past fortnight – a cocktail reception at the National Gallery; the launch of a new Mont Blanc store in Bond Street; a charity cookout for Shelter.

She'd have loved to have accompanied him to some of them, but she knew it would be just impossible to then drag herself out of bed at 6.15 when the alarm sprang into action. The prospect of dealing with 1300 kids every morning certainly put late-night fun out of the equation during termtime.

She'd tried teaching on a hangover early on in her career, in the days where Abi and she would suddenly decide to go clubbing, just because they were young and living in London, and that's what young people living in London were supposed to do, but she soon realised that no amount of frolicking the night before was worth the pain of enduring the next day in the classroom. This was a lesson Abi had yet to learn, but then spending a day mooching about the top-floor art studios fiddling with bits of clay sounded like a much easier prospect to Jayne than intense investigation into Hamlet's motives for pretending to be mad. Not that she would ever voice this opinion out loud.

They'd set aside a couple of nights in the run-up to Christmas just for them. Will had told a sternly disappointed Michaela that he wasn't sure how him being at the opening of the new polar-bear enclosure at London Zoo was going to enhance his reputation for being a TV chef, and instead they got a takeaway, a couple of bottles of nice wine and bribed Rachel to stay away for the evening. She'd had plans with Kyra anyway, but wasn't going to pass up the opportunity for Jayne to clean her bathroom for a fortnight, so had made a cursory effort to look mildly put-upon before leaving with her already-packed overnight bag.

The remnants of some rice and half a naan bread littered the coffee table. They'd made a superficial effort at tidying up by moving the balti-stained plates into the kitchen, but to do more was a bit beyond them at that moment. Lying back on the sofa, glass of wine in hand, Will put his feet into Jayne's lap and kept nudging her until she started to rub them.

'So I was standing next to this sculpture, which I swear looked as though someone had bent a few pipes together, when these two elderly women came up and stood next to me. They were really well dressed, you know, like they had lifelong membership to the Arts Council or something, both carrying their bags like this,' he stuck out his forearm and mimed having a handbag hanging over the crook of his arm, 'and they each had a glass of champagne. And one of them said, 'Now this sculpture I do like, look Maria,' and I thought, oh hello, here we go, what arty farty nonsense are they going to start spouting now? And the other one said, 'Oh yes, Polly, it's the perfect height for resting your flute on.' And they both put their empty glasses on top of the sculpture and left! I actually thought I was going to spit out my drink and I looked around but no one else saw it and I wished that you were there laughing with me. Promise you'll come to the next one?'

'As soon as term ends, I promise, you'll have your partner in crime back.'

'Excellent, because I've missed her.'

'Are you getting all soppy on me?'

'A little. I mean I'm loving doing these shows and going to these parties and things, but Michaela drags me around shaking hands with different network heads and magazine editors and all I really want to do is skulk in a corner with you and laugh at everyone else.'

'Okay, I'll come to anything after next Wednesday.' Jayne waited a little while before she said, with a tone she hoped sounded indifferent, 'um, has anyone ever asked about me?'

'What do you mean?'

'I mean, in all these interviews you're doing, has anyone ever asked if you're seeing anyone?'

A pause. 'A few people.'

'And?' He was really maddening sometimes, just dragging out information that he knew that she desperately wanted to hear.

'And, the first time it happened, I opened my mouth to say yes and to tell them about you and then Michaela cut in and said that I'm not married yet, so um, yes, I was still single.' He added these last few words as a very quiet, sheepish mumble.

'Single?' Jayne shrieked, all efforts to be nonchalant and casual vanished, along with the convivial atmosphere of the evening.

Will sat up and took her hand, which she snatched away, 'Well, I never actually said that I was single, no, of course I'm not, but Michaela thinks it's better while I'm just starting out if people think that I'm, well, available. It might make me more, um, popular.'

'Right. And me being around would, by that reasoning, make you unpopular.' Her voice had risen a few decibels, 'and you agreed with *Michaela*?' she knew she was being petty now, spitting out Michaela's name in a whiny nasally voice that she heard herself doing and despised herself for it, but couldn't help it. They'd always had each other's backs, that was what was so great about them as a couple, and now here he was, on the verge of making a real name for himself and the person who had supported him through all of it was just supposed to blend into the background.

'So what does this mean? Are you breaking up with me?' Jayne's eyes started filling up; the wine, the candles, the sudden revelations, all of it started getting too much for her, and then she couldn't control it any more and started sobbing. She tried to cover her face with her hands, embarrassed at her emotional reaction.

'Oh my God, you nutter, of course not! You are by far the most amazing thing that's ever happened to me – here, come here,' he pulled her into him, the mixture of tears and snot making the front of his shirt damp, but he either didn't notice or, more likely, didn't mind.

Burying his head into her hair, which was coming loose from its topknot, he continued, 'Of course I'm going to start telling everyone about you – that's why I want you to come out with me – it's just that–' he adopted the same nasally whining voice that Jayne had just used, which she couldn't help giving a little smile at. '*Michaela* thought that it should be a gradual thing, me being part of a couple, which is why she wanted me to be pictured on my own at things for a while. Jesus, Jayne, break up with you? You're the only sane thing in this crazy world!' He put his finger under her chin and raised her face so their eyes were level. 'Heart you, Jayne Brady.'

She sniffled and attempted a small smile, 'Heart you too.'

'Would you like me show you just how much I heart you?' he whispered.

'I think that would be the best thing to do. I'm not sure I quite get it,' she replied as he began unbuttoning her shirt. 'Make sure you're very thorough, though,' her bottom lip still protruded, 'I'm still very unconvinced.'

Chapter 13

'So, what's the plan for Christmas Day?' Rachel asked, scraping yoghurt from the pot onto her granola as she perched on the arm of the sofa. 'Is Granny coming up on Christmas Eve as usual?'

Jayne had set up a wrapping station on the living-room floor, with all the gifts she'd been stockpiling since October laid out all over the rug, along with a variety of coloured ribbons and rolls of paper depicting toy soldiers from the *Nutcracker*. Inch-long pieces of sticky tape that she had pre-cut were now hanging off the side of the coffee table. She started measuring out enough paper to cover the two-foot-long golf putter she'd bought for Dave, Will's dad.

It reminded her of the wrapping party she went to a few years ago – the PTA had organised it – and in an attempt to ingratiate herself with the mob, which she'd so far failed miserably to do, she'd gone along. The premise was to bring along items that were difficult to wrap and they could get some expert advice from a friend of the president of the

PTA who worked in the gift-wrapping department at Liberty's. All this was to be done over a glass or two of mulled wine – cue much bonding and festive merriment between staff and parents. Except everyone else had turned up with things like bottles of bubble bath, or champagne, and she'd arrived engulfed by a giant inflatable cactus. She hadn't been to a PTA do since.

'Yep. Christmas Eve.'

'Did you book that same driver that she had last time – she seemed to like him?'

'Um, no.'

'Why not? Wasn't he available? Who did you get, then?'

'Um, Stanley's driving.'

'Who's Stanley?'

'*Stanley*. Crystal's Stanley.'

'Why would he be driving four hours to drop Granny off and then four hours back again on Christmas Eve?' Rachel asked in amazement.

'He's not driving back again,' Jayne mumbled back, wincing in anticipation at her sister's outburst.

'What do you mean?'

'He's staying for Christmas. And so's Crystal. Okay, then, so that one's done, what do you think?' Jayne held the bizarrely wrapped golf club aloft.

'You better be joking, Jayne, or I swear I'm going to batter you with that.'

'Rach, look, I've been speaking with Crystal a bit over

the last few weeks, and I seriously think Stanley's mellowed her out.'

'Since when have you been having cosy chats with Crystal?'

'Since she called me on the day of Will's first TV show. You know, when we were on our way to the bar.'

'What and now you and her are best friends?'

'No, we're not best friends. She's just called me a few times and we've been messaging. She asked what we were doing for Christmas; do you realise we haven't spent Christmas with her in over ten years?'

'For good reason.'

Jayne put the wrapped golf club to one side and started tying a ribbon around the handle of a beauty hamper she'd got for Erica. 'Look, I know you find it harder to put aside all the crap we've been through, but I honestly think she's trying to make amends, and before I asked her to come, I talked to Granny about it and she agrees that Crystal seems really different lately.'

'Granny said that?'

Jayne paused. Helen hadn't in so many words said that Crystal had metamorphosed into a kind and gentle soul, but she had said that Stanley had collected her a few times from Pine Grove and brought her back to his and Crystal's for tea and that Crystal wasn't rude to her – for the first time in her daughter's adult life. So that's sort of the same.

'Look, Rach, Granny's really happy that we're all going to be together. Come on, it's Christmas, it's going to be fine.'

'Aren't we supposed to be in the Helmand Province or somewhere at the moment?'

'I think she's told Stanley that we left the army.'

'And we're just supposed to go along with that, are we? Just nod and smile whenever he asks us about life in the barracks?'

'It's the first lesson of hostage training, keep a survival attitude and be positive. Make the captor your friend, don't give too much away and remain calm at all times. Remember that and we'll be fine.'

'I hate you.'

'I know.'

'So who else is invited to this freak show?'

'Will's dad and his wife Trish, Bernard, Abi, us and the Devon lot. So there'll be ten of us.'

'And Kyra.'

'Oh, is Kyra coming? Does she not have family she'd rather spend it with?'

Rachel raised one eyebrow at Jayne's fake breeziness that had an unmistakable bitter edge to it. 'She's fallen out with her parents and her brother is taking his kids to Portugal.'

'Right. Okay, then.'

'What's that supposed to mean? *Okay, then?* You've invited Abi – why can't I invite my friend?'

'I never said you couldn't! It'll be nice, eleven of us. All together. Having fun.'

'Yep.' Rachel repeated sarcastically, 'Fun, fun, fun.'

**

Five days later, Will had swapped his fetching Michaelangelo apron for his reindeer one that was kept in a drawer for the other 364 days of the year and lovingly retrieved every Christmas morning. *'Deck the halls with boughs of holly, fa la la la la, la la la la!'*

Will loved everything about Christmas. His mum had created all these rituals that happened at the same time every year, and most of them had revolved around food. She'd pull up a stool for him to stand on next to her, both of them wielding wooden spoons, stirring the aromatic mixtures of the Christmas desserts, from the traditional Italian panettone and panforte to the Christmas pudding his dad always insisted on. She always used to slip in a ten-pence piece to the mixture – it used to be five pence, but when the coin changed size she was always worried he might choke on it, hence the increase in value. Then they made a magic reindeer food together, which involved mixing muesli with silver glitter to leave out in a bowl next to a can of Fosters for Santa. Apparently the reindeers would probably be sick of carrots and it was a little-known fact that Santa actually preferred beer rather than sherry.

He smiled at these memories as he heard the buzzer go. He'd been very supportive when Jayne first suggested inviting her mother and Stanley for Christmas, voicing only a tiny percentage of his reservations. He just really hoped that Crystal behaved herself. Jayne seemed to think that being flanked at all times by a pair of feisty eighty-year-olds would keep her in check; he really hoped she was right.

And Rachel and Kyra were a couple of unknowns as well. If they brought their A-game with them, then they'd all have a great time, but they could just do that thing they sometimes did where they just whisper to each other and ignore everyone else. Adding a fiery red-headed Irish woman to the mix could go either way as well, not to mention his own dad, who hadn't seen Crystal since she unceremoniously relieved him of over 400 pounds and made all his clothes smell of incense. His new wife, Trish, was nice enough. She didn't seem offensive in any way, so at least she and Bernard could be relied on to keep the day from capsizing completely. Jesus, he sighed, sticking a clove into the ham, happy frickin' Christmas.

Glistening ruby-red pomegranate seeds sat regally on top of the braised red cabbage, which Jayne was passing around the table as Will carved the turkey. Rachel sat next to him popping a bacon-wrapped sausage and a stuffing ball onto each plate before passing them down the table.

'Granny, try this cranberry-and-orange sauce. I helped

zest the oranges,' Jayne said, passing the small glass bowl to Helen, who was elegantly dressed in a turquoise shift dress with matching jacket. Around her neck hung a collection of different beaded necklaces in a combination of outrageous colours – her way of saying that pensioners shouldn't just wear pearls.

'If I keel over and die, you and Rachel can share my Wedgwood collection,' she twinkled, taking a generous spoonful. 'Thank you, darling. Crystal, cranberry sauce?'

Crystal put her phone down on the table to take the bowl from her mother. 'Mmmm, lovely. Well, this all looks great. Now we know what Britain's favourite chef cooks for his own Christmas Day!'

'I wondered when someone might bring up the elephant in the room!' said Stanley good-naturedly.

'Now now, Stanley, that's no way to talk about your stepdaughter! Jayne take no notice of him!' chortled Crystal.

Amidst sharp intakes of horror from the people at the table who didn't know Crystal and dismayed sighs of resignation from those who did, Rachel looked at her watch and announced, 'and that took four and half minutes. Congratulations Crystal, a new record.'

'I was kidding! It was a joke! Jayne knew it was a joke, didn't you darling?'

'It's fine, honestly.' Jayne shrugged. She had hoped that she wouldn't need to use her skill of letting her mother's barbs and backhanders wash over her, that maybe Stanley *had* quelled her talent for saying the first thing that came into her head, but evidently the honeymoon period had worn off and social ineptitude was just her default factory setting. Will rested his leg against hers under the table as if to silently will her to stay strong.

Dave stood up, glass in hand, cheeks already a little flushed from the pre-dinner champagne. 'I'd like to make a quick toast, if no one minds? Will, lad, I'd just like to say that I'm very proud of you, always have been, and if your mum was here now, she'd be made up at all this success you're having now. Jayne, we think you're really smashing and Trish and I are thrilled to pieces that you've invited us round today – thrilled to bits we are. So here's to a very happy Christmas and a really grand year ahead. Thank you for all of this, it's really wonderful, really is. Happy Christmas.'

He hurriedly sat down and Trish patted his arm proudly. It was the longest speech Jayne had ever heard him make. Admittedly when she knew him years ago he'd had other things on his mind rather than making small talk with his clairvoyant's teenage daughter, but even when Will and her had visited them in Slough he'd been a man of few words, leaving Trish to politely enquire over health, jobs and their thoughts on the traffic.

'Hear hear!' said Bernard, raising his glass, 'Happy Christmas and thank you for opening your home to a motley collection of waifs and strays.'

'Oi, Bernie, speak for yourself. I am not, nor ever have

been a waif – more's the pity, and as for being stray, well maybe you got me there. Even so, get back in your box, old man,' Abi grinned. Everyone laughed, even Bernard, whom Jayne noticed didn't even flinch when Abi used a nickname she knew he despised.

'So, what's it really like then, Will? Being famous?' Trish asked finally after the plates were cleared and the only things left on the table were a few paper crowns, a dice and a small fluorescent comb. After devouring the main course they were enjoying the same pleasant lull as families up and down the country. Kyra, Rachel and Abi were sitting at one end of the table. Kyra was telling an incredulous Stanley about a new underwater hotel in Qatar she had recently pitched designs for. He made a joke about it being a shame that Rachel's military training was with the army, not the navy, which might have been more helpful to her, which led to inquisitive expressions from Abi and Kyra that Rachel batted away with a subtle shake of her head and eyes that said, 'seriously, don't ask'.

Dave and Jayne were discussing the merits of academies versus state schools, a topic Jayne knew very little about, but felt that as a teacher it was a subject she should pretend to have strong feelings about. Meanwhile, in an effort to quash any more of her daughter's offensiveness Helen had been topping Crystal's wine glass up with water whenever she looked away, so rather than being inebriated, Crystal was just healthily hydrated.

'Um, I don't know really,' Will replied, 'Not many people

know who I am, so it's not as though I can't go to the supermarket or anything.'

'That's such a lie!' Rachel said, overhearing Will and breaking away from her own conversation to butt in. 'You get stopped all the time, and even when people aren't actually asking you to sign things in the street everyone is staring at you.'

'No, I don't think–'

'I'm afraid I've got to agree with Rachel, Chef. I'm at the coalface of it everyday and you are now something of a celebrity,' Bernard added. 'It's certainly great for business but not really for my own self-confidence seeing the faces of disappointment when I'm the one greeting them behind the counter and not you. I think I'm merely days away from developing a debilitating body-image issue.'

'Oh behave, you silver fox you,' said Abi, relishing Bernard's embarrassment.

'Is it all champagne and glamour when you're backstage on the TV shows?' Trish was making no attempt to disguise her delight at having a stepson whose picture had appeared as a thumbnail in the *Radio Times*.

Will didn't really know how to break it to her that being backstage in a television studio was about as glamorous as being back of house in a hotel – all long, bare corridors with hastily pinned-up bits of paper telling you whose dressing room was whose. Or in the case of the panel show he'd just filmed, which show it was hiring the studio that day. Like Trish, he'd expected to see A-listers in silk robes getting their make-up done in front of mirrors bordered with bulbs, glass of bubbles in one hand while a string quartet played some soft jazz in the corner.

'I haven't really seen much glitz, I'm afraid, Trish . . . but that's probably because I've been too nervous to look properly,' he hastily added after seeing her face fall. 'I did have a gin and tonic with the other guests and the band after *The Late Night Show*. Does that count as glamorous?'

At the mention of gin, Crystal perked up a bit, chiming in, 'I haven't seen many pictures of you in the paper yet, though, Billy.' Jayne noticed Will shuddering at the nickname that only she got away with using, 'Every morning when Stan comes back from the newsagents and brings me the papers I have a look through expecting to see you snapped somewhere. But apart from a couple of pictures in the diary pages of *OK* magazine, you haven't really made much of an impression on the press.'

'Surely that's a good thing?' Jayne asked, 'I can't imagine anything worse than being snapped every time we went out the front door.'

'Why do *you* need to worry about it? No one's going to want to take your picture, not when you're standing next to *him*.'

'I think what Crystal means is that so far you've managed to retain an anonymous dignity, so thankfully you're not going to have to deal with the monstrous paparazzi any time soon.'

Helen's attempt at glossing over Crystal's comment almost worked until her daughter added, 'No, that's not what I meant, mother,' leaning forward on her elbow, she jabbed a finger in Will's direction, 'I mean, look at him, now look at you, Jayne. You're lovely, you are, a real salt-of-the-earth type of person, but when it comes to looks, the words 'punching' and 'weight' spring to mind.'

'The words 'punch' and 'face' spring to mind,' muttered Will under his breath, but loud enough for everyone to hear. 'Right who's for Trivial Pursuit?'

Abi followed Jayne into the kitchen, where she had disappeared to after making some half-hearted murmurs about making coffee. 'Are you alright, pet?'

Jayne whirled around, her eyes bright, 'Of course I am! Don't be daft, she doesn't upset me. I just feel a bit pissed off that I thought she'd be different and so unleashed her on everyone else. What's she doing now?'

'Stanley and your gran are giving her a talking to. I wouldn't be surprised if she's standing facing the corner when we go back in. But seriously, for the rest of the day don't worry about her. I'll keep her occupied.'

'Are you sure you won't be too busy keeping Bernard occupied?' Jayne teased.

'Ha, I'm having so much fun making him blush, he's such an easy target! He's so lovely, though, isn't he? What's his story? Is he divorced? Widowed? Gay?'

'He's never been married. I think there was someone

serious years ago, but he has his fair share of female 'companions' that he goes out for dinner with and the odd weekend away.'

'Oo-er missus.'

'Indeed. He's a dark horse, is our Bernard. But such a nice guy.' Jayne started filling two cafetières with boiling water, 'Can you get the milk jug out of that bottom cupboard? Anyway, it should be me asking you how you are doing, your first Christmas in England. How does it measure up?'

'It's a lot more civilised than I'm used to, that's for sure! But I thought I'd miss being home, but now that most of my brothers and sisters are married it makes sense to have one year on, one off – gives my ma and da a chance to put their feet up and hear what's happening on the telly rather than just watching the moving pictures while all hell breaks loose around them.' Abi leant back against the counter and crossed her arms, watching Jayne pile cups and saucers onto a tray. 'Are you sure you're okay? You're quite quiet today. Is it just your ma, or is something else bothering you?'

'No, honestly, I'm just a bit, you know, it's just a bit weird, all this–' Jayne spread her arms out and let them drop limply to her sides. 'You know what Crystal just said about me not being photographed–'

'I thought you just said you're not taking any notice of her?'

'I'm not, it's not her, it's something Will said that's just been niggling at me. I know I'm just being really paranoid, but he said the other day that his agent woman has told him to tell people that he's single.'

'Ri-ght . . .' Abi said slowly, 'and what did he say when she said that?'

'I don't know, really. He hasn't told anyone about us yet, which I'm quite pleased about because you know I'm quite a private person, but also, it just makes me wonder if the agent is advising him to do that because I'd let him down in some way?'

'That's rubbish. Think about it from her view. She's got this good-looking guy on her books and, yes, he probably does get more interest if sad, delusional women thought they stood a chance with him. Once a girlfriend pops out of the woodwork, they might lose interest, and if the viewers lose interest, so do the networks, and now all she's got is a good-looking bloke who no one wants to book. Take it as a compliment that you've bagged the guy everyone currently dreams of being with. Seriously, Jayne, shut up, give me a hug and go and serve everyone cold coffee.'

Jayne pushed open the lounge door with her bum in time to hear Will solemnly ask in his best question-master voice, 'Which tree provided the apple for Adam and Eve?'

'Apple tree! The apple tree!' shouted Trish. Everyone collapsed in laughter at the poor woman's expense. Her cheeks were glowing scarlet as she looked around the room saying, 'What? What did I say?'

'The Tree of Knowledge,' purred Kyra from the beanbag that she shared with Rachel, their outstretched legs clad in a matching black-leather skinny trousers that brought back bad shopping memories for Jayne.

'Right answer, but it wasn't your question I'm afraid, Kyra, so no cheese this time, better luck next time, fingers on buzzers please as we go into the next round,' He seemed to be enjoying this rather too much, but at least if the cookery lark dried up, then Jayne thought he may have a future as the host of *University Challenge*.

'What is a group of bears called?'

'Ooo, ooo I know this, is it a hug?' Dave shouted.

'Wow, you two really are made for each other, aren't you?' Crystal drawled from her armchair, where Abi, true to her word, was perched on the arm, as close as she could get to her without actually sitting in her lap.

Will was laughing so much he clutched his stomach, 'Dad, do you seriously think that a group of bears is called a hug?'

'Isn't that where the term bear-hug comes from?' Dave replied innocently. Trish's head was nodding her support.

'I'm throwing this open to the room, not for cheese, just for fun. Jayne, your chosen career disqualifies you from this round, I'm afraid, but everyone else, you have five seconds, four, three . . .'

Huge platters of cheese and biscuits with carafes of port sat on the coffee table as everyone loaded up their plates, amidst many procrastinations of still being full from lunch. Crystal was the first to leave to go back to their B&B, citing sheer boredom for her early exit from the festivities. As she left the room, so did the blanket of unease that seemed to follow her around like a storm cloud, so the remainder of the evening relaxed into a stress-free few hours.

Stanley had apologised to Jayne again about Crystal's behaviour, offering up bewildered excuses as to the apparent transformation in his young wife. He didn't seem to realise that he was the one deserving of the pity and sympathy, not her. Jayne watched him sat amiably at the dining table playing canasta with Helen; she really hoped that Crystal would leave him with a modicum of his dignity still intact, but knew that this was extremely unlikely.

Will sidled up to Jayne, passing her a plate of sliced Brie and Edam, knowing that she didn't like the 'mouldy ones' like Stilton. 'Do you know what? Kyra's actually really nice when you get talking to her,' he said.

'Really?'

'Really. She's just been telling me all about her childhood: she grew up in Singapore, how cool's that?'

'Pretty darn cool.' Jayne cheerily replied. Really? Really? If the never-ending legs and kink-free hair wasn't enough, she now threw in an exotic upbringing too.

'I think the day's gone quite well, all things considered,' he continued, popping a grape into his mouth. 'Dad and Trish seemed to have fun. As they were leaving Dad even had tears in his eyes. I think this whole TV thing is a bit overwhelming for him.'

'Bless him, he's so proud of you.'

'I'm really glad they were here today. Actually I think everyone seemed to have fun. Did you?'

'Of course! And thank you for not saying what I know you wanted to say about Crystal coming. But you and Rachel were right; it was a rubbish idea, and one that I won't be repeating next year. Miserable old tramp.' Jayne leant over and kissed him. 'Happy Christmas, you delicious specimen of a man, you.'

He smiled, 'Happy Christmas . . . Jayne.' He laughed as she pretended to head-butt him.

Chapter 14

They'd been in Westfield for five and half hours, with only a short pause for two double espressos and a low-fat blueberry muffin each. But that was three hours ago and Jayne was slowly losing the will to live. Shuffling after her sister, who ran from rail to rail, her eyes darting left to right, up and down, giving each the briefest of once-overs before announcing that they were moving onto the next store. 'I think I'm going to go back for the navy-blue one with the sash,' Jayne ventured, more out of a desire to end the day, rather than a burning love for the blue one with the sash.

'Hmmm, no. I can't let you go to the National Television Awards in a dress from Coast. Oh, look, there's Ghost, let's go there.'

'Ghost is Coast with only three letters changed.'

'Jayne. Can you please start taking this seriously? I've given up a whole Saturday to take you shopping–'

'Shut up! You love this! It's hardly a massive sacrifice

for you. You'd probably be here anyway, even if I wasn't here!'

'You're not understanding the huge-ity of this!'

'Huge-ity is not a word.'

Rachel ignored her and continued, 'Jayne, in four days' time you're going to be walking up a red carpet next to Will. Will, who all the heterosexual women, and all the homosexual men, have currently put at the top of their 'Man I'd like to sleep with the most' list. You have to look amazing, and in order to look amazing, you have to take this seriously.'

Jayne fingered the nude silk under the plastic that she'd been too afraid to remove in case she tripped while carrying a cup of tea and spilled it all over it. It was the single-most expensive item she'd ever bought. But it was beautiful. As soon as she'd drawn the zip up and looked in the changing-room mirror she knew. She'd never felt that before about an item of clothing, but then clothes shopping for her normally just consisted of nipping in quickly to M&S for a pack of five high-leg knickers in her lunch break. If this was the thrill that Rachel got every time she bought a new designer outfit or pair of shoes she could see how shopping could become addictive.

Looking down at the fabric, she glimpsed her hands, which she almost didn't recognise as her own. Rachel had insisted on her having a hot-oil treatment and a French manicure, and they looked amazing. She had made a vague attempt at asking why it was necessary to have soft-looking hands, but she knew there was no point arguing with her sister when she was on a mission. Beneath her Ugg boots, Jayne had had a matching pedicure too. Even though she was wearing closed-toe sandals tonight, apparently it was all about you yourself knowing that you looked beautiful from head to toe. 'Make sure you wax your lady bits as well,' Rachel had ordered. 'There's no point you looking all glam on the outside and then underneath being a hairy mammoth.'

At half past four she was finally ready to go. Her hair had been lovingly teased by the hairdresser on the high street into hundreds of cascading, tight black curls that hung loose around her shoulders. The delicate nude tones of the floor-length gown had subtle diamante edging along the bust, which admittedly she was a little paranoid about at first. 'Shouldn't I be trying to hide the girls, rather than draw attention to them with fake diamonds?' she asked Rachel and Abi as the two of them bustled around her, plumping up the skirt and removing imaginary bits of fluff.

'Absolutely not! You are all woman and you are gorgeous!' Abi defiantly replied. If Will's wide eyes and open mouth was anything to go by when she glided into the living room, where he was waiting in a new Tom Ford tux, he thought so too.

'Wow, wow, wow. You look sensational!'

Holding her skirt out at the sides, she bobbed a small

curtsey. 'Why thank you, kind sir, you scrub up quite well yourself.'

She had ignored Rachel's pleas for her to leave her glasses behind; she was firmly putting function over form as far as eyesight was considered. On a practical level, she reduced the risk of falling flat on her face considerably if she could actually see where she was walking, but also, she wanted to take in every moment, to see every famous face up close, not as distorted blurs.

She couldn't quite believe that they were going to an awards ceremony. When *Good Morning* received the news that it was nominated for *Most Popular Daytime Show* Michaela's PR machine went into overdrive, making sure that Will's place on one of their three tables was secure. He hadn't told Jayne quite how disappointed Michaela was that he wanted Jayne to be his plus one and not her, but she'd heard his end of the phone call behind the hastily closed kitchen door. Disappointment may be the wrong word, she reasoned, more like white-hot rage. Of course she'd offered to sit this one out in the name of keeping the peace, while inwardly begging him to choose substance over style, and thankfully he said that not taking her was never an option.

He looked so handsome in his tux. She didn't think she'd ever seen him wear cufflinks before – she actually didn't even know he owned any. Against his earlier reservations, he'd visited Fernando again earlier in the day to get the gel-to-hair ratio just right, and as their car drew up to the hordes of clipboard-carrying officials, autograph-book-clutching fans and jostling photographers, they looked at each other, took deep breaths and smiled. 'Ready?' Will asked.

'Ready.'

The flashes almost made Jayne take an involuntary step back. She remembered the pre-show warnings to viewers with photosensitive epilepsy that were broadcast before celebrity entertainment shows and now realised why. A constant stream of harsh white flickers assaulted her eyes, while shouts of 'Will!', 'Will, over here!' seemed to come from all directions, invisible strings pulling them everywhere.

Beautiful women in evening dresses held microphones, cooing Will over to them with their siren songs, wanting to know where his suit was from, how he's feeling tonight, who he wants to win, where was his suit from, how is he feeling, who he's tipping to win, who designed his suit, how he feels to be there, which show does he think will win. Two minutes of identical footage for every single network.

Just behind them a massive wave of excitement surged from the crowd as a Hollywood A-lister and her musician husband emerged from their limousine. Stewards with curled wires that ran from their ear down inside their shirt collars tried to make some room on the bustling red carpet, flapping people back with their rolled-up running orders, speaking into buzzing handsets. Jayne watched the organised mayhem with undisguised awe. The serenity of the actress was breathtaking: her poise, her easy candour with the paparazzi, who begged her for 'just one more shot'. At what point did dealing with all of this become so effortless?

Will and Jayne tried to stand back to allow the pair to glide through the throng, and as they came shoulder to shoulder the actress broke her composure and gasped: 'You're the chef from YouTube! I loved your videos, we even made the goat's cheese bruschetta for a dinner party and everyone raved about it for ages.'

'Turn around! Can we have a picture?'

Jayne felt the actress put her slender arm around her shoulders as she turned to face the swarm of lenses, the four of them stood in a line. Will between the rock star and the movie starlet, she on the end. The thunderous click of hundreds of shutters all released at the same time was deafening. Absolutely unbelievable. It all happened so quickly, even after the power couple had been ushered along the red carpet, Will and Jayne stood in a stunned silence, unwilling to take a further step in case it all dissolved into a daydream.

Will broke the silence, 'Shit a brick.'

'Oh my days.'

'That was insane.'

'She touched my shoulder. Will, she touched my shoulder!'

He grinned like a lunatic, nodding his head, before

shaking it in disbelief. They made my bruschetta, MY bruschetta. At a dinner party. *They* made *my* bruschetta!'

'I'm calling everyone I've ever met to tell them about this.
They're not going to believe this! It's one thing to even come
to something like this and then to have someone like *that*
put their arms around us!'

'Let's go in first, find our table and then text everyone
we know.'

In the end, *Good Morning* lost out to an after-watershed
talk show but nothing could dampen Jayne's high spirits.
She beamed the whole way through the awards. Applauding
wildly whenever anyone won, sitting open-mouthed and
star-struck whenever a television personality walked past,
regardless of whether they acted in the country's most-pop-
ular soap, or introduced each new cartoon on Cbeebies.

She drank in the heady atmosphere of glamour, marvel-
ling at the long, shimmering dresses and the short,
gusset-skimming ones. She accepted flute after flute of
expensive champagne and declared to Will in the taxi home
that it had been the single most exciting night of her life.

Normally Will put his phone on silent during the night,
but the number of mojitos he'd knocked back coupled with
the post-2am bedtime meant they were both rudely woken
just after 6am with his shrill ringtone. Rubbing his eyes
and flinching at the narrow stream of sunlight that filtered
through the middle of the curtains that he hadn't quite

pulled together he answered gruffly, 'Yes? . . . Michaela, what the . . .?'

Jayne rolled over and squinted at him, wiping the sleep and clumps of last night's mascara from her eyes.

'You're kidding me? . . . No way! Ha ha, no, we were literally just standing there and she started talking to us! . . . That's awesome . . . okay, yes, I'll keep it next to me.'

Pressing the end key, he looked across at Jayne, who had now sat up in bed, the covers pulled up to make a vague attempt at covering her nakedness. 'You're not going to believe this. That was Michaela. You know that picture we had taken last night?'

'Which one?'

'The one with possibly the most-photographed couple in the world?'

'Of course,' Jayne yawned, 'I was being facetious.'

'It's been picked up by the American press and it's on every entertainment site everywhere! Like, literally everywhere. Michaela said that I should sack her and do my own PR if this is what I can pull out of the bag. Come on, where's your iPad? Are you ready to see yourself standing next to the world's most famous actress?'

Jayne's heart started thumping; it hadn't really registered with her that the reason they were all standing huddled together was for a photograph that might then appear somewhere. For her the thrill began and ended with that moment. She felt a bit foolish for not realising that her claim to fame was being captured for mass circulation. She ran naked to her dressing table and grabbed the iPad, legging it back across the cold bedroom floor and under the covers next to Will.

'Oh my God, what if I look awful? What if I'm blinking?' Jayne could feel and see her hands shaking a bit as she held the screen, waiting for it to connect to the Internet.

'You looked amazing, shut up. What are we looking up first?'

'Why don't we just Google Will Scarlet and see what comes up?'

'Okay. I'm so glad it's just us here. I don't want anybody else to know I Googled myself.' Will was hugging his knees with excitement as the search pages loaded. 'I've got a Wikipedia page! How the hell have I got a Wikipedia page?'

'Oh my God, you're mentioned on thousands of web pages!' Jayne scrolled down the screen in disbelief, shrieking, 'Will, look, you're on all these websites – there's pages and pages of them!'

'Click on images and see what comes up.' His voice sounded a little unnatural, as though he had something stuck in his throat. Jayne put her hand over his and he tightened his grip on her fingers. Suddenly the whole screen was taken up with Will's face. The first one, with hundreds of thousands of hits, was the picture from last night with him between the two A-listers.

'That's the one! Click on that one to make it larger so

we can see you as well, oh my God, Jayne, this is unbeliev-able!' The picture zoomed out and it showed a grinning Will flanked by the picture-perfect husband and wife. The photo ended at the actress, her right arm out of shot.

'Click on another one, you're not in that one. Look, there are loads of variations of that picture. I'm looking slightly away in that one – what about that one?' Jayne clicked through the picture gallery, seeing more than fifty slightly different versions of the same pose. In one the musician was obviously talking, another the actress had dipped her head slightly. Will had thrown his head back laughing in another.

The only thing they all had in common was that Jayne had been cut out of all of them.

She'd only moved from the bed once in over two hours, and that was just to get the iPad charger and plug it into the socket where her bedside lamp usually went. She was like a woman possessed, tapping and flicking and scrolling and uncovering this life of Will's that neither of them really knew existed. Of course she knew that his YouTube videos had been watched millions of times, and it was the success of that which had led to his television career taking off, but she had never really thought beyond that. Now she realised how utterly naïve she'd been not to grasp that simmering underneath the surface was this ever-expanding online pres-ence.

The internet had a life of its own, and if you existed in a technology-less bubble, like she usually did, you would have no idea what was smouldering all over it. She was part of the generation that had snuck in just before every activity demanded a computer to help you do it. Handwriting essays in college, visiting the library and using the Dewey decimal system to locate the right book were all second nature to her – most of the kids she taught now wouldn't know how to find the actual library, let alone be able to pinpoint the appropriate book.

She could whizz up a document in Word, do an Excel spreadsheet if her life depended on it, although she couldn't imagine any situations where that would be the case, and used the internet to read *The Telegraph*, check emails, occasionally Facebook and to find flights and cheap holidays. To suddenly discover that Will, *her* Will, occupied a fairly substantial chunk of the web was confusing, disturbing and downright weird.

The internet was not a tangible thing, they had no control over it, and no input in it either. She always knew when he was appearing in a magazine because he would say to her, 'Today I'm doing an interview for *Waitrose*,' and she would say, 'that's lovely darling, have fun.' In the same way that she would tell him that she had a departmental meeting about the latest Ofsted report, and he would wish her luck and send her on her way with a hot thermos and a cling-filmed pack of sandwiches.

It's not as though she's stupid, she kept telling herself, so how did she not know that this would happen? That people they had never met were creating Wikipedia pages about her boyfriend? How the hell did they know that he was born on the 14th July? And that he won prizes for sculpture in junior school? She didn't even know that!

There were blogs set up about him, with stills from every TV appearance he'd made, from his segments on *Good Morning* to the chat shows, to the rare paparazzi photos that have been taken of him at parties. And his notoriety wasn't limited to England either. Something called *The Aardvark* from New Zealand had run a piece about him, same as *The Times of India*. Scores of global sites had referenced him, some of them from the angle of his food, printing the recipes alongside a short clip, most of them, though, seemed to completely ignore his culinary skills and concentrate instead on how he looked. In the last twelve hours since that fateful shot with one of America's most famed exports, his online presence had been given a healthy shot of adrenaline.

For over two hours Jayne felt as if she'd been holding her breath. Will had looked through the sites with her for a while before shaking his head slightly and saying, 'it's insane, isn't it?' and then showering and popping down to the deli to speak to Bernard and Sylvia about a new range of fresh pastas he was wanting to trial. It wasn't that he wasn't as overwhelmed as she was. Jayne could tell the whole thing terrified him, but he'd just prefer not to know about things that didn't directly impact him. She wished that she were more like that. If she were, maybe she wouldn't now be feeling so sick.

'Are you *still* looking at that?' Will said, walking across the room and pulling the curtains open. The sharp burst of sunlight rebounded off the screen. 'Put it away, have a shower and then come for a walk with me, the sun is shining, it's the perfect weather to walk a dog.'

'We don't have a dog.'

'I know, but it's that kind of weather. Come on, let's go out for some air, and then grab breakfast down by the river. Come on!' Will grabbed the end of the duvet and pulled it off onto the floor. Jayne put the iPad on top of where her pants should be if Will hadn't ripped them off with his teeth when they'd stumbled through the door last night.

'Oh, so you're being all shy now? Bit late for that. Get up! I wrote a song, it's called 'Get Up', it goes a little like this,' he started singing in a dramatic deep baritone, 'Get up, get up, you lazy, lazy lady, get up, get up and get ready.'

'Lady doesn't rhyme with ready,' Jayne retorted, pretending to be grumpy, but Will's good mood was annoyingly infectious. 'Are you not in the slightest bit bothered about all this?'

'You know I've never bought into the whole celebrity thing, it's a pile of nonsense – everyone's shit stinks. Seriously don't waste your time reading it.'

'You won a prize for sculpture and never told me.'

'I did what?'

'You won a prize for doing a sculpture when you were nine and you didn't tell me.' Jayne realised, saying it out loud for the second time, how utterly ridiculous she sounded.

'Firstly, how the heck did you know that, and secondly, would it have made a difference to you saying yes to going out with me?'

She allowed herself a small smile, 'Your Wikipedia page told me and, yes, I may have thought twice about dating you. Most artists are mad as fruit bats.' They were interrupted by his phone. He looked down at the screen and started backing out of the room, 'I have to get this, it's Michaela, get washed and dressed you slovenly slattern.'

As she lathered her hair with the stupidly expensive miracle mask conditioner Rachel had gifted her for Christmas, saying, as she'd handed it over, 'I got you this because your hair is starting to take on a life of its own,' she couldn't stop thinking about being photo-shopped out of the pictures. There was just one of her that she could see that slipped into one random photo gallery, and even then it was only a side profile of her face, so you could just see one eye and a nose sticking out behind a mass of curls.

Of course, she could understand the fact that she wasn't going to sell magazines. She was an English teacher from the West Country, for goodness sake, but to not even have one journalist or one blogger even asking what her name was made her feel a little bit, well, invisible. Even the caption under the one solitary picture of her read *Handsome TV Chef Will Scarlet and friend*. And friend. *Friend*. Not even girlfriend. She'd been demoted to the status of Duncan. Not that she wanted people to follow her around the way they did Will, peering around the end of supermarket aisles giggling, taking pictures of him on their phones. She was much too private for that, but it would have been nice to feel a little bit part of this whirlwind that was happening around him, not to just be standing on the periphery of it watching with everyone else.

Chapter 15

'On the cover?'
    'Yep.'
'Of *Esquire*?'
'Yep.'
'On the *cover*?'
'Yep. I know.'
'Jeez. That's massive.'
'I know.'

They both sat side by side on the only bench in the playground watching in silence as a group of sixteen-year-old girls started jostling each other. Hormone-ravaged chests bumping and screams of 'she said you said she said you said' rising above the jeers and shouts from the small group of teenagers forming a circle around them.

'Looks like a fight,' Abi said.

'Yep. We should stop it.'

Neither woman moved. 'On the *cover*?' Abi asked again. 'That is amazing, isn't it, that's going to catapult him to super-stardom. I mean, he's kind of on his way there now, but to be on the cover of one of the world's top men's magazines is brilliant. 'Cos up 'til now, he's only really had coverage from all the women's titles. This shows that now the men want to get involved too. That's big. Oh bugger, looks like it's going to kick off over there. Jayne, you should really stop it.'

'Why me? I'm enjoying the sun.' Jayne tilted her head back and closed her eyes. The shouts increased. 'Five bucks says Michelle Whittaker's involved.'

'You know I love a flutter as much as the next man, but odds-on bets aren't my thing.'

A sudden ear-piercing scream audible above the general braying made Jayne's eyes spring open. 'Fine. You know I can't just sit here while they batter each other to death. Thanks for helping.'

'You're welcome,' Abi said to Jayne's back as she watched her friend burrowing through the jeering crowd to prise the two scrappers apart before sending them off to see the head in the main building.

'No one tells you at teacher-training college about spending your break-time duty breaking up fights, do they? Especially between girls! They always say that boys scrap and girls are just catty, but now they're worse than the boys most of the time!' Jayne huffed as she sat back down on the bench. 'That's the third fight this week I've had to referee. I have half a mind to just let natural Darwinism take over: survival of the fittest and all that.'

'There speaks a teacher who should maybe look at changing careers,' yawned Abi. 'Are you up to anything nice this half term? Will around?'

'Actually, yes, we're going away. We're going to this little hotel in the Cotswolds and he's picking me up after school this afternoon, bags are already packed and we're shutting the door on the world for two glorious nights and two fabulous days.' Jayne sighed and smiled, 'It was completely his idea. I think he realises that I've been finding it all a bit difficult having people fawning over him all the time, and all the press sniffing around him, and so he wanted us to just get away from it all. It's really sweet, actually.'

It had been three or four months since Will had received the phone call that had changed the rules of the game again. She had come through to Will directly, which Jayne knew would have annoyed Michaela immensely. Jayne still didn't know how she had got hold of his number when he had become fastidious with his privacy settings. But then, in the same way that the uber-famous can command the city's top tables at a moment's notice while mere mortals have to make do with being added to a very long waiting list, celebrities have ways of getting round pesky logistics.

He'd been in the pub with Duncan when she'd called; her sultry Californian accent ringing quiet bells of recognition with Will, but it wasn't until she'd mentioned meeting him at the television awards that the penny had completely dropped. 'I would love you to cater my birthday party for a few friends', was how she'd pitched it, using a tone that wasn't used to replies of a negative nature. After a few blustered attempts at batting away the commission, Will had heard himself agree to an initial meeting at their Kensington townhouse.

'A few friends' had turned out to be a woefully conservative understatement. On the night, Will had found himself cooking for the great and good of the silver screen, many of whom had flown over the Atlantic just for the evening. He'd said, with more than a dollop of incredulity, that a constant stream of instantly recognisable faces had glided through the kitchen door to commend him on his food and ask for a card.

To date, he'd catered over twenty of these events, even being flown by helicopter to a remote Scottish castle to host a private cooking class for one young starlet and her friends. He'd regaled a stony-faced Jayne on his return with accounts of flirty banter and barely-disguised propositions. She'd suggested that he should save the rest of the story for Duncan, as she possibly wasn't an appropriate target audience, to which he'd laughed and mocked her for being unnecessarily jealous.

The starlet had uploaded pictures of herself onto Instagram, wearing an apron and little else, sitting on Will's lap, which he'd laughed off as 'a bit of fun for the camera'. Jayne hadn't wanted to make too much of a fuss about what was clearly nothing more than a gratuitous photo opportunity, but it had hurt like a stab wound at the time.

A crowd of boys chasing a runaway basketball ran past their bench as Abi shook her head, 'I still can't quite believe that you're still leading a normal life while he's become England's darling.'

'Do you know what? It's kind of surprised me too,' Jayne shrugged. 'I think everyone just assumes he's single and so even when we go out together and there are photographers there, no one really bothers with me, which is great, so no one actually knows we're together. It's funny thinking that most of these kids and their parents know who he is, and yet have no idea that their English teacher lives with him. It's kind of cool.'

'I'd want to shout it out from the rooftops, though,' Abi pinched her nose, 'This is a public service announcement – you know that gorgeous fella you're all lusting over, well guess what, people, he's with me.'

Abi had this way of making Jayne relax with a little quip or silly voice, or even just some good old-fashioned common sense. Maybe it came from growing up in such a large family; there was simply no room for pretensions or affectations with so many brothers and sisters to sit on you until you became genuine again. She didn't treat Will-Scarlet-the-TV-personality any differently to Will-her-best-friend's-boyfriend-who-owned-a-shop. Unlike Marco, who tripped over his tongue every time he was in the same room as Will, which seemed to be a lot more often than before.

Helen was another one completely unaffected by his fame. She'd come up to London the month before and she saw first hand just how crazy Will's life had become. They'd gone to afternoon tea at the Ritz, which, in hindsight, maybe wasn't the best choice as there was permanently a paparazzi or two loitering on the pavement opposite, not even bothering to try to conceal themselves behind trees or white vans like they did in movies. But it was Helen's eighty-fifth birthday and so her granddaughters and Will thought it would be a nice surprise. Again, probably through complete naivety, they hadn't anticipated the two photographers who had snapped their entrance to the hotel multiplying into ten by the time they emerged a couple of hours and four trays of petits fours later.

'It's like being in a circus, isn't it?' Helen had remarked after being manhandled into a taxi. 'Don't these people have jobs to go to?'

'This is their job,' Rachel had replied.

'What? Taking pictures of people leaving restaurants? What a bore.'

Since the National Television Awards, Will had also branched out into presenting his own food show on a Saturday morning on ITV. He still did two cookery slots on *Good Morning* during the week, but now his main focus was the hour-long show that was taped during the week, to be aired at the weekend. Most of it was based in the studio cooking and chatting with guests, but there were a couple of segments that were filmed on location. Will would travel to a different part of the country each week unearthing their local delicacies – real Bakewell tart from Derbyshire, Welsh cakes from, well, Wales – that sort of thing.

It was on one of these trips to discover the origins of Gloucester cheese that Will had found a gorgeous little hotel housed in a Georgian manor house in the heart of the Cotswolds. Surrounded by little villages whose high streets had dolls-house shops sitting alongside clothing stores selling nothing but Barbour jackets and wellies, the hotel was as far removed from the frantic pace of London life as it was possible to be, without being at sea.

Thankfully the extra cash that Will was now bringing in meant they could afford to hire a car for this trip, rather than borrow Duncan's Ford again. Arriving at a posh country estate covered in dog hair and bits of old Quavers was not the look Jayne was necessarily going for, so being in an almost-brand- new BMW was quite the treat. A white-gloved valet opened her car door, bowing slightly as he welcomed 'madam' before collecting their bags from the boot. If any of the staff recognised Will they didn't give anything away, treating both of them with the polite, yet distant, courte-ousness the English used to be famed for.

'It's huge!' Jayne exclaimed after a butler in tails had

shown them to their suite. 'Oh my God, Will, it's got a claw-foot bath! I love this! We are so having a bath together!'

'Now you're talking.' He dropped his satchel onto the bed and pulled Jayne in for a kiss. 'Isn't this great? It's so peaceful. Which reminds me. Where's your phone? Okay, and here's mine. We're turning them off and we're not turning them back on again until we get back to London on Monday. Now turn the taps on, you're filthy and I need to scrub you down . . .'

Jayne rested her head against Will's chest, lying in between his legs, which were slippery with the water and the ylang ylang-scented bath oil he'd upended under the running tap.

They were both content to just lie there in the water; he making patterns along her upper arm with the oil, swirling his finger like a figure-skater while she started toying with the few bits of chest hair that covered his left nipple. It was dusk outside and the shadows from the flickering flames of the tea lights they'd scattered around the bathroom were dancing on the walls.

'Baby, can you pass me that little pot at the end of the bath? I think there might be some soap in it. Can you look?' Jayne shifted position to reach the small ceramic pot and lifted up the lid. In it was a little turquoise-blue box, tied with a neat white-satin ribbon.

'No, it's not soap, it's just another box.' She said, delicately popping the lid back on and setting the pot back down again.

'Maybe the soap's inside the other box? Can you check?'

'Why would they wrap the soap up in a box with a ribbon?'

'Um, I don't know, darling. Can you just, maybe, open it and see?' Will's voice was wavering somewhere between amusement and exasperation.

Jayne pulled both ends of the ribbon and it fell away into the water. Lifting up the lid, she saw the most perfect round diamond that she'd ever seen. Its smooth surface shone with hundreds of tiny flawless reflections beneath it. She gasped. Will took the box from her wet trembling hands and picked up her other hand.

'Jayne Brady. I adore the bones of you.' His eyes started filling as he saw tears flowing freely down Jayne's cheeks as she understood what was about to happen. 'You complete me. You make me a better person and I want to hear your laughter every day for the rest of my life, making me smile. I want to have children with you who grow up to be just like you, filled with fun and kindness, and compassion. We're on a crazy adventure at the moment, but it wouldn't be anything without you by my side. I want to spend every day of my life trying to make you as happy as you make me. Will you marry me?'

Jayne made no effort to wipe away her tears as she panted between sobs, 'Yes, yes, of course I will!'

He smiled and slipped the ring onto Jayne's finger, bringing it up to his mouth to kiss it. 'I love you.'

'Not heart?'

'Not this time.'

Their fingers were like raisins and the bath water had passed the point of being tepid and was nearing stone-cold when they finally, reluctantly, clambered out of it. Curled up next to each other on the sofa, both wearing matching fluffy white dressing gowns, they clinked glasses filled with the champagne Will had pre-ordered, being fairly convinced his question would have a happy ending. Holding her left hand out in front of her to admire the way the brilliant solitaire caught the light, Jayne voiced her amazement again at how he'd managed to conceal this surprise from her for weeks. 'If I wasn't so deliriously happy, I'd be slightly concerned at how adept you were at keeping something secret from me.'

'I have hidden depths that even you don't know about.'

'You'd like to think so, but we both know that's not true. Can I break the weekend rules for about thirty seconds to call Rachel, Abi and Helen to tell them our news?'

'For thirty seconds per call, and I'm timing you. I have plans for the rest of the evening that involve you, me, that four-poster and the Do Not Disturb sign.'

They had left the hotel only once over the whole weekend to tramp hand in hand along the narrow footpath that wove its way over the fields and country lanes surrounding the manor house. They pointed out ivy-clad cottages to each other that would once have been part of the sprawling estate – gardeners' cottages, or farm labourers', Will reckoned. Now prime real estate in a countryside haven filled with second-home owners. They both marvelled at the tranquility without drawing attention to it – to do so would have broken the very thing they were admiring.

The rest of the time they mainly stayed in their suite, or lounged around the oak-panelled library downstairs, reading funny bits out loud from old battered books they'd found on the shelves. Will was re-reading a Jeeves and Wooster while Jayne had picked out a Poirot.

'Do you think it's someone's job to choose the books to go in this library, because they all seem to be in keeping with the house – very *Upstairs Downstairs*,' she mused, putting the book down next to her pot of tea.

'If it is, I want it,' replied Will. 'How amazing would it be to have your own library! With a tray just like that one,' he indicated a silver tray with a decanter of brandy and some cut-crystal tumblers, which sat on a walnut side table. 'It's like stepping back in time.'

'My library would have a selection of wine instead. And when you enter, you get given your own bookmark, which acts as your membership card, so you can always find your place in whatever book you were reading when you last came.'

'That sounds more like a wine bar with books.'

'You say tomato.'

'Are we really doing this again?' Will teased.

'But don't you think it's a good idea? A place where literary-loving winos can go and have a drink after work and unwind with their favourite book?'

'Actually, you know what? It does sound fabulous. Throw in a plate of Parma ham and some olives and it's my idea of heaven.'

'We could call it Shakespeare & Chardonnay, or Rowling & Rioja. We should totally do that one day. Open up something like that.'

'Yes. In the ten minutes per week we currently have free, in between brushing our teeth and turning the light out, we should totally open up a wine-bar library.'

'I'm going to ignore your mocking tone, Scarlet, because you've just proposed to me and said some very nice things, but don't think that you can maintain this level of facetiousness once we're married, because I just won't stand for it.'

Chapter 16

Will discreetly pressed a ten-pound note into the valet's hand before slamming his door and revving the engine. 'Do we have to go?' Jayne whined, 'Can't we stay here forever?'

'Aren't you in a hurry to flash your rock at Rachel?'

'Oh, yes! Put your foot down.'

As they neared the M25 Jayne reached into her bag to turn their phones on. It had been absolutely blissful not having Michaela call Will every ten seconds barking another instruction at him, or his growing team of staff headed by Bernard, who now ran the deli and the cooking school, phoning him with some query. She'd also enjoyed not having to field calls from Crystal. Jayne had barely spoken to her since the doomed Christmas, returning only one call in ten. After decades of barely conversing with her daughter, her sudden interest in the minutiae of her life happening at the exact-same time her daughter's boyfriend hit the big time was incredibly suspect.

As soon as the screens came to life the two phones would not stop buzzing. They both had hundreds of missed calls, and more texts than their inboxes could cope with – both of them showing full capacity.

'Something's wrong. Loads of people are trying to get in touch with us,' Jayne shrieked, 'What if the flat's burned down? Or there's been some sort of accident?'

'Calm down and call Rachel or Bernard. They'll know what's happening. I'm sure it's fine.'

Jayne keyed in her sister's number. Rachel picked up on the first ring. 'Are you okay?' Rachel yelled.

'I'm okay, what about you? What's going on?'

'What do you mean what's going on? Haven't you seen the papers? Why was your phone off?'

'What papers? What's going on?'

'Where are you now?' Rachel sounded out of breath, as though she was pacing the room.

'We're about fifteen minutes away from home.'

'Don't come here – there's loads of photographers outside.'

'Outside the flat? Why?'

'Your engagement was in the papers and then some stories have come out about you, old pictures. Look, I don't want to explain over the phone just in case–'

'Just in case what?' Jayne's voice had risen to near-hysteria, 'Rachel, you're really freaking me out.'

'Well, I am pretty freaked out, they've run pictures of the two of us when we were children. I was followed to work yesterday, so couldn't go today. Seriously, it's all majorly kicked off here. Don't answer your phone and don't call Abi or Crystal.'

'Abi? Why shouldn't I call Abi?'

'Look, I'll explain everything when I see you. Where are you going to go?'

'We're coming home. I'm not going to be bullied by a few photographers. See you in a bit.' As soon as Jayne hung up she was faced with a barrage of questions from Will. He'd got the gist of the conversation from hearing Jayne's side of it, but wanted to know exactly what they were walking into before they got there.

'Can you type in Michaela's number and put it on speaker?' he said.

Again, it only took one ring before she answered. Everyone must be literally sitting on their phones today, Jayne thought.

'Where the fuck have you been?' Michaela's normal aura of composure had been eaten away by her rage. 'And why the hell was your phone turned off?'

'Jayne and I went away for the weekend. What's going on?'

'Your *girlfriend* has sold you out.' She spat out the word 'girlfriend' as though it was venom.

'Michaela, I've got no idea what you're talking about?'

'Why don't you ask Jayne how the story of your engagement leaked so quickly? Maybe she ought to choose her best friends a little more carefully. Also, why don't you ask her how much money her idiot of a mother got for her tell-all? Fucking hell, Will, in one weekend your bloody girlfriend has undone all the good work I've done in six months.'

'Jayne's mother? I don't understand?' He looked across to Jayne, who had paled and was staring at the road in front of them, her eyes wide and her hand pressed to her mouth. 'Look, I'm nearly at home now. I'll call you back in a bit.'

'Don't you dare cut me–' he hung up and Jayne could see that his knuckles were white where he was gripping the steering wheel so hard.

'I don't know what's going on. Let's just get home, talk to Rachel and see what's happening. It's all going to be okay. There's nothing that can't be sorted out.' He looked over at her. 'Jayne, say something.'

Her voice was almost a whisper, 'She said that Abi and Crystal have done tell-alls.'

'Look, like I said, we don't know what we're dealing with until we get home. Do you even want to go home? If there are photographers there, we can go to a hotel if you prefer. Tell me now, because we're almost there. What do you want to do?'

'Home. I want to be at home.'

They parked the car round the back of the deli, in the parking space ordinarily reserved for the delivery vans. The back door of the deli was locked, which was unusual for a Sunday afternoon – it was normally propped open to invite the fresh air into the compact kitchen at the back while they did all the prep for the week ahead. Will called Bernard on his mobile to signal their arrival. As soon as the door opened, Bernard quickly ushered them inside, bolting the door immediately behind them.

'Bernard, what's going on?'

'Right, well it turns out you two are rather popular today. Out the front is a bit of a rugby scrum, I'm afraid. Not a brain between them, though no one has figured out that shops also have a rear entrance, so you're in luck getting in without the blighters knowing. I've put the 'closed' sign up I'm afraid, Chef, they were all crowding in with no room for customers, and so I made an executive decision and shut up shop. Hope that's okay?'

'I'm going upstairs to see Rachel,' Jayne said, giving Bernard the briefest of nods before slipping past him to the stairs.

'I'm coming too. Bernard, you've been brilliant, sorry about all this.' Will put an arm around Bernard's shoulders and guided him towards the back door. 'Go home, no point being here today, we'll figure it all out tomorrow. Sorry again.'

Jayne couldn't stop retching. Rachel rubbed her back with one hand and held her hair back with the other. 'That's it, just let it out.' Jayne eventually sat back on the tiles, leaning against the bath, legs stretched out in front of her.

'Why?' She finally asked. 'Why would they say those things?'

'I don't know, darling girl, I don't know. Because they're jealous? Because people are just mean?'

'How am I going to face anyone again after this?'

'Don't be ridiculous, you've done nothing wrong!' Rachel tenderly brushed a curl out of her sister's eye. 'You do need to speak to Abi, though.'

'I can't. Not after this.'

'But she's beside herself with worry. She's called me hundreds of times. She came straight round here after it happened, she feels so guilty.'

'So she should.'

'It's not her fault. She was in bed with him when you called and of course she was so excited and told him. She had no idea that he'd then sell the story.'

'But she knew he was a dick and she hasn't even seen him for months. I don't understand . . .'

'Apparently they bumped into each other the night before in a pub, they went home together for old times' sake, or something crap like that, and then were still at it when you called the next day with your news. He quickly made some excuse as to why he had to leave and called the papers from outside her flat. It's not her fault. She's your best friend; you need to call her.'

'So then it took all of what, an hour, before our darling mother jumped on the gravy train?' Jayne muttered bitterly. Her head hurt with trying to piece the puzzle together. Apparently, after Dirk's revelation, complete with blurry photos from his camera phone that he'd taken of Jayne and Will at a barbecue last summer, articles had run in all the tabloids asking for information about the woman who'd managed to pin the elusive Will Scarlet down.

A motley selection of acquaintances had crawled out of the metaphorical woodwork, eager to exchange some juice-less titbits about Jayne for a few hundred pounds. The girl she used to work with in the bookshop when she was at school – Sara something – was one of the first. Jayne vaguely remembered her appearing on her Facebook feed a while back. She hardly knew her, but felt that she ought to make more of an effort reconnecting with people from her past, and as she was one of the few girls who hadn't gone out of their way to ignore her, she accepted her friend request. That was a mistake. She'd obviously passed on Jayne's profile picture to the papers too. Jayne thanked God that she was a decade too old to be part of the selfie-generation, or there would be so many more pictures littering the tabloids that day.

A couple of guys she'd had instantly forgettable fumbles with at university had also exchanged heavily embellished versions of their liaisons for a few quid. Blurry pictures of her wearing high-waisted jeans holding bottles of Newcastle Brown Ale ran alongside quotes like, 'She was an animated lover, who had a lot of books in her room.' Hold the front page, Jayne had thought bitterly as she'd scanned through the pile of papers Rachel had reluctantly shown her.

The reality was that Jayne actually had a pretty unblemished past. She'd never been in trouble with the school or the police; didn't have a crack-cocaine or meths habit she battled hard to conceal, and there was no string of unsuitable ex-lovers standing in the wings with their tales of debauched sado-masochistic sex sessions in dungeons. The reporters had very little to fill their column inches with. That was until Crystal stepped up to the tape-recorder.

'Hey, baby,' Will said sympathetically, stepping gingerly over her and Rachel's legs as he entered the bathroom. 'I got you a gin and tonic that's pretty easy on the tonic and a water; I didn't know which one you might need. How are you doing?'

'Just peachy,' Jayne replied stony-faced, stretching out for both glasses.

'Have you read Crystal's article yet?'

'No. I'm saving that for when I've had a few more of these,' she said, lifting the G&T up. 'Have you?'

'Yes. And I don't think you should read it. Just forget about her now. You've given her way too many chances and this should just be the end of it.'

'But what about all the other stories?' Jayne leant her head back on the rim of the bath and closed her eyes. 'Yesterday I was the happiest person in the world and now

I just feel like shutting the bathroom door and never coming out.'

'There's nothing in any of the other stories to make you look anything other than a very normal person. Seriously, darling, it's what? A few people who sat next to you in your GCSE history class, and a couple of college boyfriends. Although judging by your fashion sense in the late nineties you were rather lucky to get those,' Will nudged her, trying to coax a smile out of her.

'That's pretty much what every comment at the end of the article said too,' Jayne muttered angrily.

'There's not one person who didn't go through a dodgy-looking stage in their teens. Apart from me,' Rachel added, totally misjudging her sister's ability to see the funny side of any of this yet. 'And everyone knows that the only people that comment on these stories are people that have way too much time on their hands.'

'But that's just it, they weren't just commenting on pictures of me back then. One website ran a picture of Will and me at that book launch we went to a few weeks ago with a caption calling me a Big Friendly Giant. I actually thought I looked quite nice that night, so if they think I look like that then, what hope in hell do I have any other time?'

'The BFG. That's a literary reference, surely the English teacher in you is slightly impressed by that?'

'Will! They're talking about me! *I'm* the BFG. So no. I'm not impressed by that. I got called that at school too and frickin' hated it.' Jayne gulped back the last mouthful of gin. 'And almost every one of those articles was laced with the same thread of 'Really? *Really?* Will Scarlet chose *that?*'

'They were not.' Rachel admonished, 'I've spent the whole weekend, since you two went on radio silence, reading everything published about you and the ones that you're talking about are in the minority. Most are just intrigued that Will had been quite private about having a girlfriend, and now suddenly he's getting married. Oh, congratulations by the way.'

'Thanks.' Jayne managed a small smile and subconsciously flexed her left hand where the two-carat diamond was weighing it down.

'Oh my God, I haven't even seen the ring! Jesus Christ, that's huge!'

'Said the actress to the Bishop,' Will smirked.

'Alright Dirk. Jayne, it's beautiful, and so suits you. Any thoughts on the big day?'

'Well, the way I'm feeling at this exact moment, this bathroom looks like it may do the job, because I'm never leaving it.'

Will made a deliberate scan of the room and then shook his head, 'Nah, you'd never get an organ in here.'

'Said the actress to the Bishop.' Will and Rachel chorused. Almost involuntarily Jayne started chuckling, along with her sister and Will. The three of them had sat side by side on the floor of their cramped bathroom for nearly two hours, taking it in turns to swig from the bottle of Bombay Sapphire Will had retrieved from the booze cupboard under the kitchen sink. Jayne had swayed between self-indulgent and sobbing to self-righteous and indignant, before finally settling somewhere between the two.

'Okay. I'm ready to read it now,' Jayne slurred.

'I'll get it.' Rachel got unsteadily to her feet and rested her hand on the door handle to try and stop it moving. 'But get ready to be really, really sick again.'

Jayne sighed loudly as she clutched the newspaper in front of her and started scanning the long interview. She didn't really know why it was so long; her mother had never been one for long monologues, or welcomed in-depth discussions, so either she had broken a habit of a lifetime and the journalist had managed to break down barriers she and Rachel never could, or, more likely, there was an awful lot of rubbish in there. Will and Rachel exchanged a tentative glance as they both waited for Jayne's reaction.

The Pain of Miss Jayne Brady

The mother of Will Scarlet's new fiancée exclusively reveals the tragic set of events that led to the birth of her twins.

The surprise announcement of heart throb chef Will

Scarlet's shock engagement this weekend has led to us all asking who the woman is that has captured his heart? Today we learn that there's much more to the staid English teacher than we first thought. Crystal Brady, Jayne's mother, opens up about the biological father of Jayne and her twin sister Rachel, who doesn't even know his daughters exist.

Crystal's delicate hand quivers as she places her teacup back onto its saucer and her small voice cracks with emotion, 'I was a child on the cusp of adulthood enjoying a long and lazy summer backpacking around Thailand when my world changed forever ... I had led a sheltered, conservative upbringing, and knew nothing of the world. It never occurred to me that there might be people, men, out there that might see this unworldliness as an invitation. For over thirty years I've carried with me the shame and disgust at what had happened to me, that it's eaten away at my soul ...'

Jayne looked up at her sister. 'Hang on a second?'
'I know. Keep reading.'

Six weeks into her planned year-long adventure, Crystal Brady struck up an unlikely friendship with a fellow traveller also staying at Paradise Bungalows on Kho Pha Ngan beach.

'Hardly unlikely, he was male.'
'Keep reading.'

They spent the evening swimming in the azure waters
of the Gulf of Thailand and enjoying a barbecue around
a campfire with some of their fellow travellers. It was
on the penultimate day of the man's holiday, before he
left for India, that Crystal claims he took advantage of
her virtue.'

Rachel knew by Jayne's sharp intake of breath which part
of the article she'd got to. 'Is she saying that she was *raped?*'
It came out of Jayne's mouth as a hoarse whisper, computing
the enormity of this allegation was beyond her.
'Keep reading. That's not the worst bit.'

Three months later, Crystal made the astonishing
discovery that she was pregnant. 'When I found out I
was expecting, my first thought was repulsion that I had
a lasting reminder of that day, of that experience, growing
inside me. But then I realised that God had given me
this baby as a gift, to make up for the experience. A gift
to cherish, to nurture and to mend my brokenness. When
I found out it was twins it merely doubled my delight.'
A small tear slowly runs down Crystal's cheek as she
painfully admits, 'My parents wanted me to have a termi-
nation, but I couldn't have the blood of two babies on

my hands. Two innocent babies, made in a moment that they were not to blame for. I've never even spoken about it until now; I've always thought it best for everyone if I hide my anguish from the world, from my beautiful girls.'

Jayne looked up at Rachel from the paper, tears running freely down her cheeks. 'It's not true. It can't be true,' she whispered hoarsely.

'Of course it's not true! I was on Skype with Granny most of the afternoon yesterday and she's so upset about it. That's the opposite of what happened. Crystal had already been to an abortion clinic and Granny found the leaflet in her pocket and convinced her not to go though with it. She said that she and Pops would even raise us if Crystal didn't want to, but she absolutely could not abort us. She said that she remembers it as though it was yesterday.'

'Why did she never tell us?' Jayne asked, the tears falling as though they would never stop, 'We've asked her enough times about it all?' Her voice had risen to levels of near-hysteria; the gin had amplified, not numbed, her emotions.

'She said that she didn't want us ever to think that we weren't wanted, she didn't want us to resent Crystal or know what she actually planned to do.'

'But Crystal made it painfully obvious every day of our lives that we were a massive hiccup in her life, knowing she wanted to get rid of us wouldn't have been a massive shock. And what's all this rape business about? She told us that she and Neil had a 'spiritual connection' and that the moon had brought them together. She made it sound as though the planets had aligned purely for them to get naked.'

Jayne carried on reading. A heaviness had started to settle in her stomach and she could feel her heart pounding as she skimmed over the reporter's descriptions of where they now lived and worked. Jesus, they'd even named the design company Rachel worked for and the school she did.

'Obviously I'm proud of both my girls, but I always knew that Jayne would go on to achieve greatness,' Crystal ventures with the delight only a mother can summon. 'I call her my Plain Jayne Superbrain. I've always made sure she knows that other people's looks can fade and yet her cleverness will last a lifetime . . . I must admit I did expect her to be an award-winning screenwriter or a character actress, there are plenty of parts that don't necessarily call for beauty.' Crystal exhibits her characteristic frankness when asked about her daughter's relationship with Will Scarlet. 'When Jayne first introduced me to Will, I was as surprised as anyone,' she freely admits. 'I'm still not completely convinced that money didn't change hands,' she laughs shrilly, 'or perhaps she slipped a love drug in his drink, it's quite an odd match. But my Jayne is a perfect example of someone who

*overcomes adversity every day and relies on the power
of her brain to succeed' . . .*

Jayne threw down the paper in disgust. 'She makes me sound
like Stephen Hawking. What is this woman on? And they
paid her for this?'

'Yep. And quite a bit, I'd imagine. But anyone who knows
you would know it's all a load of bull,' Will threaded his
fingers through hers. 'So, seriously, forget about it.'

'Forget about it? What the hell? Saying that I've paid you
to be with me, or even worse, drugged you because you
clearly can't have simply chosen to be with me because I'm
evidently so frickin' hideous! Jesus Christ.' Jayne motioned
to the open page on her lap. 'And she's given them all these
photos of us as kids. I didn't even know she had any pictures
of us!'

'She didn't,' Rachel replied. 'She went round to Pine Grove
late on Friday night just after the first stories broke about
the engagement and asked to see Granny's old photo albums
for nostalgia reasons, or at least that's what she told Granny,
and then when Granny had popped off to the loo she'd
slipped them into her bag. You need to speak to her J, she's
blaming herself for leaving her alone with the pictures, and
feels a fool for being taken in by her again. She's in a pretty
bad way.'

'It's not her fault, Crystal's just a—' Jayne sighed, exhausted,
'I've actually got no words for what Crystal is. And she's

given them all these pictures from our Christmas as well! I saw her with her phone quite a few times and actually thought that it was sweet that she wanted to capture the moment. Yeah, right.'

Will took the paper off her legs, scrunched it up into a ball and lobbed it into the bin with the finesse of a pro basketball player. 'It's gone. No more. Come on, it's late, and you've got school tomorrow.'

'How the heck am I meant to stroll into assembly, sing a hymn and pretend that nothing is happening? This time last week I was Miss Respectable, Miss Boring Brady, and now I'm all over the papers! And this is just what's in print. What's on the web?' Jayne's eyes were wide with the sudden realisation that she may have just blindly crashed into the very tip of the metaphorical iceberg.

'Don't even go there. Life's too short for reading about yourself. Did I just say that? Who am I? I don't recognise myself,' wondered Rachel. 'Seriously, though, you'll drive yourself mad by looking for stuff that probably isn't there. Yes, you might get a few odd looks tomorrow, but laugh it off and flash your diamond at them – that'll soon shut them up. If it doesn't, punch them in the face with the rock facing outwards.'

'Wise words. If I do that, the day after I'll be in the paper for entirely different reasons. Seriously, though, there's no way I can go in tomorrow.'

'If you don't, the day after will be even harder. You've got nothing to be ashamed of, just go in, act normal, laugh it off and by lunchtime everyone will have completely forgotten about it,' Will stood up and pulled on Jayne's hands. 'But first, call Abi. You'll need an ally first thing and they don't come more loyal or fierce than her.'

Chapter 17

Abi's phone had vibrated for about a millisecond before she breathlessly answered it. Jayne had tried to sound outraged, or at the very least incredibly annoyed, but faced with her best friend's outpouring of earnest apologies and genuine concern she managed a sentence or two that were laced with mild irritation before bursting into exhausted tears.

Will was right, though, Jayne thought, as she inched her way forward through the ten or so photographers and reporters who were lining the pavement outside the school's driveway. She needed a friend inside the staffroom today. Ken, the school's security guard, whose sole duty up until this morning was to catch smokers and stop kids snogging each other while wearing their distinctive bottle-green uniform, had stepped up to his new role as bodyguard with alacrity. He waved her through the throng, shouting 'Mind your backs!' – a phrase she'd never really understood as it was normally said to people facing outwards, so they should really be minding their fronts. Ken tipped his imaginary cap in response to her wave of thanks, before turning his newly acquired superiority back to the bloodthirsty horde.

'How are you doing, love?' Abi asked after she'd enveloped her in a big hug at the side door of the school. She'd been the first person in the building today, waiting patiently by the entrance, not wanting Jayne to walk in alone. In the twenty-five minutes that she'd stood there she must have heard references to Jayne about once every thirty seconds from the teachers and students who brushed past. She felt so guilty that the original story broke because of her, her stomach lurched every time she heard Jayne's name mentioned.

She had been so happy when Jayne had called her with the news of the proposal, it didn't even occur to her to filter the information before sharing it with Dirk.

Dirk, who, as Will had prophecised, was indeed a jerk. Who would do that? Sell out someone for a few quid? Or even a few thousand? She couldn't imagine doing that to anyone for any amount of money. Then to not hear from Jayne for the next two days was unbearable – she'd really thought she'd blown their friendship completely. There's a moral to that story, she thought, even great sex can be very, very bad.

Jayne's face had taken on an ashen tone overnight and dark shadows under her eyes contradicted her response of, 'I'm alright.' She shrugged, 'Not really expecting the welcoming committee outside.'

'Let's get a quick coffee before assembly. Come on.' Abi took Jayne's arm and steered her through the foyer, which was filled with inquisitive eyes and tactless pointing. Abi kept up a constant stream of questions about the Cotswolds in a vain attempt to smother the murmured whispers that were rebounding around the hallway. Jayne knew what she was doing and was thankful for her friend's desperate attempts at distraction, and although she pretended not to hear the mirth and not to see the mocking stares, of course she did.

The whole day passed in a daze, her mind far away from set texts, SATS and mock exam papers. Jayne didn't really know what was worse, the brusque bluntness of her students, who asked her in no-nonsense terms, 'What it's like to shag Will Scarlet because he's so hot, Miss?' or the overly bright enquiries of her fellow staff as to what she did over the weekend and enthusiastic declarations of the weather's loveliness at the moment. What was it Stanley had said about addressing the elephant in the room?

Jayne wondered briefly what Stanley had thought of his new wife's latest stunt. She couldn't imagine he'd have been terribly impressed with Crystal's shameless cash-for-answers trick, but then knowing her mother the way she did, she didn't doubt she'd have concocted a creative spin on it, making her appear a blameless victim. Fluttering eyelashes and doe eyes concealed a quagmire of fake virtue where Crystal was concerned.

It had also crossed her mind that Neil may have read the article and recognised himself in Crystal's gushing memoir. But, then again, her mother's rendition of events bore no resemblance to the truth, so even if he had picked up the paper (which Jayne thought was doubtful, as in her mind he was a broadsheet reader and not a fan of the red tops) he probably wouldn't have experienced a jolt of recognition.

They were two lust-struck teenagers high on adventure looking for a way to mark their entry into adulthood – hardly the heart-wrenching tale of violation Crystal had billed it as. Who would even lie about that happening to them?

Jayne had battled with her perpetually itching fingers for about twenty-four hours now, ignoring their involuntary flexing at the sight of a keyboard. She really wanted to type her name into Google, but she knew that once that particular Pandora's box was opened, it might never close again. But, then again, better the devil you know. Ignorance is bliss. Knowledge is power. Out of sight, out of mind. Better to know either way. She was driving herself mad with conflicting idioms pulling her first one way and then another.

Being an English teacher she was doubly cursed. Little sayings and quotes from literature kept popping into her head, giving her constant subliminal messages. Mark Twain's 'A lie can travel half way around the world while the truth is putting on its shoes,' urged her to tell her side of the story; Jane Austen's 'A woman, especially if she have the misfortune of knowing anything, should conceal it as well as she can,' advised her put her head down and keep quiet.

Part of her wanted to crawl inside a cocoon and hibernate, but then another voice inside was encouraging her to beat Crystal, Dirk, Sara and the crappy ex-boyfriends at their own game, to do an interview that shut everyone up.

It was so unlike her to want to speak out, to court controversy, but she had such a strong feeling of being wronged she felt compelled to put it right. She'd talk to Will about it; see what he thought. The bell sounded, signalling the end of lesson time and she honestly had no recollection of even greeting her last class, let alone actually teaching them anything. How was she going to do this again tomorrow? And the next day?

'So how was she?' Will asked her as she re-entered the kitchen later that night. He spooned a heap of rocket leaves next to the mound of chunky chips on her plate before sliding her medium-rare steak alongside it. 'About as good as you were expecting or worse?'

Jayne cocked her head to one side, considering the question. She'd put off calling Helen all day and only relented and called her grandmother after Rachel had thrust the phone inches from her face, refusing to move until she had dialled the familiar number.

'She was okay. Kept apologising for leaving Crystal alone in her room and for being taken in by her. Again. I told her that I could understand it; of course you never want to think the worst of your own child. This is it, though – she said that she's had it with Crystal. She's even written a letter to the editor of *The Globe* saying that they should be ashamed of themselves for perpetrating libel and that Crystal's account should be discredited, so let's see what that does.'

Her sigh was louder than she meant it to be as she sank onto one of the breakfast-bar stools, prompting Will to reach over and stroke her arm. 'Granny said that even Stanley's moved out into a hotel because he's so ashamed of what Crystal's done.' Ashamed was actually a bit of an under-statement. He'd told Helen he felt gullible, used and manipulated.

When Crystal had first told him her version of the twins' conception he'd been horrified, pulling her close to him, stroking her hair and suggesting that it wasn't too late to get the authorities involved. The speed at which she'd shouted, 'No! No need for that!' rang dim alarm bells for him, but it wasn't until Helen had stormed round there after the newspaper article that he'd seen Crystal for what she was. 'Jeez, poor guy, sinking so much money into her house and then having to kip in a hotel.'

'I know. I'll call him in a few days when I don't feel like hysterically sobbing every other minute.' Jayne cut into her steak. 'This is great, thanks, darling.'

'It was the least I could do after dragging you into all

this. If I had just stayed a humble deli owner, we'd be bliss-fully left alone and none of this would have happened.'

'But I'd be wearing a much smaller diamond,' Jayne managed a rueful smile.

'I do feel very responsible for you being hounded now. I really didn't anticipate it getting this crazy. You know that when *Esquire* comes out it might get a bit crazier for a bit?'

'Yep,' Jayne replied in a matter-of-fact voice that did a good job of concealing her growing sense of unease. 'When is that, exactly, so I can dust off my flak jacket?'

'See? That's the Jayne I know and love! Michaela's getting advance copies on Thursday, it hits the shelves the following Tuesday. She's got a load of PR lined up around it, so I'm going to be a bit busy over the next few weeks.' His eyes flashed as he traded empathy for excitement. 'She even told me this afternoon that she got hold of some of the low-res shots that the mag's not using and sent them to some other bookers she knows and there's some interest in using me for some ad campaigns as well. How mental is that?'

'Ad campaigns? For what?'

'Like fashion stuff. Designer clothes, poncey aftershave, that kind of thing, I guess.'

'So you'd be, like, a model?'

'I don't know really. I'm meeting her on Thursday for her to show me the proofs and talk about the next steps.'

He paused and took a sip of his wine. 'Um . . . I was thinking that maybe we should move.' He tried to gauge her reaction, but Jayne deliberately put another forkful of food in her mouth to buy herself some time.

'Jayne? What do you think?'

'I don't really know what that would solve,' she ventured after swallowing. 'The journalists will find us wherever we are, and we like it here.'

'I know, but at least it will separate us from the deli, allow that to get back to normal, and we could move somewhere with a fence around it, at least! Or an apartment with a reception and security downstairs?'

'I don't think it's come to that, us needing security.' She suddenly looked horrified, 'Why, do you?'

'No, not at all, I just don't want you to feel too bothered, you know, with people following you, or around us all the time. If we lived somewhere a bit more secluded we could regain a semblance of privacy again, rather than traipsing through the shop every time we wanted a pint of milk.'

'The days of you just popping out for a pint of milk have long gone, Will. When was the last time you just popped anywhere?'

'I pop.'

'When? When do you pop?'

'I posted some invoices last week.'

'And in the 100 metres between our flat and the post office how many times were you stopped or shouted at?'

'A few. Not many. It was fine. I liked it. People are nice to me. Anyway, that's not the point. I just don't want you to get too worked up about it, that's all. We can afford to move to something bigger, better, if you want to. Just think about it.'

'I've thought about it and I'm happy here. I like having the deli downstairs, chatting to Bernard and Sylvia when you're not here, which is a lot. We don't need something bigger, or better.'

'Okay, then.'

'Okay, then.'

They both fell silent as they finished off their meal. Jayne was anticipating the storm that was slowly edging ever-nearer, and Will was wondering if apple cider vinegar might have made a better dressing for the rocket than balsamic.

**

'Can you hear me? It's stupid loud here!' Will shouted over the din of the station announcements, 'I tried to call you on your mobile as soon as I got out but your phone was switched off, so I've been waiting for you to get home.'

'Some arsehole got hold of my number and kept prank-calling me, so I turned it off until I got home safely. How did the meeting go?'

'Really good, get this – I'm going to be fronting the Autumn/Winter Diesel ad campaign and I'm going to have my own column in *The Sunday Telegraph*'s magazine! How's *that* for a day's work! Yes, sure, have you got a pen? Of course you can have a picture, hang on a second, Jayne – are you still there? I'll call you back when I'm on the train.'

Jayne hung up and turned to face Rachel, who was looking at her with inquisitive eyes. 'Business owner, chef, internet sensation, chat-show guest, TV personality and now model and columnist. Puts teaching frickin' *Hamlet* day in and day out into perspective.'

'Do I detect a bit of the old green-eyed monster?'

'No! You know I'm happy for him. He deserves this; he works so hard. I'm just feeling a bit sorry for myself, that's all. This week has been beyond crap. Everywhere I turn people are whispering about me. Some aren't even making the effort to whisper. This afternoon a few of the mums were smoking by the gates and when I walked past them, one of them called me a fat slag and they all laughed. It's like being fifteen again.'

'Don't take any notice, that put-down is both unoriginal and untrue as you're merely big-boned and have had very few sexual partners, considering your age.'

Jayne was sure that there was a compliment in there somewhere, but was too tired to search for it, so affected a mildly disgruntled air instead, replying sarcastically, 'Thanks, sis, can always depend on you for support.' Although it had only been five days since her picture, name and bra size (38E) had appeared in every tabloid going. Jayne barely remembered the life she had led before the weekend.

She was sure that at one point she used to walk to the

tube by herself, blissfully anonymous, happily unknown by everyone she passed. Now surreptitious camera phones lurked under people's coats, poised to snap her at her most vulnerable – mid-sneeze, mid-yawn, mid-blink. The stage whispers of scorn designed for her to hear; the barely concealed disdain that someone like her should dare to be with someone like him.

She sighed – at least she had Rachel to confide in. 'Don't tell him I said any of this, though, will you? I don't want him to think that I'm not happy for him.'

'Of course not. And you're being the model girlfriend, sorry *fiancée*, about everything, the odd wobble is completely natural. Your world has just been turned upside down.'

'We tried to go to Pizza Express last night, but before we'd even managed to eat a dough ball there were loads of people crowded around our table wanting pictures with him, so we left. What the hell is wrong with the world when a person can't even be left alone to eat a dough ball?'

'Indeed.' Rachel nodded solemnly and then started to smile. 'You know life's bad when you can't even eat a dough ball.'

Chapter 18

B ernard, my old chum, my old mucker!'
'Good morning, Chef, glad to see you're full of the
joys of this glorious summer day.'

'The sun is shining, the birds are tweeting, the hills are
alive, we're alive. It's going to be a magical day.' Will pumped
Bernard's hand up and down while patting him on the back
before Bernard stowed his satchel under the counter and
started tying his apron around his waist. 'The delivery for
the quails' eggs came early, so I sorted that out, the first
batch of pastries are almost baked and I also ordered some
new Kitchen Aid mixers for the school, can you let Trudy
and Karen know?'

'Will do. Do I have the pleasure of your company today
in the shop? That will be a treat for one and all.' Out of
anyone else's mouth that would have sounded sarcastic, or
at the very least vaguely ironic but, ever the gent, Bernard
meant every word.

'Sadly not,' Will juggled a hot croissant between his hands,

'I have a rare day off from filming anything, so Jayne and I are going to look around a few different wedding venues this morning and then I'm going to look at a couple of other premises for the third shop.'

'Exciting times, Boss, exciting times.'

Jayne unsteadily appeared at the foot of the stairs. She was wearing a new pair of high wedges under her tailored linen trousers that were the same vibrant red as the Estée Lauder lipstick she'd impulse-bought the week before. She'd been wearing the same just-off nude shade for about fifteen years and had experienced an unexpected lip epiphany in Boots. Ever since she had started to be followed by photographers she'd begun to make a bit more of an effort with her whole appearance, not just her mouth. Her shapeless maxi skirts, which had been her beloved companions through most of the last decade had been somewhat unwillingly consigned to the back of the wardrobe, and in their place a more mature, quality collection of clothing items had set up home. Zips had replaced elasticated waists and her fail-safe flip flops had been joined on the shoe rack by an ambitious collection of strappy sandals and heels.

'Morning, Bernard!' she shrilled as she tottered across the shop floor to pick up a smoothie bottle from the refrigerated cabinet.

'Morning, Jayne. My, you look a picture.'

She raised an eyebrow, 'A good picture?'

'A masterpiece,' he smiled.

'Are you really sure a six-foot woman should be wearing three-inch heels?' Will asked, suddenly feeling a little dwarfed.

'Don't you like them? Are you worried if we get photographed you're going to look like a short-arse?'

'It's not that . . . I'm merely questioning the practicality of them – we're going to be traipsing around places all day. I just want you to be comfortable.'

'And shorter than you?'

'That's not what I'm saying. I'm thinking of your feet, that's all. Wear your flats.'

'I want to wear these.'

'Okay, then. Wear those, but don't moan when they start to hurt.'

'I'm thirty-two, not two, Will. I'm perfectly capable of choosing appropriate footwear.' He rolled his eyes behind her back as the last remnants of his good mood fully evaporated. 'Okay, then. Bye, Bernard.'

By the third venue Jayne was wincing every time she took a step. Angry blisters had formed on the back of both feet, on the inside of her ankle where the strap rubbed and on her left little toe. It took every ounce of willpower and stubbornness not to fling the damn shoes in the nearest bin and walk barefoot for the rest of the day.

The old Jayne and Will would have had a hearty laugh at her expense, before performing a ritual sacrificial burning of the wedges in a dustbin out the back of the shop on their return home. However, the new Will was busy enquiring over the maximum numbers of guests, saying that a limit of 200 just wouldn't work for them, while Jayne was concentrating on transferring her body weight from one foot to the other, to momentarily relieve the agony.

When he'd first suggested this trip to see different options for the wedding she'd been pleasantly surprised. Obviously a wedding usually does follow a proposal, but she'd been so consumed with keeping her head above the water while her legs frantically paddled underneath she hadn't really considered the post-engagement phase.

They'd spent hours weighing up different options. She was keen to have a very intimate ceremony on a beach somewhere or on a remote Italian hillside. After all she only had a handful of people she'd want there, and thought it might be nice to revisit Will's Italian heritage, but Will's roll call of invitees seemed to expand every day. Duncan, Erica, his dad and Trish still topped the list, but hastily scrawled underneath them were the names of editors, producers, fellow presenters, make-up artists and his regular camera crew as well as all his staff in the delis and school, which now numbered twenty-four. And apparently everyone had to have a plus one as well. Her fantasies of standing in a semi circle with their nearest and dearest in some exotic paradise, barefoot of course, because after today she never wanted to wear shoes again, had well and truly disappeared.

'What do you think of this one, baby?' Will asked her as the heavily made-up wedding planner clutched her moleskin notepad to her non-existent bosom next to him. It hadn't escaped Jayne's attention that she'd barely received a glance from the woman since they met her at Café Nero in Covent Garden just after nine that morning. 'It's got a great terrace, where the jazz band can go when the guests are having canapés and we're having photos.'

'It's . . . nice. A ballroom is a ballroom, though, isn't it? They all seem to be the same.'

The wedding planner gave Will the briefest of sympathetic looks, as if to say 'you poor thing, having to deal with such a heathen for the rest of your life. Pick me, pick me!'

'How can you say they're all the same?' Will shook his head and pointed at the floor, 'This one has the dance floor in the middle, but the other two had it at the end.'

'I don't know, really, can we sit down and talk about it?' Jayne tried to remove the pleading from her voice.

'No time. Onto the next one – we have three more today,' breezed the planner, whose pencil-thin eyebrows matched the width of her skirt.

'Are you okay?' Will asked in the taxi on their way to the restaurant that evening. After a few aborted attempts at eating out, Will had decided to book a private room in the basement of a China Town restaurant for the meal with Duncan and Erica that they'd been talking about having

261

ever since Christmas and hadn't got round to actually doing yet.

'I'm fine. It's been a long day.'

'You didn't seem to like any of the hotels, though. What was wrong with them?'

Take your pick! she wanted to shout. You're inviting hundreds of strangers to my wedding; it's not in Tuscany; I'm not going to have either of my parents there; I have to wear shoes. But instead, she settled for, 'No, they're all, very luxurious. It's just a bit overwhelming I guess. It would be nice to keep it small, but that's a bit impossible, isn't it?'

'I just want the world to know how lucky I am marrying you, and so for me the more the merrier!'

'How many is 'more' exactly?'

There was a discernible sheepishness in Will's voice as he shifted in his seat, 'er . . . around 250 . . .'

'Two hundred and fifty people? We'd better not be doing the whole bride's friends and family sit on the right and groom's on the left because my lot will fill two rows, while yours will be stretching out to the car park!'

'But you know I've been whittling down the list as much as I can – everyone coming are genuinely people I really want there. Don't be angry.'

'I'm not angry.'

'But you're not happy.'

'I am happy. Look.' Jayne forced her mouth into a wide toothy grin. 'See? Happy.' The London streets slowly flashed past their windows. Summer had pushed the darkness back to past ten pm, extending the long, hot days by hours. It seemed as though half of London had made the decision to abandon sweaty tube carriages and cycle back from work, so garishly helmeted novices wove their way through traffic that was now at a standstill. Even with the windows fully down, the cab had taken on an oppressive quality, heavy with July air and unvoiced agendas.

'Um, I wanted to mention something, actually,' Will began tentatively, 'Michaela mentioned that she might be able to get the wedding paid for and a bit of extra cash that we could use as a hefty deposit for a house or something,' Will casually volunteered.

Jayne swung round to face him, her mouth falling open in disbelief. 'As in, barter our wedding off?'

'No! As in sell a few of the pictures afterwards, or slip a few branded things in. No one would even notice, but it all helps, doesn't it? A wedding for 250 people in a posh hotel isn't exactly cheap.' Jayne bit down hard on her lip to stop herself saying the obvious. 'I just thought that maybe we should think about it rather than immediately saying no. I mean, the photographers are going to want some shots and if we actually arrange a magazine to cover it, at least then we're in control of it and not the other way around . . .' He tailed off, suddenly aware of the gaping silence coming from the other side of the back seat. 'Baby, you're freaking me out, what's wrong?'

'I'm fine, honestly,' Jayne replied, 'It's just been a really strange couple of weeks. You've had months and months to get used to this, this—' she wanted to say freak show, but instead settled for the less punchy 'notoriety'. 'It's been less than a fortnight for me to get used to a flash going off in my face or someone stopping me in the street telling me how lucky I am.'

'You should listen to them.' Will grinned and elbowed Jayne in the ribs.

'See? You're not even taking this seriously!' Jayne pouted.

He slid over to her side of the cab and pulled her head onto his shoulder. Jayne immediately felt her shoulders drop a notch as she allowed her head and worries to rest against his familiar frame. 'I am. I promise. But this whole fame thing is ridiculous. It's so bizarre and surreal, the only way to approach it is with bemusement. Like you said at the beginning, enjoy it before a dancing dog knocks you off the top spot, and that's what you should do.'

'But that's so easy for you to say, Will, everyone just loves you! They literally think you're God's gift to mankind, and I'm some hairy heffalump that must have drugged you to fall in love with me.'

He raised an eyebrow, 'hairy heffalump?'

'Yes.'

'I know I'm going to regret asking this, but what is a heffalump – hairy or otherwise?'

'You know what a heffalump is.'

'I promise you I don't, otherwise I wouldn't ask, I'd just go 'oh yes' and agree, or not. Depending on what it is.'

'You must know. In *Winnie the Pooh*, the heffalump is an elephant that appears in Pooh and Piglet's dreams. You know, with the woozles.'

Will stifled a smile at her earnest sincerity, 'I know I'm going to regret asking this, but what, in the name of all that's holy, is a woozle?'

'They had a song.'

'This just gets better and better. I think I need to hear the song to, you know, jog my memory.'

Jayne glanced at the sign on the window between them and the driver to check that the light indicating that he could hear them wasn't illuminated before saying, 'Don't think that I don't know that you're mocking me, Scarlet, but I will humour you with a little snippet anyway. Purely in the name of memory-jogging, you understand.' She took a deep breath and held out her two index fingers, as though conducting an invisible orchestra.

'A heffalump or woozle is very confusel
The heffalump or woozle is very sly
– sly – sly – sly
They come in ones and twoosels
but if they so choosels
before your eyes you'll see them multiply
– ply – ply – ply . . .'

'Have I mentioned lately just quite how much I adore you, Jayne Brady?'

'Not lately, no.'

'Well I do.'

At that moment the cab pulled up outside a fairly innocuous restaurant in China Town. In its window was an array of cheap golden cats with their left paws rocking rhythmically back and forth and a collection of dusty red parasols and paper lanterns suspended from the ceiling with yellowing sticky tape. They'd decided to choose privacy over pretension for this meal, knowing that it wouldn't even be on the paparazzi's radar. And after all, a spot of food poisoning was a small price to pay for an evening without camera lenses.

Duncan and Erica were already seated in the small windowless basement room that masqueraded as a private dining area. Erica swiftly rearranged her features from disdain to delight when they walked through the door. It was obvious that she'd assumed having a famous friend meant dinners at The Ivy, not The Golden Duck.

'You look amazing, Jayne! What a gorgeous lipstick! It really suits you! Will, darling, come here, you look divine as usual! Give me a kiss, you gorgeous man.' Erica pulled Will in for a hug that lasted a couple of seconds too long.

'I need to apologise for my lush of a wife. We were in such a hurry to leave the kids we arrived here an hour early and we're already onto our second bottle,' Duncan beamed as he leant across and kissed Jayne's cheek. 'But she's probably only got another hour in her before she passes out in the corner, so bear with her in the meantime,' he added amiably.

'Shut up!' Erica replied, 'How are you both?' her expression turned to theatrical pity as she then looked at Jayne, her bottom lip protruding and her forehead deeply furrowed. 'And how are *you*? You poor thing.'

Jayne smiled the polite smile that she'd now perfected. A smile that turned upwards at the edges but that didn't quite reach her eyes. 'I'm fine. Good, I'm good. We looked at wedding venues today,' she said, brightly side-stepping Erica's obvious probing. It wasn't that she didn't want to open up a conversation about how utterly rubbish the last couple of weeks had been, in fact she could have waxed lyrical about the crappiness of the fortnight all night, but she preferred to save her tales of wretchedness for Rachel whose loyalty to her was so fierce it was sometimes scary. Not that she didn't trust Erica. Jayne didn't doubt that her concern was heartfelt, but even Abi had been receiving the watered-down, heavily edited version of 'woe is me' lately.

Wedding talk accompanied heaped plates of surprisingly tasty spring rolls, spare ribs and prawn crackers. Will relayed the pros and cons of the five hotels they'd seen that morning to a rapturous Erica and vaguely interested Duncan, who nodded in all the right places before enquiring whether there would be a free bar.

A lull in the conversation as the waiter cleared the plates

gave Erica the chance to revert to what was clearly her plan for the evening – making Jayne talk. Reaching across the table to put her hand over Jayne's she gushed, 'It must be so hard for you.'

'Um, not really. Weddings are fun, aren't they?' Jayne replied, deliberately misunderstanding.

'I have so much admiration for you facing these vicious people on the internet. What are they called again, Duncan?'

'Trolls.'

'Yes, trolls. The things they are saying about you. I would die. I would quite literally die.'

Jayne inwardly winced at the un-literal use of the word literally before shrugging and shaking her head. 'I'm trying not to let it bother me.'

'We're choosing not to read too much, actually, Erica,' Will interjected.

'Yes, that's probably for the best. I mean, I was just devastated for you reading all the horrific abuse on Twitter about you. Calling you all those horrible names, and those blogs that have been set up with the only intention of being nasty about you. What was one of them called Dunc – you know the one with the picture of Jayne as a voodoo doll with pins sticking out of her?'

Duncan shifted uncomfortably in his seat, 'Um, Eric, I don't think anyone wants–'

'Or the one that's a cartoon of a boxing glove going into your face, which they called The Brady Punch. I mean that's just horrible. And after your mother did that interview, I know Will has told us that it's all lies, but everyone has picked up on what she said, calling you Plain Jayne SuperLame. I am in so much awe of you, even leaving the house with all this going on.' Little tears started forming in Erica's glassy, kohl-rimmed eyes, 'You need to stay strong, Jayne. Stay strong. That's the only way to beat the bastards.'

'Wow, look at the duck! That looks lovely,' Will almost applauded the entrance of the duck and pancakes. He moved his leg under the table so it brushed Jayne's in a silent show of intimate solidarity, but the gesture came too late. Jayne's heart had quickened and she felt as though the walls were closing in on her, the deep-red walls slowly moving forward to squeeze her into a smaller and tighter space.

She reached out for her water and saw her hand shaking uncontrollably. It knocked the delicate stem of her wine glass, sending the red liquid gushing over the tablecloth onto her pale-blue skirt. She jumped up as everyone frantically started patting her and the table. 'White wine, we need white wine!' 'Salt!' were the last things she heard as she ran from the room and locked herself in the toilet cubicle seconds before huge heaving sobs escaped her body.

She tried to slow her breathing down, to release the tightness in her chest. Amidst her panic, a lucid thought of not wanting to pass out on the germ-ridden floor of a backstreet Chinese restaurant in Soho floated to the surface of her mind and enabled her to gain a modicum of control.

Her face and neck were wet with tears and sweat patches had started to form under her arms, staining her new silk camisole. She didn't blame Erica for what she said; she knew she wasn't being malicious, just drunk and tactless. Since as far back as Jayne could remember she'd dealt with any kind of controversy by simply blocking it out, humming a happy tune and pretending it wasn't there. Never quite managing to cultivate the full-body armour that Rachel donned every morning, she had had to resort to pure, plain avoidance of anything that wasn't rosy. And now, at the age of thirty-two she was still doing it. It was just a shame that her friends weren't.

Jayne splashed water on her skirt, trying to avoid her reflection in the mirror above the small sink. She knew she must look awful; she didn't need to see the streaks of foundation and her panda eyes to know that they were there.

'Baby? Are you okay?' Will's concern was audible through the door. 'You've been in there ages. Are you alright?'

'I'm fine!' Jayne called back perkily. 'I'll be out in a sec. The wine's not coming out.'

'Can I come in?'

'Sure, wait a sec.' She tried to dab away the most stubborn mascara stains and pinched her cheeks to give them their colour back. 'Hi!' She flung open the door and smiled.

Tilting her chin up he asked tenderly, 'Have you been crying?'

'Maybe a little.'

270

'About the wine or what my best friend's socially inept wife said?'

'Bit of both,' Jayne softly admitted. 'Mainly the wine. I liked this skirt.'

'I liked it too. But I like you more.' He gently kissed her lips. 'Don't take any notice of her. Do you not think that there are thousands of people who think that I'm a complete prat? Do you see me upset about it? No, because I only give a toss what a tiny handful of people think about me. If you start worrying what complete strangers, who you'll never meet, think about you, you'll drive yourself insane.'

'I know. I know that. But it's really difficult to just ignore the fact that these things are out there. Voodoo dolls of me? Cartoons where you can punch me in the face? What have I ever done to anybody? That's sick. Really, really sick.'

'I know. But just put it out of your mind. I've made some ready-rolled pancakes for you, with lots of hoisin sauce, just how you like them. Come and eat them before Dunc does.'

'Do they think I'm stupid?'

'Of course not! We'll just tell them it took ages to get the stain out.'

'But it hasn't come out, look.' The wine had stained the blue fabric a putrid brown colour.

'Oh. Um, I don't really know what to suggest. Have you got a petticoat on that might pass as a skirt?'

'No. Just my knickers, and nobody really wants to see me in my knickers.'

271

'I'd like to see you in your knickers . . . No? Okay, do you want me to pop out to a shop to buy you a new skirt?'

He'd only been gone about two minutes before he arrived back in the basement bathroom breathless. 'There's a few photographers and people upstairs. Someone must have tipped them off.' He ran his hand through his hair and chewed his bottom lip, 'I don't know what to do. We're sort of trapped down here, and you look like you've been at a murder scene.'

'There's no way I can go out there looking like this. Can you imagine? If the world thinks I'm a fat, ugly witch at the best of times, seeing me like this is going to make the internet melt.'

'Wait here. I'll talk to the manager and sort something out.' As it turned out, he didn't need to. Duncan had arranged for them to sneak through the kitchens into the back alley, where a car driven by his brother's friend was waiting to pick them up.

Jayne and Will were bundled into the back seat, keeping their heads low under Erica's coat as they edged through the baying crowd of hungry camera-wielding snappers and autograph-hunters lining the road. One or two people looked in through the rear windows as the car glided past and saw their two bodies doubled over in the back and started banging on the glass and pulling at the locked handles. 'Just drive!' Duncan ordered. The engine's sudden rough roar, coupled with adrenaline-filled whooping from everyone else, covered Jayne's sobs from where she lay huddled in the dirty foot-well of the stranger's car.

'That was insane!' Duncan shouted, twisting around in the passenger seat as the car sped along the river. 'Jesus H Christ, is it always like that with you, Will?'

'That was particularly mental. Jeez, my heart's still pounding!' Will replied. Shrugging off Erica's coat, he pulled himself up on to the back seat. 'Jayne, baby, baby,' he nudged Jayne with his feet, 'You can get up now.' Reluctantly Jayne slid up onto the seat, bringing her knees up to her chest and huddling into the door. If anyone noticed her reticence or caginess it was ignored as everyone else in the car relived the great escape with delighted hoots and yells. She blocked out everything except the sound of the blood pumping loudly in her ears and the rhythmic hum of the engine.

It was alright for them, she thought. To them, this was fun.

This wasn't fun.

Chapter 19

Jayne had tumbled from car to back door to bed, not even bothering to take the remains of her make-up off or brush her teeth. Surprisingly she'd slept a dreamless sleep until a wide shaft of daylight found the crack between the hastily closed curtains and announced that it was morning. Her face felt stiff, taut with caked foundation and salt water. Running her tongue over her teeth made her grimace and flashbacks of last night reignited the hammering in her chest again.

Will was still sleeping, lying spread-eagled in his boxer shorts, the duvet consigned to the floor, his mouth slightly ajar. It was easy to see why he'd garnered such an intense fan-base so quickly. He was incredibly handsome, much more so than most normal people you see on the street. But part of his appeal was that he had seemed so totally oblivious of it. Less so now, but then she couldn't blame him; being flattered all day by make-up artists fawning over your bone structure would do that to you. He was told the other day that he had the longest eyelashes one stylist had ever seen. Up until that point, Jayne wasn't sure that Will was even aware he had eyelashes.

If she was completely honest, the new, and supposedly improved, Will was not really an improvement in her eyes. She had actually liked the greying temples that Fernando had painted over, one hair at a time. And whereas before his hair had that 'just got out of bed look' because he had actually just got out of bed, now it had that quality due to about twenty minutes in front of the mirror and four different expensive products.

He'd stubbornly refused to have a manicure for about three months, before finally kowtowing to Michaela's supposed better judgement. 'It does make sense, I suppose, when I have close-ups of my hands all the time,' he'd reasoned afterwards, while surreptitiously admiring his cuticles whenever he thought Jayne wasn't looking. He drew the line at fake tan, but he had that gorgeous olive skin tone that darkened to a honey caramel within seconds of seeing sunshine, so he never needed to have that particular battle anyway.

What must it be like, she wondered, to be so beautiful that people have to have a second look just to make sure that their first impression was right? To know that whichever room you were in, you were the best-looking thing in it. Even if the attention was good attention, not the vitriolic hatred she was now experiencing, but the kind of grovelling adulation Will enjoyed, she was sure she'd find it claustro-phobic. But he didn't seem to. He still swore that he wasn't really aware of it most of the time, but to Jayne that line was starting to feel a little practised.

Thank God there were only two more days of term left; the word 'exhausted' did a disservice to the way Jayne felt. It had been a month since Crystal's article and interest had started to ebb away from her onto the next victim, so the photographers had gradually peeled away, been sent onto other assignments, but one solitary man, with a Marlboro in one hand and a camera lens in the other, persisted in turning up every day with only a pack of twenty and a *Racing Post* to keep him occupied until she arrived. His familiar leer had even started haunting her dreams – when she managed to sleep. Her misery was obvious. It was etched on her face as though with an indelible marker, and yet still he raised the camera to his face and clicked away with gay abandon as she hurried past every day. Today was no different.

Kyra had given Rachel a relaxation CD filled with 'posi-tive reinforcement messages' and 'affirmations for a happy life' to pass on to her, and it was testament to just how insular Jayne had become that she hadn't even questioned why Kyra had ever needed to be in possession of such a CD in the first place, she'd just wordlessly accepted it. Apparently she was meant to breathe in for four counts and out for eight while picturing a rainbow emerging from behind the clouds, bathing her in its magical light. She'd listened to the whole CD on the journey in, trying desperately to find a rainbow amongst the clouds and to slow down her quickening pulse with longer breaths, but it was impossible.

She knew what this was. She'd seen her A-level students have them before an important exam; she just needed to calm down, to inhale and exhale. The worst thing you can do is to give in to the rising sense of panic, she knew that. She'd said it often enough. Just close your eyes and breathe. And search for that blasted rainbow. It didn't help that Abi wasn't around; she'd left school a few days early to go back to Ireland for a family party – so Jayne was well and truly on her own.

She'd just about got through the morning, well, almost. One more lesson to go and then lunch. She really hoped that Will and Rachel wouldn't be out again tonight; she didn't want to only have the clouds for company. Again.

'Morning all,' she greeted her class. She could really have done with some eager year sevens to round the first half of the day off, not this group of beligerant year elevens. She wasn't in the right frame of mind to go into battle against a room of raging hormones.

She'd snapped, 'because I told you to,' to one girl, who questioned why she had to be the one to read aloud. But instead of doing it in her normal friendly, but authoritative, tone, which normally put an end to teenage whining, she'd let a note of desperation seep into her voice. A note that made thirty-two pairs of ears prick up; a red rag of a note that shouted 'let the games commence'.

'You think you're so special, don't you, Miss?'

The irony of juxtaposing the insult in the first half of the statement with the term of respect in the second part didn't escape Jayne and she resignedly sighed, 'No, Michelle, I don't.' Which was true. Jayne had never harboured any pretensions of being special. Growing up with Crystal had put paid to any illusions that she was in some way different to any of the other seven billion people who walked the planet just trying to get through the day.

'You do. But even your own family didn't want you, did they? You think that you're so much better than everyone else because you've managed to con someone as hot as Will Scarlet into being with you.'

Jayne kept her eyes down, staring at the open book in front of her. Her vision started to blur. *Don't cry,* she willed herself, *don't cry, not in here, not now*.

'Do you pay him? Is that it? That's what even your mum says. She said that you're paying him to be with you because there's no way you could pull him if you weren't.'

The room laughed, big, bolshy, mocking laughs. If Michelle hadn't quoted Crystal, if Michelle had chosen some other taunt or line of bullying she'd have been okay. Jayne would have been able to shrug it off, to stare her down, to rise above it and see it for what it was. But Michelle didn't, and now Jayne couldn't. Her breath quickened, her heart hammered against her ribs and she heard herself give an ear-piercing scream.

The head had called it 'taking a well-earned rest', but the real term was 'suspended with pay'. It had taken thirty-seven seconds, basically the time it took the class to type 140 characters into Twitter, for the 'incident' to be on its way to going viral. By the time Jayne had reached the deli there was a crowd of braying parents and photographers outside. Even the rear entrance was no longer sacred, with a smaller, but just as angry, mob lying in wait for her. Bernard was standing in the middle of them, a friendly face in the midst of such anger. He opened her car door and bundled her inside the shop. He could see immediately that any type of fight or resistance had left Jayne's body. She'd felt smaller, frailer in his arms, letting him guide her up the stairs to the flat, shaking her head weakly at him as he lifted her feet up on to the sofa so that she was lying flat.

She had been so shocked at her own outburst; it was the first time in her life that she'd ever lost her temper, let alone used so many swear words in one sentence. And at a child. *A child*. It didn't matter that the child was a notorious bully, or that she hadn't been in the right head space to deal with it. She'd lashed out at a child. In one instant, one badly timed, completely out-of-character moment, she'd flushed thirteen years of teaching down the toilet, along with any semblance of empathy anyone might have had towards her. *A child.*

'I've really done it now, Bernard,' she ventured weakly.

'Tea or wine?' was his compassionate response. He knew Jayne well enough to know that she'd reached her breaking point. No amount of clucking or pity was going to hoist her out of it. There was only room for practicalities now. 'Maybe we'll start with tea and then move on to something stronger when the sun goes over the yard-arm, yes?'

Jayne could hear Bernard busying himself in the kitchen. The clank of cups and the kettle boiling were interspersed with the sound of him leaving urgent messages with a variety of people for Will and Rachel to return home 'quick as you can'.

Chapter 20

Three days passed. Three days of not leaving the flat. Three days of wearing pyjamas during the day. Three days of headlines like, 'Plain Jayne Assaults Pupil' and 'Scarlet's Woman in Abuse Shocker'. Three days of Rachel chaperoning her in the bath, checking that she didn't keep her head submerged for too long.

Michelle Whittaker's parents had threatened to sue on grounds of their daughter's 'distress', a threat that was swiftly and sanctimoniously replaced with offers involving the words 'out of court' and 'settlement'. Will was on his way back from a meeting with Michaela's solicitors now to confirm if there was anything to be concerned about in their ludicrous claim. Jayne could see that his stoicism was beginning to wear a little thin; he didn't understand at all why she'd let everything build up to such a crescendo, but then, why would he?

'So as a gesture of goodwill, the solicitor called them to offer a thousand pounds—' Will raised his hand to stop

Jayne from furiously interrupting – 'to the charity of their choice, and their reply was even fruitier than the words you called their daughter, which obviously the solicitor recorded, which means that we won't be hearing from them again.'

It was a relief; she knew that they were just chancing it, but the thought of potentially going to court on top of everything was just too much to bear. Will obviously thought that this news would be an end to her 'blues', and wrongly deemed the time right to merrily mention a new luxurious block of flats in Kew that had just started to be marketed. The white-gloved doorman and twenty-four-hour manned reception desk had proved too difficult to ignore as he airily slid the glossy estate agents brochure across the breakfast bar to her.

'What's this?'

'A brochure of a new development near here. It looks pretty good.'

'These are nearly a million pounds! We can't afford a million pounds, Will!'

'We could with a mortgage based on my projected earnings this year.'

'But the deposit alone would be hundreds of thousands. We don't have that kind of money in the bank!'

'We could do if we accepted the magazine deal, which, thank God, they haven't retracted yet . . .'

'Are we still talking about this? I thought we agreed that we wanted to keep the day private.'

'We do. Which is why I think it's a good idea to sign up with just one magazine, so we don't have loads of different photographers all jostling for a picture. If we agree to be exclusive with just one publication then it puts everyone else off. Seriously, that's the way it works. Michaela told me.'

'Oh. It must be true if *Michaela* told you.' She knew that it had been Michaela who had generously offered her lawyer's services on the company account this afternoon, but even that wasn't enough to stop Jayne wanting to kick a wall every time her name was mentioned. *Michaela*. *Michaela*.

Just then the front door slammed and feet started clumping up the stairs, fused with excited chatter and laughter. Rachel burst through the kitchen door with Marco and Kyra in tow. Jayne's stomach lurched. Cue a round of air kisses – although the air between Marco's lips and Will's cheek miraculously vanished when it was their turn to greet each other. 'I haven't seen you for ages, Jayne! How are you?' The 'how' and the 'you' were voiced as if in italics, Kyra's head tilted to the side as she said it, a thousand other words of pseudo-sympathy hung in the air.

'Good. I'm fine thanks, Kyra. You?'

'Great, thanks, but then I'm not the one with my face all over the papers every day. Well done you for not going into hiding. If it was me you wouldn't have been able to coax me out from under my bed, I don't think!' She laughed and placed a hand on Jayne's arm. 'Rach says you're being a superstar about all of it.'

'Jayne's doing brilliantly,' Rachel revealed supportively. 'She knows it's all a load of tripe, don't you?'

'Can I just say, and I know she's your mother and everything, but what a bitch for starting all this,' added Marco. 'I felt really sorry for her at first, and then when Rachel told us the truth we were like, oh no she didn't.' His last few words were accompanied by a hand on the hip and a wagging finger. Trying not to revert to stereotype was a constant battle for Marco.

'I was saying to Rachel whether you should maybe tell your side of the story, so that people know the truth?' Kyra asked, 'That way, *you'll* get some of the sympathy and not your mum or this Whittaker girl.'

Will leapt in at the same time as Rachel, both of them saying variations of no. 'I don't think that's the right thing to do. It'll just prolong the story being in the papers.'

'Just be the bigger person and keep quiet. Don't lower yourself to their depths,' was Rachel's argument.

'But if you do an interview, it'll be completely on your terms – you can choose which newspaper or magazine to speak to, you can decide the direction it goes in and what you say,' Kyra reasoned. It pained Jayne to admit it, but Kyra actually talked sense and seemed genuinely on her side. She caught her sister glaring at Kyra, making it quite obvious that they'd been discussing this before.

'Or, like Will said, it'll keep you in the news far longer than you would be if you just lay low.' Rachel added.

'If I lie any lower I wouldn't get out of bed. A woman actually spat at me when I came back from school that day. Can you believe that?'

Marco and Kyra shook their heads sympathetically. Rachel and Will had spent a couple of hours calming her down that evening, so this wasn't news to them. She'd wanted to call the police and lodge it as an assault, until they both convinced her not to. What was wrong with these people who had made snap judgments on her based on the way she looked and who she was dating? What did these psychopathic women think, that if she didn't exist Will would be with them? These thoughts had tumbled out of her mouth, without even pausing for breath, and Will had just laughed them off, telling her not to be silly and over-react. She didn't think it was over-reacting to be a little incensed at having a stranger's spit in your hair. Rachel's initial compassion had also morphed into frustration, telling her, albeit kindly, to 'grow a pair.' *You know what?* Jayne suddenly thought, *I'm going to do it. I'm going to put the story straight and then everyone will leave me alone.*

The trouble was, she didn't know how to go about speaking to the press. She was, had been, an English teacher, not a media guru, and she absolutely didn't want to ask Michaela's advice, because she knew that it would be the same as Will's and Rachel's – keep schtum. Jayne knew that the tabloids would love her to talk to them, but they would put their own spin on everything she said, having bought in so completely to Crystal's and Michelle's tales of sorrow. The weekly magazines would sandwich her interview between a story of a woman who had horns instead of ears and a feature on the latest diet tips that involved just eating puréed red cabbage. And the monthly magazines, which she would definitely prefer, would interview her now, yet not run the story for another two or three months, such was their lead time. And she couldn't wait that long for her life to go back to normal.

She suddenly remembered the young journalist who first interviewed Will back in November. Samantha something. She was really sweet and it was her article that made people fall in love with Will. Maybe she could do the same for her?

It wasn't difficult to find Samantha's contact details; since her interview with Will was published her byline was on more and more stories nearer the top of the webpage, not buried a few screens down, like before.

Samantha answered by barking 'Newsroom!' down the phone, which gave Jayne a bit of a jolt. Her only experience of the media so far had been negative and upsetting, and yet here she was willingly calling a person whose greeting when picking up their phone is 'Newsroom!'

'Um, hello, Is this Samantha Carter? This is, um, Jayne Brady, Will Scarlet's fiancée . . .' There was a moment's pause, and the sound of fumbling from the other end.

'Hi, Jayne, how are you?' In the nine months that had

passed between her standing in their living room shrieking with excitement at getting her big break and now, Samantha's naïve exhilaration had been replaced by a more mature worldliness, making her sound as if she'd been expecting Jayne to call.

'I'm, well, I'm okay. I was just calling because there have been some stories about me recently that haven't really been true, and so I wondered if I should, well, tell my side, and you're the only reporter I've ever met, so I'm calling you first.'

'Great. Yes, that's great. But let me stop you there. I'll need to talk to my boss to see what we can offer for this. So you haven't approached anyone else? It'll be an exclusive? We don't want to get involved in a bidding war, so our offer will be final. Are you okay to hold or do you want me to call you back?'

'Um, I don't really know what you mean. I don't want you to pay me for this. Is that what you mean? You think I'm doing this for money?'

'Aren't you?' Samantha sounded shocked.

'No! I just want to tell the truth and then be left alone.'

'That's very commendable Jayne, but I think it's better to be honest and just say the amount you're looking for so that neither of us wastes our time. Ten thousand? Twenty? Give me your ballpark.'

'You're not listening to me. I don't want your money. I'm doing this to tell my side. I don't want all these people, who don't really know me, to influence what people think about me! I'm a nice person, I really am, I don't hurt small animals or children, I just try and get on with my life and hope that people like me!' Jayne's voice had risen to near-hysteria, forgetting that she was talking to a journalist with a dicta-phone held next to the receiver.

'I don't deserve this, people spitting at me in the street, shouting abuse at me wherever I go. Is it such a crime that I fell in love with someone prettier than I am? Hold the front page! I'm living in a frickin' nightmare. I just want it to end!' Shaking as the words tumbled out of her mouth, Jayne suddenly remembered who was on the other end of the line and her hand shot to her mouth. She panicked and slammed the phone down.

The phone had been ringing continuously for half an hour and Jayne had just sat there staring at it, not knowing how to make this right. She hadn't meant to go off on one like that, but the suggestion that she was anything like Crystal, or Dirk, trading secrets for cold, hard cash, just made her so angry. Was it so inconceivable that she'd want to just give an honest account of her life for no other reason than to speak the truth? She gingerly picked up the receiver, 'Hello?'

'Oh thank God! You had me worried.'

'Hi Samantha, I'm sorry about that. It's been a really tough few weeks and I just flipped out.'

'It's okay, completely understandable. Are you ready to talk now?'

It had all spilled out. Jayne had attempted to keep Rachel out of it as much as possible. She knew that her sister didn't approve of her even doing an interview, let alone being part of it, so she tried to use the words 'I' and 'me' instead of 'us' and 'we'. It was a bit challenging remembering to speak in the singular rather than plural when her whole life had been entwined with Rachel's, but she knew how intensely private her sister was.

She heard herself unravelling her history – everything from always looking for the father who didn't even know she existed, to what it was like growing up with a mother who pretended she was her sister. Fond memories of Helen's part in her life were tearfully talked about, but it wasn't until Jayne mentioned the summer when she met Will that Samantha's interest really peaked.

'So you say that his mother had just died?'

'Um, yes, but don't put that in. I don't think he'd want me to talk about it.'

'Did he cry a lot?'

'Really, I don't want you to write about that. I shouldn't have–'

'Did he have bad dreams about it? Wet the bed? Do you think he views you as the mother he didn't have?'

'We're the same age! And no to all of your questions. I don't want to talk about this. Do you know what? I don't want to talk any more.'

'But Jayne, it's going so well. Please, keep talking–'

'No, this was a bad idea. I shouldn't have done this. I don't want to do this article any more. Please forget I ever called.'

'I can't do that now, Jayne, my editor is very excited about this. We're leading with it tomorrow.'

'But I don't want you to! I'm not taking part in this any more.'

'*You* called *me,* Jayne. You called me and now the story is running.'

'Can I at least see it before you print it? I need to see what you're writing.'

'Sorry, we don't give editorial consent before publication to anyone. And anyway, it's all your own words. I can't make up what you didn't say. I trust you've been recording this conversation as well, so you know what you said?'

Jayne knew that Samantha knew that she hadn't even thought of doing that. Why hadn't she thought of doing that? Because she was stupid. A stupid, stupid woman who thought she could play this game. But she couldn't. She was just a little pawn being shuffled around a board that other people controlled. Other people who were far cleverer and more together than she would ever be.

Chapter 21

Jayne Brady is a woman teetering on the brink of suicide, 'I'm living in a f***ing nightmare, I just want it all to end,' she emotionally confides to The Globe *in this explosive exclusive interview. Talked back from the edge by our own Samantha Carter, Jayne opens up for the first time about the mental abuse and neglect she suffered at the hands of her mother; the father she yearns every day to meet; the estrangement from her twin sister and how she saved fiancé Will Scarlet from the grief that was set to destroy him.*

What the hell were you thinking?' Jayne didn't think she'd ever seen Will so angry. Veins were popping out on either side of his neck and his face was flushed red, 'You weren't, you weren't thinking. You can't have been, because no sane person in their right mind would have said this stuff.' Jayne winced as he threw the paper at the living-room wall. She was sitting at the table like a naughty child, her head bowed low and hands clenched in front of her, while he paced the room behind her like an angry animal, flinging admonishments at her. You're stupid. You're careless. You're insane. She knew she deserved every accusation. It *was* stupid, careless and insane.

Downstairs the door slammed shut. 'Where is she? Where is she?' The fury in Rachel's voice shook the walls as she came hurtling up the stairs. 'What the fuck did you think you were doing?' Rachel cried as she flung open the living-room door. 'How did you think this would make anything better?

'Please don't shout at me. I know it was a mistake—'

'A mistake? A mistake would be buying full-fat milk instead of skimmed. A mistake would be going out without a coat in October. This, this—' Rachel thrust the newspaper inches from Jayne's face. 'This is a complete disaster.'

Tears started running down Jayne's cheeks. 'I'm sorry, I don't know—'

'No, you don't know,' Will jumped in, 'you don't know what massive damage you've done. I hadn't told anybody about Mum dying, and then you just blurt it out – and to tell the world that I was falling apart—' he picked up the crumpled paper from where he had thrown it down on the table and read out loud, 'with grief so raw he had started walking down a path of self-destruction.' What does that even mean?'

'But I didn't say that! I mentioned that she'd died and then as soon as I said it I told her not to write it!'

'Oh that's okay, then. You told a journalist something, but then told her not to write it. Because journalists do that. They ask you questions and then ignore your answers. Jesus, Jayne, how could you be so gullible?'

'And what the hell is this 'estranged twin sister' garbage all about? Reading this article you wouldn't even know you had a twin sister, it's all 'my childhood this, I did that, me, me, frickin' me.'

'But I didn't think you'd want me to talk about you!' Jayne blurted out between sobs.

'So you just thought that you'd erase me from your past – Rachel won't like me doing this, so I'll just pretend that she doesn't exist. Nice. Thanks for that. I've done nothing but listen to you go on and on about how you hate what's happening, you despise the attention, you don't like the women hanging around Will, you don't like his new hair, or nails, or clothes–'

Will interrupted, 'You don't like my hair or nails?'

'And that's the part you're concerned about?' Rachel said incredulously, swinging her attention to Will for a second before turning back on her sister. 'And this is how you show your gratitude? By rewriting history without me in it?'

'But that's not how it was – she twisted everything I said.'

'Again, that's what journalists do, ' Will jumped in, 'They don't want a story where everyone pulls together and gets on with life while skipping hand in hand through a forest together – they want tales of deceit and heartbreak and grief, and that's just what you gave them. Jesus, Jayne, you're not a dim person, how could you be taken in so much? And what I don't understand is that you approached her! It's not even as though she caught you off-guard staggering home from a pub – *you* called *her*. Which makes you doubly stupid.'

'Yes! Yes, I'm so stupid! I know I'm stupid, will you two just back off, just back off and leave me alone!' Jayne ran out, the door shuddered as it slammed loudly behind her. She ran into their bedroom and pulled a small bag out from under the bed and stumbled over to her dressing table, frantically pulling out drawers, gathering up a few knickers and bras, some t-shirts, a couple of skirts. As an afterthought she also grabbed her passport. She kicked the wedges out of the way and knelt down in front of the wardrobe, digging away in the bottom of the cupboard until she found her old denim jacket and her flip flops. She then paused at the two framed pictures on her bedside table.

One was of her and Rachel. They must have been about six or seven, standing in just their Care Bear swimsuits next to a half-filled paddling pool that still had a hose sticking out of it. Helen was taking the picture and her long shadow stretched across the grass to the side of where the girls were standing, grimacing into the sun, their little arms wrapped around each other's waists. The other photo was of Will and her – he was giving her a piggy-back and she had her head thrown back laughing. He'd just been running through the park with her on his back, neighing like a horse and stamping his foot. She'd laughed so much she'd cried. That was before. Before he cared who saw. She hurriedly grabbed both frames and pressed them down on the top of her bag.

'So that's the answer, is it? You're running away?' Rachel came out of the kitchen as Jayne ran past with her holdall. 'You're running away, leaving us to deal with the aftermath.'

Will stood in the doorway of the living room, 'Jayne, what are you doing? Why have you got a bag?'

'I just need to go away for a couple of days. I can't handle this any more. I'm no good at it. I hate everything about this whole situation. I hate you being famous. There, I've said it. I hate you being famous. It stinks.' The three of them stood in the hallway, each in the doorway of a different room. 'I just need some space to think.'

'Think about what? You screwed up. Twice. We'll deal with it and move on. What's there to think about? You're being dramatic.'

'As usual.' Rachel added sullenly.

'See, that's just it!' Jayne shrieked, 'You can't see that everything's changed. We were so happy, and then it all started shifting, and I can't deal with it. I can't deal with people mad at me for loving you. I'm fed up with justifying to people all the time why you're with me. I don't want to live like this. I don't want to sneak out of restaurants through the kitchens. I don't want my students asking me what it's like to sleep with you. I don't want parents whispering about me and pointing. I don't want strangers taking pictures of me on their phones and uploading them onto Instagram for people to laugh about how awful I look. I don't want strangers spitting at me in the street or telling me that I'm punching above my weight. And I don't want a massive wedding with hundreds of people I don't know in a ballroom that also does conferences. I just want to be us again. Jayne and Will and Rachel. Just us.'

For about a minute no one spoke. It was the longest, most tranquil, minute that had ever existed in the flat when all three of them were at home and awake. Will and Rachel stood staring at Jayne, who felt at once exhausted and exhilarated after blurting out everything that had been making her chest feel tight for the last few months.

She inhaled deeply and picked up her bag. 'So I'm going to go away for a couple of days and clear my head. Work out what to do next.' She hesitated for a moment, bag in hand. This was the part where Will would walk over to her and wrap his arms around her, bury her head in his chest and smooth her fizzing hair. Tell her in soothing tones that it was all going to be okay. That the rest of it meant nothing without her. That they could pretend the last year hadn't happened and go back to the way it was.

Instead he scuffed his shoe along the skirting board and said quietly, 'Maybe that is for the best. Sort your head out and then we'll talk.'

He couldn't have shocked her more if he had slapped her

around the face. She had never expected him to agree that she should leave. They were meant to be opening a bottle of wine right now, the three of them bustling around the kitchen collecting a corkscrew and glasses to share a drink and work together on making this right.

Jayne looked at Rachel, who shrugged sadly, 'If that's what you want, then do it.'

No! Jayne wanted to shout, it's not what I want, I want either of you, both of you, to tell me it's all going to be okay and to stop being so ridiculous and to unpack my pathetic little bag. 'Okay, then,' she said with far more grace than she felt, 'I'll see you in a few days.'

Bernard gave her a cheery wave as she rushed through the deli, before noting her white knuckles gripping a bag. He looked as though he was going to say something, but then decided against it, believing that other people's business was just that. Jayne pushed through a couple of customers and jostled a pushchair out of the way of the door.

She strode purposefully towards the station – purposefully but purposeless. She didn't have any idea where she was going; she hadn't planned any of this. Her first thought was to get to Helen, she'd make it all okay, but she knew there was nowhere for her to stay at Pine Grove. Helen's room at the residential home was already crammed with the contents of her four-bedroom house. Glass cabinets filled with painted china figurines and easels with half-finished canvases of seascapes took over what little floor space there was. There was no room for a runaway granddaughter as well, much as Helen would have loved there to be.

Abi. Abi would make this all okay. Jayne felt a pang of guilt that she'd done a pretty good job of alienating her best friend in the last couple of months since Dirk lit the first fuse. She'd pretended to forgive her, made all the right noises when pressed about it, promised that she didn't blame her, but their friendship had certainly waned in recent weeks. Cordiality had replaced affection and the warmth that had characterised their friendship over the last decade had given way to politeness. She'd done a sterling effort in distancing herself from everyone, Jayne grimly recognised, as she scrolled through her phone for Abi's mobile number. The second Jayne heard her friend's soft Irish lilt say 'hello' she felt a weight lift off her shoulders. She closed her eyes in relief and stood aside in the foyer of the station to let streams of commuters pass by. 'Abi. I need your help. Can I come over?'

'I'm back in Ireland for a couple of weeks, my love, is everything okay?' Jayne vaguely remembered Abi telling her about her parent's fortieth wedding anniversary party she was going to at the start of the summer holidays back in County Mayo.

'Oh bugger. Sorry, I mean bugger for me, but that's great for you. How's the family? I bet your mum's pleased to have you back.'

'See, that's what I love about you, Jayne Brady, you're

obviously going through something, yet you're asking about my mam. She was just asking about you too, actually.'

'Why, has she seen the paper?'

'What paper?'

'*The Globe*. The interview.'

'No. What interview? Oh Christ, has your ma been talking again?'

'No,' Jayne admitted sheepishly, 'This time it was me, and I've screwed up royally.' Noticing a few furtive looks from people using the ticket machine she was leaning against, Jayne turned her back slightly, so she was huddled into the wall. Speaking in a low voice she added, 'I was just calling to see if I could stay with you for a few days, but don't worry, I'll find somewhere else.'

'Don't be daft. Oh dammit, I've got my spare key with me, otherwise I'd say you could camp out at my flat until I get back. Look, this might sound crazy, but why don't you come here?'

'To Ireland?'

'Why not? You said you want to get away for a bit, and believe me, County Mayo is the last place any paparazzi are going to look for you.'

'But disaster seems to be following me all over the place. I don't want to inflict that on your poor family!'

'Oh behave, like we care. Where are you now?'

'Richmond station.'

'Oh so you got quite far, then?' Abi chuckled, 'You can

tell that you're a novice at this. Okay, so get to Gatwick and get an Aer Lingus flight to Knock. Text me and tell me what time you get in and I'll get Barney or Liam to pick you up.'

'Knock as in knock knock who's there?'

'The very same. And don't you even think about taking the piss out of our place names when you English have villages called Lower Soggy Bottom or something like that.'

'You're wonderful. Thank you.'

'Don't go getting all soppy on me, just get the flight. Then you can tell me all about your royal screw-up over a couple of bottles of moonshine.'

Chapter 22

'Wow.' Abi let out a low whistle, 'You're an eejit.'

'I know.'

'I know you know, or you wouldn't be here.'

'But I don't know how to make it right,' Jayne took a deep breath. 'Or if I even want to.'

'Of course you want to. You and Will are made for each other; you're both mad as fruitbats.'

'But I want the old Will, not Will Scarlet, 'hello there, pretty lady, of course I'll sign your breast'.'

'Does he actually sign people's breasts?'

'Probably,' Jayne pouted, taking a gulp of her wine. 'Actually, probably not. But in my head he does.'

'But that's just it. In your head it's so much worse. He's still exactly the same as he always was, just more people know him now.'

'He dyes his grey hair black.'

'As do you.'

'Touché. He has his nails filed by a man called Stefan.'

'Lucky him. Next gripe?'

Against Jayne's will a little laugh escaped, 'How do you do this?'

'What?'

'This. Making me laugh when I want to cry.'

'When you cry you make this face,' Abi wrinkled her nose and crossed her eyes, 'and so I'm going to do all I can to save the world from seeing that. Hang on, my phone's buzzing.' The name on the screen made Abi smile, 'Hello there . . . yep . . . she's here with me now . . . Yes, in Ireland. Just having a bottle of wine, talking about the situation in Palestine . . . Okay, yep, I'll call you later.'

'Was that Will?' Jayne asked as soon as Abi had hung up.

'Nope.'

'Rachel?'

'Nope.'

Jayne's heart started pounding and panicked she burst out, 'It wasn't a journalist? Do they know I'm here? Did you tell anyone?'

'I'm going to pretend you didn't just insinuate that I'm talking to the press behind your back, Jayne Brady, or you and I are going to fall out big time.' Abi stuck her nose in the air, feigning an air of indignance. 'If you must know, it was Bernard.'

'Bernard? As in Bernard who works in the deli Bernard?'

'Yes. The very same.'

'How does he have your number?'

'How do you think? I gave it to him. We call each other a bit. Have the odd bite to eat. Glass of Merlot. Occasionally kiss each other.'

'With *Bernard?*'

'Yes, with Bernard.'

'But you never said! Since when?'

'To be fair, you've been pretty busy dealing with your own life to really notice what's been under your nose in the last few months. I don't blame you, it's been manic for you, but Bernie called me after the whole Dirk debacle and was very sympathetic, took me out for a drink, then dinner, and what do you know, we've started sort of, well, seeing each other.'

'You're sleeping with Bernard!'

'Well, not exactly, we're taking it slowly.'

'You. *You're* taking it slowly? The woman who thinks taking it slowly means removing the dress before the pants?'

'The very same. He's revolutionised my thinking. I'm a new, purer woman because of him.'

'Well, I'm lost for words. How could I not have seen this? I feel awful for not knowing! But you guys make such a great couple. I'm really happy for you.'

'So, on the bright side, we won't be needing our plus ones at your wedding, so that's two less lamb shanks you need to budget for.'

'If there even is a wedding now. After my outburst telling

Will that I didn't want the wedding he wants, I'm not sure it's still on.'

'Shush. Of course it's still on. Just have another day or so here, breathe in the mountain air, let the dust settle, then go home to a man who adores you. Right, another bottle?'

The next morning Jayne was woken by a gentle knock on the door followed by the entrance of a breakfast tray. 'Morning, sleepyhead. I've brought you some tea and some orange juice.'

'Mrs Sheeran, you're a superstar, thank you so much, what time is it?'

'Just gone ten.'

'Oh my days, I don't think I've slept that much in years! You must think I'm so lazy!' Jayne said apologetically as she sat up in bed.

Abi's mum laughed as she opened the curtains and let the sun flood the room with light. 'Not at all, obviously your body needed to rest. I've got some bacon grilling downstairs, so after your shower come down and have a bacon sandwich to set you up for the day.'

'You're a legend,' Jayne smiled, 'Thank you so much.' She looked over to the other single bed in the room where Abi had slept. The covers were neatly doubled back and her pyjamas were folded on her pillow. 'Where's Abi?' she yawned.

'Gone to the newsagents on the corner for some milk

and her da's tobacco. She'll be back soon. Come down when you're ready.'

As Jayne lathered her hair with the lemon-scented shampoo left in the tray of the shower she realised that she wasn't feeling the same sense of unease that had plagued her for months. She'd been carrying an ever-present anxiety around with her like a trusty purse, and now it wasn't really there any more. As much as her tantrum in the hallway at home had been fraught with tension at the time, she felt a huge sense of relief that she'd vocalised all the thoughts that had been eating away at her, keeping her awake at night and poisoning her days.

Talking to Abi last night had helped so much too. She'd really missed her lately; no one else managed to blend such complete honesty with humour the way she did. Everything was going to be okay, she could feel it. She'd call Will this morning, sort it all out, stay for the party tonight and fly back in the morning.

Jayne flung her head forward and wrapped her head in a towel turban and draped the bath sheet that Abi's mum had left folded on her bed – like they do in hotels – around herself before stealthily creeping along the hallway back to her room and picking up her phone. Will was usually like one of those blue-chip companies that promise to answer your call by the third ring, but today his mobile went straight to answer phone.

'Um, hey, it's me. The stupid one.' She hoped this sounded

tongue-in-cheek rather than just accusatory. Damn answer machines. 'Um, just checking in. I'm okay. Not dead or anything.' Why did she say that? That sounded as if she didn't think he'd care. Of course he'd care. 'I thought we should talk before something happens and we can't any more.' Shut up. Shut up, Jayne, now that sounds as though you're actually going to top yourself. Or shoot him in the face. 'I really do love you, you know, even though you're, you know. And um, call me back when you get this. If you're not too busy.' Why? Why did she add that little dig at the end? No need for caustic little asides, she was meant to be being the bigger person here and instead had recorded a message that made her sound like a suicidal sociopath crippled with animosity. That's the way to win back the man you love and adore.

'Jayne, are you in there?' Abi hammered on the bedroom door, 'Are you nearly done? I need to talk to you.'

'Yep, hang on a tick.' Jayne tightened the towel around her before opening the door to her breathless friend. 'Hey, what's the hurry? Is the bacon burnt?'

'Has Will called you? Where's your phone?'

'I've got it here. Why? What's happened? Is something wrong? Is it Rachel? Or Helen?'

'Jayne, stop,' Abi placed a protective hand on her friend's arm. 'Everyone's okay, but there was something on the front cover of a few of the papers, a picture.'

'Of me? Where? At Matt Malloy's? I didn't see anyone?

Oh God, did they take a picture of me playing the trumpet?'
After three bottles of rough house white the pair of them
had taken advantage of the pub's resident jazz trio being on
a break at the bar to hop onto the makeshift stage and
mime playing their instruments. 'Why did I think that was
a good idea? I blame you, you always get me into trouble
like this. Oh well, could be worse. I was seconds away from
picking up the horn, imagine the caption on that!'

Abi was still. 'Jayne, the picture's of Will.'

'There's always pictures of Will, what do you mean?'

'He's with someone.' Abi took a deep breath; it was as
though the words were forming inside her mouth but she
didn't want to let them out. 'The one who's always with
Rachel. The blonde one.'

Jayne had never really understood the phrase 'blood
running cold' before that moment, but as she heard herself
squeak the name 'Kyra,' she suddenly knew exactly what it
meant.

'Show me.'

Abi gingerly held out a stack of six newspapers. The same
pixelated picture of Will nuzzling Kyra's neck was on the
front page of three of them, and within the first five pages
of the other three. He was holding a bottle of beer with one
hand while his other was reaching up to tuck her hair
behind her ear as he leant in. It was a simple act of intimacy
that stabbed Jayne in the chest harder than if Kyra was
straddling him.

'I'm sorry, Jayne. I thought you'd want to know.'

There it was again, the pulsing in her ears. *Scarlet the Harlot!* one headline cried, while others had more eloquent variations of 'you dirty two-timing dog'. Jayne sank down onto the bed, staring at the picture in disbelief. This was Will. *Her* Will. Dependable, loyal Will, who waited, what, twelve hours before tucking another girl's hair behind her ear, the same way he'd done to her on their first date. Well, that was obviously quite clearly his modus operandi. Simple, really, most men go straight for the lips, or the zip, not Will, no, he likes to start small, start with the hair, that'll get them.

Abi perched on the bed next to her. They must have sat like that for a few minutes, each giving the moment the gravitas it deserved. Only yesterday Jayne had been making flippant remarks at how the wedding might be off, or not comprehending how to make it right, yet they had both known inside that these words were just filling the silence, they weren't serious considerations. Of course it would all be okay. Except now, after this, it really wouldn't be.

'I need to get dressed.' Jayne said finally, standing up, clutching the towel to her.

'Okay. I'll be downstairs,' replied Abi, moving towards the door, 'I'll make some fresh tea. Or I'll open a bottle of something. Whatever you want, just tell me and I'll do it.'

'No, tea would be good,' Jayne said quietly. She stood in the middle of the room, intending to dress and yet finding the very act of finding clothes and stepping into them a bit beyond her. As soon as Abi had gently closed the door behind her, Jayne dropped numbly onto the bed. She picked up the top paper again to torment herself by having another look and her heart raced faster than it ever had before.

It was obviously a nightclub, with bodies pressed together in a way that happens only in dark, loud places. The sound of mirth and hilarity sprang out from the page. His beer was almost empty, but Jayne realised by the way he was holding it, his little finger tucked around the bottle's neck, coupled with the way he was leaning, that it wasn't his first. Kyra's head was slightly tilted away from him, a gesture that some would interpret as coyness, but Jayne knew it was an affectation, a gesture of mock bashfulness, a 'what? little old me?' stance that made her want to scream.

And they weren't even being mindful of who saw them, which she could understand from Kyra's point of view. Of course she'd want this little charade to be played out in public, but Will was usually ultra-careful. The doomed dinner in China Town was one of the few nights out together in months. But then, Jayne reasoned, if she had looked like Kyra maybe he wouldn't have been so quick to suggest 'another night in'.

Perhaps their hermit-like existence together wasn't romantic, or deliberately sacred, like he'd made her believe. Maybe it was just because she wasn't photogenic enough. Her wide afro might obscure his cheekbones, she thought resentfully, or her glasses might rebound the flash and block him out in a big haze of light.

This wasn't supposed to happen. She wasn't supposed to be sitting in a foreign bedroom with faded posters of Boyzone on the wall. She was meant to be waking up on a Saturday morning with him, reading their books in bed together, bantering over who would fling on enough clothes to be deemed decent and go downstairs and bring fresh pastries and strong coffee up to bed. Like they had every weekend for the last two years. It wasn't supposed to be like this.

It was torture studying this photo, yet she couldn't seem to drag her eyes away from it. Something about it didn't seem right. Well, nothing about it seemed right, but something niggled at Jayne. She brought the paper closer to her face and dropped it suddenly with a gasp. There was a shadowy figure laughing in the background of the picture; a blurred silhouette that Jayne knew almost better than her own outline. More than Kyra elbowing her way into Will's drunken line of sight eight hours after she'd left, even more than Will being fickle enough to wave goodbye to his fiancée before pressing 'next' on his dating buzzer, the thing that brought on a violent wave of nausea was the fact that Rachel was looking at the scene unfold in front of her and finding it funny.

'I was sick in your bin, but I washed it out,' Jayne walked into the kitchen and laid her head on Abi's shoulder.

'Don't worry about it. I've been sick in that bin more times as a teenager than I can remember. It's what it's there for. That's why I made Ma buy one that wasn't made of wire mesh – there's nothing worse than sieved vomit.'

Jayne managed a small smile at her friend's attempt to lighten the mood as Abi's mum bustled past her, momentarily pausing to place a hand on her shoulder on her way to swill out her coffee cup in the sink. 'Morning, pet. Abigail tells me that you're having some trouble of the heart. Well, you're in the right place, with four daughters and three sons passing through this house, I've witnessed my fair share of misery caused by love, I can tell you that for nothing.' Placing the upended cup on the draining board, Mrs Sheeran wiped her hands on a tea towel hanging from a hook at the end of the counter. 'Do you want to talk about it, or just trot on and try and put it out of your mind?'

Faced with such genuine concern from a relative stranger, Jayne suddenly found herself wracked with grief and fat tears poured down her face. She couldn't believe she was standing in an unfamiliar kitchen in Ireland sobbing and heaving as though a dam had opened and all the pent-up anxiety and stress from her entire life had burst through.

'There there, my love, come here,' Mrs Sheeran held Jayne close, tenderly stroking her hair saying, 'Just let your heart break, pet, I promise you, it won't kill you.'

These were the words she'd longed to hear from her own mother her whole life. She'd been desperate to have this moment with her for thirty-two years, to have her kiss her scraped knee better, or tell her in a wise no-nonsense tone that everything would look better in the morning. Any one of thousands of parenting clichés that spill from the lips of mothers all over the world every day would have done. Just one.

This is what had made Rachel's betrayal so much harder to understand. The two of them had a bond beyond friendship or normal sibling love; they'd barricaded themselves together against the world, and now Jayne was completely alone. Well, as alone as one could be when staying with a huge Irish family reunited for a family party.

'I'm okay now, I'm sorry, so sorry,' Jayne pulled away and blew her nose into a tissue that Abi was holding out to her over her mother's shoulder. 'This is meant to be a really happy day for all of you, and look at me snivelling and bawling. I'm okay, honestly, thank you. I'm so sorry.'

'Have a seat for a minute,' it was more of a gentle order than a request as Mrs Sheeran pulled out one of the pine kitchen chairs and patted the floral cushion that was tied to the spindles at the back of the seat. 'I'm not saying this to interfere, but Abigail has told me a bit about your man, and what he's been doing. Sounds like quite the go-getter,' her eyes twinkled. 'Forgive me for stepping in where I might not be welcome, but I wanted to pass on some advice from someone who might know a bit about what you're going through.'

Taking Jayne's hands in hers she looked her straight in the eyes and said, 'Everyone grows up with dreams, of course they do, dreams to cure horrible diseases, dreams to be in the movies, dreams to be on stage, dreams to be the best bricklayer in the world. These dreams are what make us get up in the morning, they fire us up, they make us excited to be alive. And then, when you meet the person you want to spend your life with, you either accept their dreams and help them reach their goals, or you both reassess your individual dreams and weave ones together that work for both of you. Or sometimes . . .' her fingers stroked the top of Jayne's hands. 'Sometimes, a person's dreams are so important to them, they don't want to change them or they find they can't bend them to fit in with their partner's dreams, and yes, that's okay too, because we each have to walk our own path. When that happens, when two people have such different dreams, you have a choice. You can either decide that one person's dreams take precedence, and the other one sits back and is supportive from the sidelines, while putting their own goals on hold for a while, or, you let them go and realise their dreams for themselves. And when they've done that, they may well realise that success is so much sweeter shared, and your lives will entwine again, or, they may not. But that's a choice no one can make for you. If your man's dreams are the polar opposite to yours then, pet, you need to think long and hard about your own path. Can you try and knit your dreams into his, or try and alter his to fit your own, or is it time to walk away?'

'I . . . I don't know,' Jayne stuttered.

Mrs Sheeran laughed, 'I'm not asking you to decide now! Take your time, search inside your heart and see what will make you both happy, because you want him to be happy too, yes?'

'Of course I do! Well, no, not right now, but yes, I do.'

'Well, then. Now why don't the two of you pop down to Sheila's and get your hair done nice for the party later?'

'Oh no, I couldn't come to the party, I'll just stay here if that's okay? Or if I'm in the way I can go to a hotel?'

'Will you stop it? Like we're going to leave you here all day and night crying into your pillow! You're coming with us and that's the end of it. Now get out of my kitchen the both of you. I have three hundred vol au vents to fill, unless you want to help me mash up the egg into the mayonnaise? No, didn't think so – be off with you, then.'

Jayne's phone was burning a hole in the bag at her feet. She hadn't dared to turn it on yet, not wanting to see the number of missed calls or pleading text messages. Or worse, see that there weren't any. She knew that Will must know that she'd seen the photo because she'd heard Abi through the toilet door furtively whispering to someone, she assumed it was Bernard, telling them that she was 'devastated but bearing up,' and that she was going to stay in

Ireland with her for another couple of weeks. She hadn't even thought about what she was going to do from tomorrow onwards, let alone talk to Abi about it, so she felt a rush of relief that the decision had been made for her and all she needed to do was remember to breathe in and out, nothing more.

The sprightly sixty-something hairdresser interrupted Jayne's thoughts, 'So I was thinking of piling it all up on top like that, but then I thought, no Sheila, where have you ever seen such gorgeous hair before? You haven't, so I'm just going to leave all the curls loose around your shoulders, it looks like a beautiful black halo, don't you think?'

'I don't feel particularly angelic at the moment,' Jayne admitted with a hint of a smile, 'so anything you can do to remedy that would be very welcome.'

'Well you look beautiful. What are you girls wearing tonight?'

'Oh Jeez!' Jayne covered her face with her hands, 'Abi, I have absolutely nothing to wear to the party. I came with two changes of slob clothes! What am I going to do? I can't borrow anything from you. I'm about a foot taller!'

'Our Cameron's girlfriend's about the same size as you. I'll call him and ask if you can borrow something.'

'Won't she mind? She doesn't even know me!'

'But she knows me, and I know you, so it'll be fine.' Abi started punching in numbers and secured a borrowed dress. 'Done.'

'Thank you fairy godmother.'

'You're welcome, Cinders. Thanks, Sheila, we'll be off now.' Standing on the pavement outside of the hairdresser's that had sun-stained posters in its window of women from the eighties sporting slicked-back crops and streaks of pink and purple eye-shadow, Abi said, 'Right, look. Rachel's been trying to call me all morning but I've cut her off each time. I really think you need to speak to her.'

'No.'

'Why not?'

'She's a back-stabbing cow who laughed seeing her so-called best friend kiss the only man I've ever loved, or indeed, ever likely to love. I'm not talking to her. Or him. Any of them.'

'You should hear what she has to say.'

'Why? So she can say that it wasn't what it looked like? She was laughing because she'd just heard a joke and he was helping retrieve something from Kyra's ear?' Saying Kyra's name out loud made Jayne shudder. Even her name was more exotic than her own, which conveniently for journalists, rhymed with Lame, Plain and Shame. 'Seriously, Abi, I'm not ready to hear their cover-up story. It is what it is, and I just need time to figure out how I'm going to get over this, but talking to my sister about it is not going to do anything except upset me again, and I've cried more this morning than I have done in the last thirty years.'

'Okay. I understand that, but I think I need to at least

tell her that you haven't topped yourself. She's called about twenty times since we were in Sheila's.'

'Fine. Tell her that your razor blades haven't been touched, but no more. I'll see you back at your mum's, I don't really want to listen to the conversation, if you don't mind.'

'Sure. But know that if you go back now, you'll be put to work making ten tons of coleslaw.'

'There are worse things in life,' Jayne replied bleakly.

Chapter 23

Jayne had been dispatched to the local village hall to start hanging the vibrant bunting that Mrs Sheeran and her other daughters had spent many evenings cutting and hemming into neat triangles. Lisa and Aoife, two of Abi's sisters, were sent on the same mission – each of them perched precariously on step ladders of varying heights, trying to remember from Girl Guides which knot would be the most secure.

Lisa had brought her speakers along with her and put her iPod on shuffle. An interesting array of songs had been belting out for half an hour: Broadway show tunes mixed with eighties dad rock blended with nineties house music. Jayne was glad of the distraction. Admittedly Will had popped into her head about once every few seconds, but having a task to do, and questionable music to do it to, meant that while she couldn't control the number of times she thought about how miserable she was, at least she couldn't wallow in it. Not yet. She'd save that for tomorrow.

She wondered why Abi wasn't back yet, but then dismissed the thought. In all likelihood she'd gone back to the house and been furnished with another job that needed doing.

'Afternoon, girls!' came a cheerful Irish accent, 'Where would you like the band to set up?' Jayne swivelled round as much as being seven steps up a ladder would allow and saw the same house band from the pub last night wander in with their instrument cases and amps. She quickly turned back around and busied herself with the flags. She vaguely recalled playing a shaky rendition of *When the Saints Come Marching In* before the trumpet's real owner had retrieved it from her with a jaunty shake of the head and a wry smile. That was before her world had well and truly fallen apart.

Rows and rows of flowery chintz and fabric polka-dotted flags decorated the once-bare ceiling as Jayne turned her attention to the matted ball of fairy lights recovered from the Christmas-decorations box in the attic. She was sitting cross-legged on the floor weaving the plug through endless loops of the twisted wire when a shadow fell over her. 'It's you, isn't it?' a deep voice said, with a soft Irish burr.

Jayne steeled herself for an insult about her weight, and punching above it, but it never came. 'You're the mystery trumpet-stealer.'

She smiled, relieved, 'Hardly stealer, merely temporary borrower.'

'You say tomato.'

Jayne felt a pang. Will and she had had exactly the same banter on the day they'd met. She could feel her eyes start to tingle with the now all-too-familiar warning that tears were about to start, so she hurriedly looked down and concentrated on the next knot. 'Do you need any help there? Looks like you'll still be unravelling them when the guests arrive!'

'No, I'm fine, honestly. Shouldn't you be doing a sound check or something?'

'A sound check? As in one two, one two? How many concerts in village halls have you gone to?'

'That would be none. But when I saw Bon Jovi at Wembley they did that.' Jayne added with sheepish shrug. She really didn't want to keep talking, but the trumpet-player had now sat down on the floor next to her and had taken up the other end of the matted mess of wires and lights.

'I don't think I've seen you around here before. Are you on holiday? If so, why are you sat in a village hall undoing lights when you should be hiking up the mountain or eating ice cream by the river along with the rest of the tourists?'

'I'm visiting a friend.'

'A boyfriend?' He asked cheekily.

'A friend that's a girl. Not that it's any of your business Mr Trumpet Man.'

'Aye. None of my business at all. I'm just wondering

whether to talk to you as a normal person or to use my charm, quick wit and repartee on you, that's all.'

Jayne couldn't help laughing at the sheer audacity of the greying musician, who was now sitting opposite her, arching one eyebrow comically. 'Quick wit and repartee? I fear it would be wasted on me. I'm in the middle of one of the worst days of my life.'

'Granted unknotting fairy lights is not the best use of a young person's time on a sunny July day, but there's no need to be dramatic about it.'

'Funny. That's what my fiancé,' she paused, 'ex-fiancé, used to say to me.'

'He sounds like a wise man, except he doesn't because he's your ex. Stupid, stupid man.'

'My thoughts exactly. Stupid, stupid man.'

'Stupid is as stupid does.'

'If there was a town called Stupid, he'd be the mayor of it.'

'Chief Stupid of StupidTown.'

They broke into big grins. 'I'm Jim.'

'Jayne. So, Jim, you're a trumpet-player.'

'Actually no, I'm a history teacher. Who plays the trumpet in pubs and village halls. I need the outlet for my creative expression. And the money.'

'I teach English, so I know what you mean. On both counts.'

'You're a teacher too? See? I knew you were a kindred spirit the first time I saw you.'

Jayne rolled her eyes. 'Are you like this with every unsuspecting girl who wanders into your path?'

'Like what? He asked innocently, eyes and arms open wide.

'Alright James O'Malley?' sang Abi as she sauntered in, weighed down by tupperwares filled with triangular sandwiches and sausage rolls. 'See you've met my friend, Jayne. Didn't take you long to sniff out some new blood in the town.'

Jim held his hand to his chest, 'I'm wounded, Abigail, wounded I tell you. If you'd only accepted my proposal back in high school I wouldn't need to fill the void you left in my heart.'

'Be off with you, you crazy eejit.' She stooped and kissed his cheek with obvious affection, 'I saw you last night at Matt Malloys, but you were either up on stage or chatting up some poor woman, so I didn't come over.'

'Poor women, my arse, they were fans, Abigail, fans. It's tough being this gorgeous to the opposite sex, that it is.' They all shared a smile. Jim with his small, but noticeable, paunch and long, messy hair, which had gone beyond the salt-and-pepper stage into full-blown grey with a few strands of brown, could never be called 'gorgeous to the opposite sex' in the traditional sense of the phrase, but his humour and self-confidence were obviously compelling to the long line of women he'd evidently snared. Including, Jayne realised, her best friend, who was exhibiting the common signs of being in the company of an ex-sleeping partner – hair flicks, coy giggles and intermittent arm-touching. Poor Bernard, she thought, what has he got himself into?

Jim made his excuses after a short while and jumped up on the small stage to join the rest of his band mates. 'Well?' Jayne said to Abi as soon as Jim was out of earshot.

'Well what? He's an old friend.'

'Not him, I can see what he was,' Jayne rolled her eyes, 'What did Rachel say?'

'You've got it all wrong.'

'See!' Jayne shrieked, 'I knew this would happen. You'd speak to her, buy into whatever rubbish she'd tell you and then convince me to go back. Well the evidence is pretty compelling.'

'It's actually really not. Call her. Call her now and listen to what she has to say. And then, for God's sake call Will and sort this out, because they're both going out of their minds and you all need to talk.'

'No.'

'Jayne, you're being stubborn.'

'Me?' Jayne yelled, before seeing all the other helpers in the hall turn to look. 'Me?' She had lowered her voice to an irate whisper, 'I'm now the bad guy? I'm not the one with my tongue in Barbie's ear. How did I become the bad guy? I actually did call him this morning before I knew about his bed-hopping and his phone was turned off, so obviously he has no interest in talking to me. I don't want to talk about this any more. Are you going to help me with these lights or what?'

'I'll help you only if you promise to call them tomorrow. It's fine that you don't want to do it today with everyone around, but tomorrow, when it's all calmed down, you'll call them?'

'Fine.' Tomorrow was far enough away for her to put it out of her mind. Except that she couldn't.

Even though she'd never been to Ireland with Will, even though he'd never met any of the people in this town, everywhere she looked there was something that reminded her of him. God, even seeing Abi's dad polish his shoes before they left for the party reminded her of the little canvas bag of polish, duster and brush Will had tucked away inside his wardrobe that came out before a big TV appearance. The only time she'd seen the shoeshine kit before he became famous was on the morning they were going down to Torbay to meet Granny for the first time. She remembered being really touched that he thought the occasion special enough to warrant exchanging his trusty Converse for proper shoes, and to even polish them beforehand. But then he was thoughtful like that. Before he went to a nightclub to celebrate his supposed new-found singledom. That wasn't very thoughtful.

The little village hall was crammed with well-wishers. Kids in their party clothes ducked squealing between legs, sliding across the dance floor on the seats of their newly pressed Sunday best. Family and friends holding paper plates brimming with titbits from the buffet table that ran the length of the room were noisily catching up. The laughter and chatter were almost as loud as the chirpy jazz tunes coming from Jim and his buddies on the stage.

Seeing her glance over, Jim tipped his brown felt trilby at her and winked. Why couldn't she be more like that? Topping up what he lacked in aesthetic appeal with self-confidence? If she were more like Jim she'd never have found herself in this mess. Who were her bullies, anyway? They were bored, lonely women huddled in front of a computer with nothing or nobody to occupy them. Screw them. Screw them all.

Now that she didn't have a task to occupy her with apart from 'having a good time' a blanket of pure misery had descended over her. She stood with her back to the wall looking out at everyone else having fun. Abi was being twirled around by one of her brothers, doubling over guffawing as they got their arms entwined together. What she lacked in rhythm she made up for in enthusiasm. It reminded her of the tango lesson she and Will had taken, not realising at the time of enrolment how austere and serious tango was. They'd heard that it was the dance of sex and passion, so thought they'd give it a go, but their teacher had yelled at them to stop smiling as it was ruining the dance, which made them giggle even more. They'd ended up cutting the lesson short and finding a hot and sweaty Latin club in the basement of an Argentinian restaurant, where they could laugh and thrust their limbs together as much as they wanted.

Jayne tried to make herself look as inconspicuous as possible, dreading the moment when Mrs Sheeran would coerce one of her sons or many nephews to ask her to dance. The moment was coming, she just knew it. Jayne cemented a small smile on her face and started tapping her toe along with the music, to try at least to give the impression she was enjoying herself.

As the song ended, Abi's father gave a nervous little cough into the microphone. 'Ladies and gents, friends and family, Maureen and I would like to thank everyone for coming today to celebrate with us as we reach the milestone of forty years of marriage. Someone said to me tonight that serial killers get less time than that, which I thought was nice.' The room laughed with him. Jayne didn't think she'd ever heard Abi's dad say so much in one go before, but then with a house filled with seven children, all just as talkative as Abi, and a wife who had the right words on tap for every occasion, why would he need to add to the noise?

'Some of you here tonight were there the very night Maureen and I met. We were at an open-air concert in the city. She came right up to me and my friends,' he nodded to a couple of old men near the front, 'and she said to me, I'm waiting for my friends, can I sit with you until they come? We said sure, and she sat down, drank our beer, ate our food and then said, 'I'll be back in a minute'. Well, I watched this little slip of a girl weave her way through the crowd, a few thousand people were there that day, and I watched her walk right up to the front of the audience, and start walking up the stairs to the stage, just as the man on the microphone introduced the next act. I couldn't believe it. What is she doing, I wondered? Then, to my surprise and delight, she took the microphone from him, the band started, and she began to sing. Well I have never heard anything like the birdsong that came from her mouth. With every note I fell more in love with her and she searched my eyes out in the crowd until they locked with hers and sang the rest of the song to me.'

He paused in the story to wipe a small tear from his cheek as Mrs Sheeran slipped her arm around his waist, 'and we've been inseparable since that day. We married six months later and, after seven children, we're as happy now as we were on that day in the park.' The room erupted into spontaneous applause and whistles, which grew even wilder as Mrs Sheeran took the microphone from her husband, gently kissed his forehead and started singing Billie Holiday's *It Had to Be You*.

Her smooth voice cracked with emotion as she faced the man she'd woken up to every morning for forty years, the man she had eaten dinner with every night, given birth to seven of his children with, while he held her hand and cheered her on. The man she'd given up her dreams for, knowing that the life they would have together would mean more than a fleeting moment of success. They held hands as she lovingly sang the words that Jayne found so touching, so raw and powerful she couldn't do anything but sob, and for the first time, she wasn't even thinking about who was looking.

'I've wondered around, finally found
somebody who
Could make me be true
Could make me be blue
And, even be glad just to be sad thinking of you,'

I need to call him, I need to speak to him and tell him that he screwed up, but it's okay, we're going to be okay, Jayne thought as she blindly pushed her way through the crowd to the door at the back of the hall. I need to hear his voice and he needs to hear mine.

The car park was bathed in a half-light, the summer's evening was closing in and the only sound outside was the intoxicating melody emanating from the hall. She half-ran, half-walked along the lane back towards the housing estate. A fierce determination had set in, surpassing the sense of self-pity that had dominated for most of the day. She just needed to get to her phone, which she'd wilfully slammed in a drawer seconds before leaving for the party – an act of defiance that no one but her knew about, but had made her feel good at the time.

With trembling hands she opened the drawer and her heart gave a jolt as she saw the volume of missed calls from Will and Rachel. For a horrible moment, as she had taken the stairs two at a time, she considered how deflated she would be if a blank screen had greeted her. Which one should she call first? Will, it had to be Will. Rachel would understand why. This time he picked up on the second ring. 'Where the hell have you been?' he shouted. As a greeting, it was unexpected. Jayne was prepared for crawling remorse, not anger.

'Where have *I* been?' This wasn't the conversation-opener she'd been hearing in her head all evening. It flipped a switch and whatever graciousness she was planning to impart immediately vanished. 'Where have *you* been, more like! Oh no, don't tell me, sticking your tongue in Kyra's ear, that's where!'

'Grow up, Jayne. Abi's told you what really happened, you can't seriously still be pissed off about it now?'

'Abi hasn't told me, actually,' Jayne replied, affecting an air of superiority, desperately grappling for the upper hand in the conversation. 'I told her that I didn't want to hear your excuses for what is actually pretty obvious.'

'Yes, yes, you're right, Jayne, of course, you know best. I mean, why could you possibly want to know the truth when the story you've concocted in your head is so much juicier? Why am I always the bad guy in these scenarios that are actually pretty innocent?'

'I fail to see how nuzzling my sister's best friend is inno-cent, but there we go, maybe we have different interpretations of the word innocent.'

'Can you just get down from your high horse for one minute and listen to me? Or call Rachel and get her to explain what was really going on.'

'Rachel? You mean my sister, who thought you getting off with Kyra was funny? You mean *that* sister?'

'You have this so wrong, Jayne, so wrong. But then, that's fairly typical of you at the moment, isn't it? Just making up stories about people and believing your own version of events instead of seeing things that are right in front of your face.'

'Billy, I–'

'I'm not Billy! Jesus, Jayne, I haven't been Billy for nearly twenty years. I'm Will. Will Scarlet. If it's Billy you want to be with, then you're going to be pretty lonely because he doesn't exist.'

'He does! He's just been taken over by this megalomaniac, who's starting to believe his own hype. And as soon as Billy realises this he'll be back.'

'Is that what you think? That I'm a megalomaniac? You seriously believe that it's me who's changed? I'm not the one who's turned into a neurotic agoraphobic who refuses to leave the house! Who spends every minute, when she thinks I'm not looking, trawling through the internet looking for reasons to be even unhappier! Where's the fun, carefree woman I fell in love with?'

'You want to know where that Jayne has gone? Do you?'

'Yes, yes, I do.'

'You killed her, Will.' There. She said it. And then there was silence as the phone went dead.

Chapter 24

She had sat doubled over on the side of the bed with her head in her hands for almost ten minutes. How had that conversation even happened? He was meant to be remorseful and repentant, apologising for causing the misunderstanding – she was supposed to be empathetic and forgiving. Instead they'd had the worst argument they'd ever had, flinging words at each other like weapons that could never be recalled. She didn't even recognise this couple that they'd become, who Billy had become. Well, screw him. Screw him and Kyra and Rachel, and all of them. Jayne stalked over to the petite pine mirror on Abi's dressing table that had small pictures of Ronan Keating cut out from magazines tacked all over its frame and calmly picked up a bright-coral lipstick and ran it over her lips. Screw them all.

**

'There you are!' A flushed Abi threw herself at Jayne as she walked back into the hall. The party had been turned up a few notches since she had left and the dance floor was crammed with sweaty bodies pulling and pushing each other, twirling and jumping and clinging onto each other. 'Come and dance!'

'I need a very large drink first. Or lots of very small ones.'

'You, lady, are talking my language!' Abi grabbed her arm and wove through the crowd to the two trestle tables disguised as a makeshift bar that Abi's underage cousins were taking it in turns to man. 'Six jaeger bombs, my good man. We're on a mission, and it's not going to be pretty.'

**

This wasn't Abi's bedroom. Jayne's eyes widened as they darted around the room, her body lying deathly still. Where curtains should be was a large blue-striped bedspread tacked up to the window with a sentry line of tarnished drawing pins. Her nose wrinkled; tobacco mixed with booze combined with sweat and dirty laundry baskets. Her head pounded, and yet she had to try to move it, she had to confirm her worst thoughts. Straining her eyes as far left as they could go without moving her neck too much she could see unkempt grey hair spilling over the pillow next to her.

Moving her hands millimetres at a time under the covers, desperately trying not to make ripples in the duvet, or any sudden movement, she ran her hands slowly down her body. The relief she felt at touching the fabric of her clothes was overwhelming. She couldn't believe she had got herself into such a state that she wouldn't have been surprised to find herself naked in a strange man's bed. Now how could she leave without waking him? Or sneak back into Abi's house with no one seeing? Ever so gradually, she started moving one leg towards the edge of the mattress, sliding it over the bobbly lint-ridden sheet until it was outside the cover. Gently lowering it to the ground, she began softly sliding the rest of her body out too. Jim shifted in his sleep, gave a loud fart and drifted off to sleep again.

She had no idea what time it was, but guessed by the number of cars on the road and the fact that the shops were already open that it was around nine or ten, which would make sneaking back in to the Sheerans unnoticed impossible. She could pretend that she had got up early to go for a jog? In her best friend's brother's girlfriend's sequined party dress. Or, she could have got up early to surprise the family by buying them breakfast and she had merely flung on the nearest clothes in which to do it? Yes, that will have to do, she thought, as she hurried into the bakery and bought all the pastries they'd baked that morning.

Ignoring the front door, which was never used, Jayne went round to the kitchen door. It had a mat outside it with the words *Back-door guests are best* printed on it. She'd found this so hilariously smutty on her first visit to Ireland a decade ago it had stuck in her mind ever since and she'd regaled a delighted Will with the recollection a few years later. They'd scoured online stores and every bric-a-brac shop they'd ever passed for one for themselves, but never could find a replica. The fleeting thought of Will jarred in her chest and she had to steady herself before turning the handle.

As the warm air of the house rushed to greet her she gasped. Sitting at the kitchen table with Mrs Sheeran and Abi was Rachel. But this wasn't the Rachel she'd left behind, this Rachel was barefaced, devoid of the war paint she'd perfected over the last twenty years. Her hair was scraped back from her face and as she looked up at the opening door, Jayne could see dark circles under her bloodshot eyes. Her sister leapt up and flew at her. For a second Jayne thought she was going to slap her, but instead she flung her arms around her and buried her head in Jayne's neck. 'Oh my God, Jayne, I've been so worried. Where the hell have you been?'

'Rach? What are you doing here? When did you get here? Why are you here?'

'We'll give you girls a bit of space to talk. Abigail, my dear, come on through and leave them to it. There's tea in the pot.' Mrs Sheeran flapped Abi out of the kitchen with both hands and discreetly closed the door behind them.

The sisters stood facing each other, both leaning against

opposite kitchen counters. Jayne stared down at the floor, concentrating on a half-filled dog bowl that sat on the worn-out lino. 'What's happening to you, J?' Rachel finally said, her voice a mixture of disbelief and compassion. 'This isn't you.'

'It's not what you think,' Jayne sullenly ran her toe along the line where two halves of lino met.

'We all seem to be saying that a lot to each other lately.'

'This is different. It actually isn't what it looks like.'

'Just like the picture in the paper of Will and Kyra.'

Hearing Kyra's name linked to Will's with just an 'and' in the middle of it made Jayne involuntarily shudder. 'It's nothing like *that*,' she spat defiantly, raising her eyes to stare at her sister.

'What exactly do you think happened that night?'

Jayne shrugged her shoulders and pursed her lips. 'It's there in print.'

'And we both know how reliable that can be.'

'So you're telling me that he wasn't nuzzling her neck? That I'm mistaken – he just lost his footing and fell into her hair? That you were standing there laughing about it because someone had told a joke that you found funny? Is that what was happening? Oh, silly me, do I feel stupid?'

'Sarcasm is an ugly defense mechanism, Jayne, it doesn't suit you. Will is in bits about this, you know.'

'Yeah, he sounded really cut up about it on the phone last night,' Jayne sarcastically retorted.

'That's why I'm here. He came off the phone in tears. I've never seen him like that. And now you're off shagging about with God knows who. Will's going to be devastated.'

Jayne's voice went up an octave as she blurted out, 'You can't tell him! I mean, nothing happened, but he can't know about this!'

'Why wouldn't I tell him, Jayne? You've been a right bitch to him for months! Are you jealous? Is that it? Do you look at him making a success of himself and you can't handle it?'

Jayne gasped, 'Do you really think that? That I begrudge him this success? It's not that at all, it's not about me, it's him, and all the craziness that now surrounds him. Do you have any idea what it's like to have everyone you meet wonder what on earth your boyfriend sees in you? To have every outfit you wear scrutinised and laughed about by strangers? To feel like you should be grateful that he picked you?'

She knew that she was being hysterical now, but couldn't stop herself. Rachel was quiet, letting her sister getting worked up, knowing that her frenzy would reach a crescendo before it started ebbing away, and she just leant back and let it happen.

'Do you know what? I thought we could get over this, that somehow he would say, you know what, Jayne, I love you more than I love fame, and I'm going to give it all up for you, and then we'd go back to being the way we were. I actually thought that could happen, and then I saw the picture in the paper and I realised that it's impossible to go back, it's gone too far. If he can do that with *her* just hours after I leave, and then not even be sorry about it, then he's not the man I love.'

Very calmly, and with a composure Jayne was lacking at that moment, Rachel walked across the small kitchen until she was standing shoulder to shoulder with her twin, both of them facing the breakfast table, which was still littered with cereal boxes and bowls with milk pooling in the bottom of them. 'You know the calendar that's on the wall in our kitchen?'

'What?' Jayne said, not understanding the turn the conversation had taken.

'Our calendar. The 26th July had been circled for a few months, with the word *Anniversary Party* on it. Do you remember seeing that? Or me asking you a while back to keep the date free?'

It was vaguely ringing bells for Jayne, 'Um, sort of. Why?'

'Kyra had hired out a bar in Chiswick to celebrate her one-year anniversary and she wanted you and Will to come. You stormed out the morning of that party. Will wasn't going to go, actually. He was sitting staring into space for hours after you left and I made him get washed, dressed and literally booted him out of the door to come to the party with me, because he knew it meant a lot to me.'

'Why would you care if he went to Kyra's party? And I

didn't even know she was seeing anyone. Who's her partner, anyway?'

Quietly Rachel replied, 'I am.'

'You're a lesbian?' Jayne cried, swivelling around to face her sister, 'When did that happen?'

'About thirty-two years ago, in theory, but only a year in practice.'

'But how can you be a lesbian?!' Jayne was incredulous, how could she not have known this? She knew that her sister was a lot more private than she was, but hiding her sexuality from her own twin for their whole lives was not possible. 'You love men!'

'I tried to love men, which sounds like a massive cliché, but I tried to convince myself that it was just because I hadn't met the right man, but it wasn't, and I've been with enough men to know that.'

'But a *year*? You and Kyra have been together for a *year*?'

'I was going to tell you after a few months, when I realised that she was pretty special to me, but then the longer it went on I couldn't find the words to tell you, and then everything started kicking off with Will and then you got yourself all worked up and became so insular, and I didn't feel like I could talk to you about what was going on with me when you had so much going on in your own life.'

'You and *Kyra*?'

'Me and Kyra.'

'*Together?*'

'Yep.'

Jayne opened her arms and Rachel nestled into them, squeezed tight against her sister's body. They stayed like that for some time, each taking in the enormity of what this meant. The implied, but unsaid, accusation that Jayne had been too self-absorbed to see what was under her nose the whole time was crushing to her. They were all each other had, and for Rachel to feel that she couldn't confide in her the single-most important detail of her life was too much for Jayne's already fragile state and she allowed fresh tears to cascade down her cheeks.

'I'm so sorry, Rach, so sorry.'

'So in that picture, Will wasn't nuzzling, he was actually just saying goodbye as he wanted to go home in case you came back. And as for me laughing, yes, I probably was – because, for the first time in my life, I felt free and light, and unfettered, and able to just be me.' Rachel wiped a tear away from her sister's cheek, 'You've always been the more outgoing one, the cleverer one, the one who makes people laugh by doing something daft, and I've always just tagged along behind. You think I'm so strong and capable, but it's all a façade, Jayne, I'm only like that because I know that you need me to be.'

'What a frickin' mess I've made of everything.'

'No arguments here.'

They shared a rueful smile. 'How can I make it all better?'

'Well, you can start by having a shower and getting

changed, the mermaid-sequin look is a little too glam for eleven o' clock in the morning.'

'Wow, the old Rachel would never have said no to sequins before lunch. Now you're a lesbian are you going to be all Doc Martins and dungarees?'

Rachel gave her a playful shove. 'Well, if I am, I know whose wardrobe to raid.'

'Touché.'

'And while you're in the shower, I'm going to book us both on a flight home. The sooner you and Will talk to each other the better. You were both put on this planet to be with each other, there's no question about that, and this is a tiny blip in an otherwise very nearly perfect life together.'

'Very nearly perfect. I like that.'

'Now go! You stink. You're never going to win back the man of your dreams smelling like a boozed-up harlot.'

'Sir, yes sir.'

Chapter 25

The cabin crew had just finished their half-hearted attempt at informing a planeful of disinterested passengers about the brace position when Jayne's mind started to wander.

Rachel's head rested on her shoulder; the early start and belated soul-cleansing had obviously exhausted her into a peaceful slumber. Her words 'when you had so much going on in your own life' kept floating to the forefront of Jayne's thoughts, jabbing at her conscience. While she had been so wrapped up in the changes in her own life, she'd completely ignored everyone else. If anything, Will used to accuse her of being too attentive to others, too involved in people's lives, telling her to butt out and mind her own on quite a few occasions, and look at her now. To know that Rachel had been going through such a huge turmoil of emotions while she'd been prattling on about uneaten dough balls was horrifying.

And Abi and Bernard. *Bernard.* She'd toasted so many

new relationships with Abi over the years with a lukewarm glass of cheap white and a handful of pub cashews, but when it really mattered, when she'd met someone who actually made her glow from the inside, Jayne was too absorbed in her own drama to even notice.

She ran through, for the hundredth time, the speech that she wanted to say to Will, about her decision to support him in whatever he wanted to do, and how she was going to grow a skin so thick a hundred voodoo dolls couldn't do her any damage. How she was going to take a step forward and be with him every step of the way on this new adventure. Whatever he wanted to do, she was going to be right there next to him, holding his hand, because she knew that if the situation was reversed, he'd be her loudest cheerleader. She just hoped it wasn't too late.

Their flat was so still Jayne had a sudden horrifying thought that he'd packed up and left already. There was no hum from the radio or low buzz of the TV that usually signalled Will's presence in the apartment. Passing a square little watercolour on the stairs Jayne allowed herself a sigh of relief. Will would never leave behind the last canvas that his mum had ever painted.

She then had a horrible premonition of walking in and finding him in bed with someone else. After all, she'd found herself in a similar, albeit completely innocent, position that very morning – a fact that Rachel and Abi had thankfully agreed that no one else ever needed to know about. She'd made Abi swear on Ronan Keating's life that Jim wasn't going to try and supplement his paltry teaching and guitar-playing income by going to the papers about his night of no-passion, but Abi was adamant that an ageing lothario he might be, but he was as decent as they come. She'd followed that up with, 'like Will.'

Hearing the front door rub against the fraying piece of carpet held down by layers of masking tape that he'd been meaning to fix for years, Will peered over the bannister. 'Hey.'

'Hey.' As reunions go, this one was slightly more sombre than she was expecting, but then she could hardly blame him. In the last twenty-four hours she'd accused him of being a megalomaniac adulterer; maybe it was going to be slightly harder to get him to overlook that than she'd thought.

Putting her bag down on the floor beside her, they both stood on the landing. Jayne noticed how bloodshot his eyes were, and the beginnings of dark circles blemished his usually flawless skin. His hands were in the pockets of his tracksuit bottoms, which Jayne had only ever seen him wear when he had flu. 'I'm sorry,' Jayne said simply.

'Me too.'

'I said some horrible things.'

'Yes, you did.'

'I didn't mean them.'

'Yes, you did.'

'Okay, well, maybe I meant them at the time, but I was being irrational, and I see that now.'

'So now you're being entirely rational?'

'Yes.'

'So if we were to talk about all this, and I mean properly talk about all of this, you wouldn't go crazy again and storm out, or accuse me of kissing someone else, or paint me as any kind of villain?'

'No, I wouldn't.' In response to his arched eyebrow she added, 'I promise.'

He described the attention as intoxicating, which she thought was a good word for it, covering as it did all the emotions from euphoria to overwhelming paranoia. Up until the picture with Kyra, the press and public loved him. He'd felt that he was infallible, universally adored, which he didn't think would have affected him so much, but he couldn't help but like his newfound celebrity persona, and she couldn't blame him, either.

Part of the reason she'd toyed with the idea of acting way back when was to pretend to be a person that people admired, or fleetingly thought had talent. But like a trip switch that suddenly plunges everything into darkness, that one blurry shot in a backstreet bar in Chiswick catapulted him from England's darling to a two-timing slut in the space of an hour. That's all it took for the nation's opinion of him to nosedive and he suddenly had a glimpse of what she'd been dealing with for the last few months.

He'd tried so hard to ignore the hateful comments tagged onto the end of all the articles, each of them variations of, 'the next picture we see of Will Scarlet he'll be snorting coke off a hooker's belly, watch this space'. Even the mildest ones offended him deeply, insinuating that he was nothing more than a heartless playboy and that he was clearly the reason for his fiancée having a nervous breakdown.

Rachel had told him before she'd left for the airport that she'd be fine about him telling the media the truth, to explain that Kyra was monumentally not interested in him and she was the reason why, but he refused to bring their private relationship into a public forum just to save his skin, which made Jayne love him even more.

'The thing is,' he admitted, 'I just love cooking, and you know what? I really do enjoy all the TV-presenting, inspiring people to cook more, teaching people how easy it actually is to mix a few ingredients together and come up with something so much cheaper and more delicious than you'd get from a packet from the freezer. But it's just such a shame that so much crap comes with being on TV.'

'But it doesn't have to, does it?' She innocently asked. 'Call me naïve, but isn't it possible to walk a middle road somewhere: one where you're not going to the opening of a new nail bar just to get your name out there, and instead just concentrating on food-related stuff? Once the press realise that actually you're pretty boring, really, they won't hound you, or us, so much.'

'So I'm pretty boring am I? I thought we weren't name-calling?'

'You know what I mean! Michaela's agenda of fast-tracking you to super-stardom meant that you went into overdrive, making sure that you were everywhere a camera might be, and fair play to her, she really knew what she was doing, but somewhere along the way she, and you a bit, forgot that actually underneath the hair dye and clear mascara—'

Will opened his mouth to object, and then decided, actually, it was a fair comment.

'—underneath all that gumph, you're a chef. A really passionate chef. So there's no reason at all why you shouldn't still do the TV. In fact, why not talk to the network about launching a programme that you really want to do, but for the love of all that's holy we need to stop the public's fascination with you, with us, because a woman needs to eat dough balls.'

Will raised one eyebrow, 'I'm not even going to try and decipher that last comment. But everything you said before makes a lot of sense. Who was I kidding? Poster-boy for Diesel? Cover of *Esquire*?'

'You don't need to pretend to me that it wasn't fun, Will, it's okay to say, 'you know what, Jayne, I had a blast'.' She shrugged, 'And you know what? it wasn't all miserable for me, either. I stood next to Hollywood royalty, for Christ's sake, even if no picture exists to prove it. So don't beat yourself up over any of it, but it was starting to get out of hand, and I think if we're going to come out the other side of this we just need to reassess what makes us happy.'

They were sitting next to each other on their bar stools, choosing the less-confrontational side-by-side seating arrangement over sitting opposite each other and staring into each other's eyes. Will slowly leaned and gently shoulder-barged Jayne. 'You make me happy,' he said finally. 'Well, you did, before you started going loop-the-loop.'

'And when you didn't enjoy having the excess of your cuticles trimmed, you made me happy too.' She barged him back.

His voice became more serious as he quietly asked, 'What do you want to do about the wedding?'

'What do *you* want to do about it?

'I asked you first.'

'I asked you second.'

'I made a banana cake earlier, why don't we have a coffee and figure out what we're going to do.' He jumped off his bar stool, giving her head an affectionate ruffle as he passed. She watched him take the small Tupperware of ground coffee beans out of the fridge and set it alongside two matching mugs with comedy moustaches on them that they'd once bought each other as 'just because' presents, and right then she knew it was all going to be okay.

Chapter 26

Twelve months later

Sitting still and contemplating life was not something Jayne had ever really felt comfortable doing. She wished she were one of those women who started each day with a fifteen-minute meditation that centred them and realigned their chakras, or whatever it was that sitting cross-legged and 'omming' was meant to do, but she wasn't. The second her eyes closed she either fell fast asleep or the mother of all to-do lists floated stubbornly to the forefront of her brain, rendering any kind of relaxation impossible. Surrendering your consciousness to the universe was hopeless when there were smear tests to book and overdue dry cleaning to pick up. She couldn't even visit the bathroom without a book, magazine, or the back of a bleach bottle to read, which showed just how much she despised having time to think. But this morning, being alone felt completely the right thing to do.

They'd hired out a local taverna the night before, in a small cobbled piazza away from the main thoroughfare, and big glass jugs of the local red kept being thumped down on the table with alarming regularity by the jovial owner. So when Jayne woke early, completely devoid of any lingering reminder of the amount she'd drank, it was a welcome, if a bit surprising, start to the day. Abi was still fast asleep next to her, and as tradition dictated, the men had spent the night elsewhere in the vast, ancient villa. Jayne felt an overwhelming need to get out and inhale the Italian air, and just sit still for a while, doing nothing and thinking of even less. It was going to be a crazy day and she reckoned she had about an hour until the house started creaking awake from its slumber.

They had been allocated the vast attic suite that she supposed was once where a few housemaids laid their heads after a busy day serving the Italian elite. But in the last fifty years or so, their narrow single beds and chamber pots had been replaced with a sumptuous sleigh bed that Abi was currently spread-eagled on.

Will had found this villa on a website and knew instantly that it would be perfect. It was remote enough to feel private, yet only twenty minutes away from the picture-postcard town of Maratea with its forty-four churches. Ever since they'd got the booking confirmation through they'd spent their evenings devouring every guide book going, while working their way through the case of twelve bottles of Basilicata wine Will had ordered from a posh wine merchant to get them in the spirit.

Tiptoeing along the old knotted floorboards that were punctured with shafts of light from the old kitchen below, Jayne held her breath for fear of waking anyone else up. Floorboards gave way to flagstones on the ground floor – big square slabs, no doubt sourced from a local quarry when the house was being built a couple of centuries before. They felt refreshingly cold to her feet as she was still carrying her sandals in a bid to cloak her temporary escape in silence.

The air was beautifully fresh; although it was September, no one had told Italy that this should signal a move into autumn, and the sun still resolutely bathed the rural hillsides in a strong white light during the middle part of the day. But now, just a couple of hours after sunrise, and later when they would all gather on one of the villa's cliff-top terraces a couple of hours before sunset, it was perfect.

The steps down to the villa's private stony beach were man-made in the sense that hundreds of years of people walking the same route had created ideal shoe-sized rivets in the craggy hillside, which Jayne navigated with unchar-acteristic dexterity.

She felt alive and free, and so unbelievably happy. To think that it was just over a year ago that she and Will had almost called time on their relationship over things that now seemed completely trivial. How she'd let an ignorant sixteen-year-old and the comments section on websites dictate the path her life should take was now shocking to her. The direction of her anger had swerved about like an out-of-control sniper, first aiming at Will for getting them into the situation, then at Crystal for escalating it, a quick veer to the hate-filled strangers for making her feel inadequate and ugly, and then finally, the red dot had focused on her own forehead for allowing herself to feel that way.

It had taken months to actually mean it when she shrugged her shoulders, or to be able to put real weight behind the words 'screw them', but in time she'd nailed it. And she knew that she'd had to. For all of Will's procrastinations, she recognised that he enjoyed having a toe in the spotlight, and as much as he'd made all the right noises and offered to give it all up for a life as a humble deli-owner, she knew she could never have asked him to do that. So when he'd been approached to present a new TV series tucked away on BBC2 on Sunday afternoons, he'd jumped at it. A niche, but loyal, audience of passionate amateur cooks had replaced the ardent attention that Will's foray into ad campaigns and primetime TV had commanded, so thankfully the balance had shifted. That's not to say that they'd dropped off the radar completely, but the media are a fickle lot; when you're only ever photographed going in and out of your own home or the local Sainsbury's it's amazing how quickly the photographers stop loitering around you.

The deli business was going from strength to strength

too, he now had four shops all over south-west London, and when the bicycle shop next to the original Richmond deli closed down, they'd bought that too. With the rhythmic noise of sledgehammers swinging through the dividing wall in the background, Will had told her that it made financial sense to enlarge the deli and put more café tables into it. She was totally unprepared to come back from visiting Helen in Devon a couple of weeks later to find this new area painted a deep-claret red, with floor-to-ceiling bookshelves and wine racks adorning each wall. Double-height ladders were fixed to rails that slid gracefully along them, while battered leather armchairs and mismatching wooden tables were dotted around.

'It's a wine-bar library!' she'd gasped, as Will wrapped her in a bear hug from behind and whispered 'Surprise'. They'd called it Pinter & Pinot and it had consumed Jayne's life, in a good way.

The weeks and months after the Michelle incident at school made Jayne reassess what made her happy, and she had decided to take a couple of years out from teaching. She missed it terribly, so had thrown herself into organising open mic poetry nights, book clubs and informal wine-tastings, where the words 'nose' and 'bouquet' were strictly taboo.

She'd also finally done what Rachel had urged her to do on the day they had both bought a one-way ticket to London Paddington eighteen years ago, and that was to forget about

Crystal. Accepting that she was merely the vehicle for her and Rachel to enter the world, and nothing else, was an emotional journey, but once she'd made it, it was like an albatross being prised off her back. It had been eight months since any kind of contact had been made between them – even Helen had distanced herself from her daughter's dramatics, telling Jayne that Stanley had moved out and that she'd managed to find him a place at Pine Grove. Her exact words were, 'Poor Prue's passing had a silver lining, but probably not for Prue.'

Firing Michaela was the last step of many in reclaiming their lives back. She didn't go quietly, either. Rachel was convinced her rage had less to do with losing a cash-cow of a client and more to do with the fact that she'd been harbouring thoughts of a carnal kind towards her protégé for months. She'd sent Will flowers every day for a fortnight in an attempt to change his mind, which Jayne had thought was a bit weird; he's a bloke, send him alcohol and season tickets to the Emirates Stadium. For such a clever woman, she wasn't very bright. Will's new agent seemed so much more understanding and quiet. The fact that he was a balding man in his fifties was neither here or there, Jayne thought dryly as she finally reached the tiny cove.

Tucking her long sundress into her knicker elastic, she gingerly edged her toes into the clear water that lapped at the tiny pebbles on the shoreline. Small silver fish darted playfully around her feet as she stood still, indulging their inquisitiveness as the sun's rays started gathering strength on her face. Closing her eyes, she lifted her chin and deeply inhaled the warm, salty air. If there is a heaven, she thought, this is what it would be like.

Despite the villa being a good kilometre up the hill, Jayne could sense that it was starting to stir. One of the early risers, not Rachel, she acknowledged glibly, but maybe Bernard, would have filled the juicers with plump oranges and put the kettles on to boil. The network of historic pipes would be clanking into action as showers were turned on in different rooms, and the heavy blue shutters would be creaking open as each part of the house started to wake up. Gathering up her shoes, she started her ascent back up the hill, her mind clear of everything except a pure blissful anticipation of what lay ahead.

She had been adamant that the chief bridesmaid should wear white as well; a beautiful flowing gown with layers upon layers of silky chiffon that clung to all the right places and skimmed all the wrong ones. Looking in the mirror at them both, Jayne's eyes started to well up. 'You look amazing.'

Abi twirled around, the sunlight catching on the delicate diamante tiara that held her veil in place. 'Do you think so? Do you think Bernie will like it?'

'He will love it. He's a lucky, lucky man.'

Abi narrowed her eyes, ' and how are you doing? With

all of *this*?' she pointed to the open window that overlooked the tree-lined terrace where the ceremony was being set up, 'I know it's the type of wedding you'd want.'

Jayne shrugged and smiled, 'Look, Hon, I'm not going to lie, this is anyone's dream wedding, but you know, a characterless ballroom near a tube station with over two-thirds of it filled with total strangers is every girl's dream too, eh?'

On every other point Will had compromised, or given in completely, but having a big fancy wedding with a guest list to match was one area that he was not budging on. Even the night before they left for Italy, while they were both padding back and forth between their chest of drawers and the opened suitcase on the bed, slowly filling it with piles of clothes, he'd reeled off another ten names of make-up artists or boom operators that he wanted to add to the ever-growing list. The old Jayne would have stamped and whined a bit, but she'd come to the conclusion that as long as by the end of the day she was Mrs Scarlet, it didn't actually matter too much how she got there. Except now, looking down on the terrace and seeing ten or fifteen of their closest friends standing around laughing, drinking aperitifs surrounded by the lengthening shadows of the cypress trees, she realised it actually did matter. It mattered a lot.

'Anyway, never mind about me,' Jayne fluffed out the back of Abi's dress, straightening the small train, 'I had a nice chat with your mum and dad before. She's definitely come round, they're having a whale of a time.'

Abi rolled her eyes, 'Sheesh, you would have thought they'd be happy not to foot the bill for a grand Irish wedding, but it was never what me and Bernie wanted, getting wed in front of second cousins twice removed and your great-aunt's neighbour. I just want to look out and see the people that I love there, not a bunch of strangers. Oh shit, sorry.'

They were still laughing at her unintentional faux pas when Abi's dad gently knocked on the door, which was Jayne's cue to leave them to it. She felt another pang of bittersweet envy as she realised that an emotional father-daughter moment was yet another wedding-day scenario that she would never get to experience.

Standing under the pagoda, the soft breeze wrapping itself around the gently billowing white drapes, Will looked more handsome than she'd ever seen him. He and Bernard were in matching linen suits, with open-necked white shirts under the jacket, where small white flowers lit up their lapels. A jazz trio were playing *It Had to Be You* as Jayne walked slowly towards him up the makeshift aisle between the two rows of chairs. This moment would be perfect, Jayne thought, if only she wasn't being closely followed by the bride.

When they reached the registrar, Abi reached back to give her the single-stem calla lilly that she'd chosen in lieu of a traditional bouquet and as she took it her eyes locked with Will's. He gave her a wink and she felt herself blush. How was he still able to make her feel like that after all these years?

As Abi and Bernard spoke their vows, Jayne glanced over at Mrs Sheeran, who had one hand clasping a tissue and the other entwined with her husband's. Next to them were two of Abi's brothers, who were the only siblings to make the journey; the others were placated by the promise of a big party back in Ireland in a few weeks' time. Rachel and Kyra sat behind them, sun-soaked and obviously totally in love. They had recently moved out of the flat and into their own little terraced house in Barnes, which was achingly chic with its reclaimed this and restored that mingling with designer Danish furniture from the fifties. Jayne admitted that she had been so wrong about Kyra, blinded by a combination of her own insecurities and Kyra's caramel highlights.

Jayne's focus shifted back to what the registrar was saying about love wrapping an invisible, but unbreakable, loop around Abi and Bernard, a loop that no one could see but everyone could feel. The loop could extend out, giving each a bit more space when they needed it, or it could tighten, bringing them back close, where they could feel the warmth of the other, their breath, their heartbeat.

Over Bernard's shoulder she could see Will wipe a little tear away from his eye before putting his shoulders back and trying to stand a little taller. No one else was managing to be so controlled with their emotions, sniffling into their tissues while whispering to each other what a passionate lot the Italians were. This is what she wanted, Jayne thought – not to repeat her vows into a microphone so that the people in row thirty-two could hear her. She knew that cancelling the hotel now would lose them the hefty deposit, not to mention the potential friendships of some strangers she hadn't met yet, but she didn't care. She wanted this.

Silver trays of delicate crystal flutes of champagne had appeared as soon as Bernard and Abi had sealed their union with a rather over-enthusiastic lip-locking. Jayne hadn't realised that Bernard had it in him, but seeing him dip her best friend back and passionately assert his right to kiss his wife changed her mind. Maybe he was the perfect match for Abi after all.

Will sidled up and planted his lips on Jayne's bare shoulder, 'You look sensational.'

'You look rather handsome yourself.'

'No, seriously, you look amazing Jayne, really beautiful.'

'They say you shouldn't wear white to another person's wedding, but it was Abi's choice, and I love it, are you sure I looked okay?'

'You look gorgeous.' He gestured to a young waitress carrying a tray to come over and took two glasses from it, handing one to Jayne, 'What did you think of the ceremony?'

'That it was the most beautiful service I'd ever been to. In fact, the whole thing is just beyond perfect.'

She opened her mouth to follow it up with some emotional plea-bargaining, when Will added, 'I thought so too.'

Her eyes widened in disbelief, 'Really?'

'Really. So much so, I think we should get married just like this.'

'Really?' Jayne shrieked.

'Really. Turn around.'

'What?'

'Turn around.'

Coming slowly down the steps of the villa onto the terrace were a frantically waving Dave and Trish. It was the first time Jayne had seen Dave in anything other than jeans and Trish had a feather fascinator fastened to her chin with elastic that was designed to go around the back of your neck. They were followed by a beaming Duncan and a sober Erica. 'What the? What's going on?' Jayne asked, bewildered, 'Why's your *dad* here?'

'They've come for the wedding,' Will smiled.

'But they don't even really know Abi or Bernard – they only met at that Christmas!'

'*Our* wedding.'

Jayne's mouth dropped open as the enormity of what Will had just said hit her. Everyone started walking closer, forming an intimate circle around them.

'Jayne Brady, would you do me the honour of being my wife?' Will's eyes danced, delighted at pulling off the biggest surprise of his life.

'But how? I don't–' She was cut off mid-sentence by Abi removing her veil and gently tucking the comb into Jayne's own curls.

'Your something borrowed,' she explained.

Out of nowhere Rachel appeared beaming and carrying a small bouquet of peonies, Jayne's favourite flower, tied together with a small blue ribbon. She handed them over and kissed her sister's cheek. 'Sorry, we were all in on it.'

Their friends had clustered around them, smiling self-satisfied grins at each other; she was obviously the only one in complete ignorance. 'But how? How did this happen?'

'I did all the paperwork in the UK and then when we arrived here, when you thought I was playing golf, I was meeting the registrar.'

'But what about the big do you wanted? I feel bad you're not going to have that!'

'Don't! Everything I said in the last few months was just a wheeze to put you off the scent of this. I don't even really know what a boom operator is, let alone know one I'd like to witness our nuptials, and if you'll have me as your husband, I'd really like to marry you now, please.' Jayne burst into laughter as Will picked up her hand and kissed it. He took a little ring box out of his inside pocket. 'Your something new.'

'And I'm your something old.' Jayne swivelled round at the sound of a delightfully familiar voice. There standing completely clad in orange with a wide-brimmed straw hat, adorned with fragrant fresh flowers was Helen, her hand resting comfortably in the crook of Stanley's arm. Finally detangling herself from her granddaughter's wild embrace, Helen pushed Jayne towards the pagoda, where the registrar stood smiling at this wonderfully eccentric bunch of English people. 'Now don't leave the poor man waiting, my darling, it's been twenty years already.'

The sun was just disappearing over the hills as the fairy lights strung through the trees came to life. Bernard, Abi and Will, during their secret wedding-planning meetings in the months leading up to this, had decided that they should have one long table for everyone to eat together, in the spirit of an Italian street party. The white tablecloth was now adorned with heavy silver cutlery and little glass jars with flickering candles gave off a romantic glow.

Pots of aromatic herbs held the menus in delicate clips, displaying the names of the dishes that Will was adamant had to be present at the big Italian feast. In neat swirling handwriting the words *Garlic bread * Lasagne * Tiramisu* were clearly printed.

Jayne picked one of the menu cards out of the holder and laughed, 'This was our first meal together!'

'It was also the moment I fell in love with you again.'

Jayne took Will's outstretched hand as they looked around their small but perfectly fitting group of friends and family. 'I can't believe this!' Jayne gasped, 'It's incredible, thank you so, so much.'

Will's grip tightened, 'Well, you once said to me, when you came back from Ireland, that our life was very nearly perfect, and, to be honest, I just felt that wasn't quite good enough . . .'

Epilogue

So if you can all come next week armed with pithy insights on the genre of magical realism I would be eternally grateful. The set text is Angela Carter's *Nights At The Circus*, so do me a favour and at least read the back of it before entering the lecture hall. Until next time.' Picking up his jacket from the lectern, he then stuffed some books back into his rucksack. Mandy, his wife, despaired at him using the same battered Adidas rucksack for work and the gym; she had even bought him a leather satchel for Christmas in the fervent hope that his frayed sports bag would be consigned to the bin, but he'd never been one for following fashion. If it did the job and wasn't a lurid shade of neon, it was good enough for him.

He took the stairs of the auditorium two at a time, stopping occasionally to pick up a discarded empty can of Red Bull or chewing-gum wrapper, tutting at his students' nonchalant littering. It was the same at home with his two teenagers; it would be impossible to ever lose them – you'd just have to follow the detritus they casually dropped as they went about their business.

He sighed when he saw a folded newspaper on the last row of seats. Facing a couple of hundred yawning undergrads is one thing, but to know that some of them are actually reading a tabloid while you're trying to inject some literary charm into their lives was a step too far. He picked the paper up and wrinkled his nose in distaste. *The Globe* – car-crash journalism at its best. What anti-immigration, anti-royalist, far-left mixed with far-right witterings made the press today? Oh look, apparently eating only a diet of pickled beetroot can cure cancer. Who knew?

Flipping the paper over, his brain started whirring at a thousand spins a second as he gaped at a young blonde girl staring back at him. She was sitting on the steps of a Thai beach hut, squinting into the camera, but it was definitely her. Losing your virginity was not a moment you'd be likely to forget, particularly when the girl was as full on as Crystal was. He'd often thought about her, wondering why she had never written to him as he'd made sure that he'd earnestly pressed his address into her hand before leaving. He'd been such a nerdy child and to have this assertive blonde girl quite literally throw his books to one side, pin him to the bottom bunk and straddle him had been the first, and last, time he'd ever been seduced like that.

He quickly scanned the article; apparently her daughter

had got married to a famous chef in a tiny ceremony in Italy and didn't invite Crystal. Getting to the last paragraph made him sharply inhale and grab the back of the bench to stop himself stumbling over.

Jayne always blamed me for not having a father, but what could I have done? I was fifteen, pregnant with twins, alone. Knowing that she has just got married without any parents there just breaks my heart.

The small thumbnail of two mixed-race girls, one slender like Crystal, the other slightly larger, with an out-of control afro, confirmed it to him. They were the spit of his own two teenage daughters. He sank onto the bench, his heart pumping blood loudly into his ears. How could he have lived his life not knowing that he had these girls out there in the world? He sat there for almost an hour, staring down at the picture, seeing two beautiful women who were half him and wondering what kinds of lives they had had without him being part of it.

With trembling hands he reached into his jacket for his phone and started punching in Mandy's familiar cell number and suddenly stopped. He knew what he had to do instead. He dialled directory enquiries and heard himself calmly ask for the number of *The Globe*.

He felt a little sorry for the woman he'd been put through to, Samantha something or other, when he'd introduced himself; he thought she was going to hyperventilate with excitement until he'd ruined her day by telling her that under no circumstances was he going to talk to her on or off the record. He just wanted to reach his daughters.

It had taken thirty-six years for him to find them and it took precisely six minutes for them to call him back.

Acknowledgements

A huge amount of thanks have to go to my lovely agent Luigi Bonomi and the team at LBA for their constant support, advice and unwavering belief in me. My editor, Charlotte Ledger and the fabulous team at Harper Impulse deserve a lorry-load of love for seeing the potential in me and for holding my hand through this whole magical process. Being surrounded by amazingly talented editors who love romance as much as you is a wonderful thing.

Being one of the winners at the Montegrappa First Fiction award at the Emirates Literature Festival set this wonderful dream sequence into action, and I will always be eternally grateful to Isobel Abulhoul and her team at the Lit Fest for having this platform for aspiring authors to realise their dreams.

Closer to home, thank you to my fabulous husband Ed for never letting me have a minute of peace until I'd started writing this novel. You believed I could, so I did. Your endless support and copyediting even though 'chick lit is not really your thing' was appreciated more than you'll know. I also owe a huge thank you to my parents, Tim and Carol, who encouraged me to write stories from the minute I could hold a pen and never doubted that one day I'd be writing the acknowledgements to my own book. Thank you to my sisters Hannah and Davinia who have had to listen to my stories for almost four decades. I love you all 60-80.

A huge amount of gratitude has to go to my beautiful friends and first draft critics, Lisa Stratford, Jasmine Collin and Anya White who read, re-read and inspired me, Marites Tugade for being wonderful, and my gorgeous writer friends Rachel Hamilton and Annabel Kantaria for their invaluable advice and for pouring a steady stream of Prosecco into my mouth.

And thank you to Amélie, Rafe and Theo, who make the world a whole lot brighter. And louder. So, so much louder . . .